Caroline Bingley

Caroline Bingley

A Continuation of Jane Austen's *Pride and Prejudice*

JENNIFER BECTON

A WHITELEY PRESS BOOK

A WHITELEY PRESS BOOK

Copyright © 2011 by Jennifer Becton
http://www.bectonliterary.com
11   1 2 3 4 5 6 7

ISBN-13: 978-0615549507
ISBN-10: 0615549500

Printed in the United States of America.

Cover: *Woman with a Fan* by Hamilton Hamilton. (PD-US: Image in the public domain.)

The characters and events in this book are fictitious or used fictitiously. Any similarity to real people, living or dead, is coincidental and not intended by the author.

OTHER WORKS BY JENNIFER BECTON

THE PERSONAGES OF *PRIDE & PREJUDICE* COLLECTION
Charlotte Collins
"Maria Lucas": A Short Story
The Personages of Pride & Prejudice *Collection*

৽৩৫ ৫৶৽

THE SOUTHERN FRAUD THRILLER SERIES
Writing as J. W. Becton

Absolute Liability
Death Benefits—Coming January 2012
"Cancellation Notice": A Southern Fraud Short Story

৽৩৫ ৫৶৽

For

Every reader of *Charlotte Collins*.

Without you, this book would not exist.

Thank you.

Well! Evil to some is always good to others.

੭੭੬ Jane Austen ੭੬੭

One

ഛ One ഇ

December 1812

Banished.

The word echoed through Caroline Bingley's mind with each beat of the horses' hooves, and she felt the stab of her own mortification with each bone-jarring jolt of the hired carriage in which she was imprisoned. Her brother Charles's own hand had locked her away in this dreadful post chaise, which was presently being drawn by a second-rate pair of horses, and the entire conveyance was bound for the worst place she could imagine: her mother's home in the north of England.

Caroline glanced at the woman seated beside her. This, ostensibly, was her traveling companion, for it was quite improper for a woman of Caroline's status to voyage alone. In truth, their current mode of transport—two women traveling alone by post— was verging on impropriety as it was.

She thought her companion's name was Rosemary, but she had not taken the initiative of remembering. After all, Charles had been the one to employ the impertinent widow to accompany her while in transit and to act as her companion once in the tedious, unvarying society of Kendal, Cumbria.

While she could not blame Charles for hiring a servant to attend to her while navigating the public roads and dealing with the unsavory individuals one often encountered at posting inns, it was

1

beyond the needs of propriety to have retained her for the duration of her stay in the north. Caroline did not need a chaperone; nor had she reached that unfortunate stage in life wherein she required the services of a paid companion. She was no doddering fool, but a wealthy young woman of sound mind and good judgment.

Caroline lifted her chin against the humiliation and anger rising within her breast. The presence of a companion was an insult to be sure!

To think that she had become a prisoner in her own life—with the right to make her own choices stripped from her—was intolerable. No, she had chosen neither the voyage nor her companion, and she certainly would not have elected to embark on such a long journey so late in the year when the weather was apt to turn foul.

Ha! It was all a good joke. This was no journey. This was a prison sentence, and Rosemary was her jailor.

Rosemary.

Caroline winced at such a gauche name. She certainly hoped that her memory had failed and that the woman's name was not Rosemary, for she did not like the pert flavor of that particular herb in servants any more than in a roast of beef. Besides, her parents must have been quite inelegant to name their daughter after such an ugly, sprawling plant, and Caroline had no patience for inelegance.

Unfortunately, the name seemed to suit both the woman's piquant personality and her gauche posture, for Rosemary was currently slumped in her seat, asleep with her head lolling in rhythm to the motion of the carriage as strands of strawberry blond hair swayed across her forehead. A woman of her age—why, she must be nearly thirty!—should not sit so indecorously.

Caroline leaned forward to scold her, to remind her how a lady ought to recline, but then she sat back and sighed. What was the point of correcting her now? They were going to the country, where posture was unimportant. For who of worth would be present to observe and reward such correctness of bearing?

She considered the woman and her vexing ability to rest despite the ruts and bumps of the byways they traveled. How could Rosemary possibly sleep at such a time? It was just the sort of incommodious thing the woman would do. For her own part,

Caroline found that she could not possibly relax. She sat perfectly erect, hands crushed together in her lap, looking with great regret in the direction from whence they had come, back toward the remnants of her dreams and desires. Now her life was in shambles, and the winter-worn roads that led her inexorably into a dismal future did nothing to lull her into the forgetfulness of sleep.

Here was the sad state of her situation: Caroline not only failed to win the regard of Mr. Fitzwilliam Darcy, the only gentleman she had ever admired, but she had lost him to Miss Elizabeth Bennet, a headstrong young woman of neither breeding nor fortune. As a result, Caroline's thoughts of becoming one of the wealthiest women in England and mistress of the great estate of Pemberley had been ruined. Indeed, she had forfeited the most excellent society of Mr. Darcy and endangered the shy companionship of his sister Georgiana.

To make matters worse, she had also been unsuccessful in thwarting her brother Charles's unwise marriage to Miss Jane Bennet, and now, it seemed, no one would forgive her for having been opposed, and justly so, to both matches.

Though Caroline had never believed such a possibility to exist, her beloved brother had ostracized her, sending her away for the sake of family harmony or some such nonsense.

Her crimes?

Attempting to elevate her family's position by seeking an advantageous marriage? Hoping to prevent her brother from marrying a young lady so beneath the status to which he should ascribe?

Indeed.

But what had she done that any woman of sense would not have done? Would not the sainted Miss Elizabeth Bennet herself have shifted the heavens in order to prevent her sister Lydia's disastrous match to that scoundrel Mr. George Wickham? Caroline believed so, and as she had done nothing out of the common way in attempting to separate her brother from Miss Jane Bennet, she did not believe she deserved the censure she had received. Why, Mr. Darcy, who had been chief in instigating the entire scheme, had already been forgiven by all involved.

It was utterly unfair.

Tears of frustration welled in her eyes.

'Twas a centuries' old struggle in which she had been engaged, a struggle whose outcome had not been in her favor.

Society dictated that the Bennet girls must aspire to such gentlemen as Charles and Mr. Darcy. For was it not the duty of all children, be they male or female, to marry as well as possible for the benefit of their families?

In the same way, family loyalty had ordained that Caroline must wage a campaign against them. For was it not the duty of every family of wealth and consequence to guard against the infiltration of low-class fortune hunters?

Caroline had been forced to act after Charles had shown his admiration for Miss Bennet at their first meeting at that silly little public assembly in Meryton. Upon developing a deeper acquaintance with the lady in question and her rather wild, country family, Caroline had become concerned that her brother might have fallen in with a lady, kind though she may seem, who only sought his fortune.

She had shared her concerns with Mr. Darcy, and he had agreed wholeheartedly with her assessment. In fact, he had been the one to declare that Miss Bennet seemed to emit no real feeling for Charles, and they both shared reservations about her low-born relations.

After much strategizing, it was decided that it would be best to remove Charles from Hertfordshire before he could become the victim of a one-sided marriage to a fortune hunter wearing a dowdy country frock.

Being naturally humble, Charles had been easily convinced of Miss Bennet's indifference, and he had allowed himself to be taken to London. After learning of Miss Bennet's true feelings, he could not forgive himself for having doubted his own. His anger at Caroline's interference had been complete, and try as she might, she could not convince him that she had been acting in his best interests. She had wanted to protect him.

Caroline's cheeks moistened with tears, and she swiped them away as she considered the other charge leveled against her: her abhorrence of Mr. Darcy's decision to marry Miss Elizabeth Bennet.

As to that, she could not claim such innocence. She had considered Mr. Darcy to be her ideal match. He was everything a gentleman ought to be if he possibly can. He was handsome, well-spoken, dutiful, and rich, and he had accumulated his fortune in the most acceptable manner—through inheritance.

Caroline's own fortune, though substantially smaller than Mr. Darcy's, would assure her lifelong comfort, but her wealth was tainted: her father had earned the bulk of her inheritance through trade, a fact that Caroline always sought to conceal.

A union with Mr. Darcy would have ended the necessity of concealment and raised Caroline in the esteem of society.

And so she had sought the good opinion of a gentleman through those arts—flattery and a bit of flirtation—that all women use, and through conversation and comparison she had sought to make him aware of the obvious inferiority of any woman other than herself for matrimony.

In this, she had failed, and now she was truly a prisoner of society's whims, for though she was wealthy, she was not free.

Again, Caroline turned to look along the muddy road toward the past, as if merely looking in the direction of Pemberley might somehow transport her back in time, might change her circumstances, might win her the gentleman she had admired.

But it was not to be.

The carriage only swept her further from the comforts of her brother's household and from her dreams of permanency of station and home. Caroline braced herself against the seat, wishing she had thought to demand extra cushions when they had stopped to change conveyances at the last posting inn, for there was nothing more irksome than to arrive at one's destination with a sore posterior. She glanced about the coach for a cushion, and seeing no other suitable option, she folded her lap robe and positioned it beneath her. Fortunately, it was warmer today and dry, so the covering was not necessary to ward off the cold, though her feet were a bit chilled. The robe did little to absorb the shock of the carriage, but at least she had taken some action.

Hoping to forget the jarring of the rented carriage and her circumstances in general, Caroline forced her attention out the window. Only now, she looked ahead toward her destination, her future. Yes, even in winter's gray gloom, the countryside was quite lovely—rolling hills and all that—and had she been in the right company she might have said something poetic about the picturesque landscape of the Lake District. But the dozing Rosemary was hardly proper company, so Caroline remained silent, finally finding consolation two hours later when the coach crossed the arched stone bridge into Kendal and then bumped its way into the drive of the final posting inn.

Feeling quite bruised all over, Caroline pulled the robe from beneath her, attempted to smooth the wrinkles, and folded it into a neat square. She touched her hair, knowing it must look a fright, and adjusted her bonnet to hide the greater part of the damage.

As they drew closer to the inn, Caroline felt her heart leap a bit in her chest at the prospect of seeing her dear mother again.

Her mother, Elthea Knowles Bingley—now Elthea Knowles Bingley Newton—was the very best of women, always kind, generous, and self-effacing. If the meek were to inherit the earth, as the Scriptures said, her mother would certainly be a beneficiary. She was ever thinking of others above herself, a trait of which Caroline could not quite approve.

The post chaise pulled in front of the inn at Kendal, and Caroline spied her mother and Mr. Augustus Newton, her husband, awaiting them at the window. Her mother waved and then disappeared from view, likely rushing heedlessly to greet her in the stable yard instead of remaining inside and out of the cold and mud.

The postilion halted the team, and the horses sighed at the pleasure of resting. Caroline decided that was as good a sign as any that it was time to awaken Rosemary from her slumber. She issued her a gentle nudge to the shin. Her companion's eyes fluttered open, and she scowled as she reached down to rub her leg. "Can I be of assistance, Miss Bingley?"

"We have reached our destination."

"And that required a kick to the shin?" Rosemary asked with narrowed eyes. "Mr. Bingley is not paying me enough to be kicked."

Impertinent woman!

"Do not be dramatic. I am wearing slippers, not boots, and it was only a nudge to rouse you from slumber."

Rosemary mumbled something under her breath and then glanced outside. Then, she said, "Oh, it is lovely. In the face of such a lovely place, I have found it in my heart to forgive you."

Caroline was on the verge of telling her that she was looking at nothing but another dreadful posting inn, and more, she had not begged her forgiveness, but the postboy opened the coach door and assisted her out of the conveyance and into her mother's arms.

"Oh, Caro!" Mrs. Newton whispered as she wrapped her pudgy arms around her daughter and held her close. "How pleased I am to have you here."

Caroline was briefly inundated by feelings of so tender and unfamiliar a nature that she could not name them. She inhaled deeply of her mother's scent, and tears welled once more in her eyes. She closed them tightly and willed herself to keep her rampant emotions in check.

She was not generally prone to so many displays of feeling in such a short time. Nor was she often compelled to share every tribulation and fear she experienced, but she was tempted to do so now as she rested in the comforts of her mother's embrace.

Caroline steeled herself against these emotions, for she simply could not tell her mother the humiliating truth of what had occurred.

૭ర్వ Two ૭ర్వ

On that dreadful October evening, Caroline had endured long in
the company of her sister Louisa and her husband Mr. Hurst at the
inn in Scarborough, where the three of them had come to tour.
After some weeks of incessant shoreline walks, Caroline had
become bored, and thoughts of her brother and Mr. Darcy had
begun to assail her.

The course of her musings often returned to her last glimpse
of Mr. Darcy on the morning she, Louisa, and Mr. Hurst had
entered the carriage bound for the shore, while her brother and Mr.
Darcy, who claimed some mysterious business in town, had stood
on the stone staircase at Pemberley to see them off.

As Caroline turned to offer them a departing wave, a most
overwhelming feeling of inevitable change had crashed over her.
Her brother and Mr. Darcy stood at the foot of the immovable
Pemberley, but it was as if the whole building had somehow shifted
or perhaps the earth itself had changed position in the heavens.
Yes, something indefinable—and yet somehow also tangible—had
altered since Miss Elizabeth Bennet and her companions had
visited Pemberley, and Caroline had known then, as the carriage
carried her away, that her circumstances would never again be the
same.

But what precisely was occurring? She must know.

So distracted was Caroline with thoughts of her former
companions that she had taken up Mr. Hurst's custom and began

ignoring Louisa, who was opining again on the virtues of the seaside for improving one's complexion, when there came a knock at the door of their private sitting room.

"Oh, why must they bother us in our private chamber after such a pleasant meal?" Mr. Hurst moaned from his chair in the corner where he had been feigning interest in a newspaper.

"It is quite damaging to the digestion and such an inconvenience for someone to knock at this hour," Louisa agreed. "It is rather a jarring sound indeed."

Caroline's only reply had been to bid the servant to enter, for he might possess a letter bearing news of what had occurred since she left Pemberley.

To her greatest delight, the servant said, "A letter, ma'am." He presented the missive on a silver tray, bowed, and exited the room as swiftly as he had entered.

"Oh bother!" Louisa said as she touched a hand to her forehead. "Is it from Charles?"

Caroline checked the handwriting on the direction and nodded as anticipation welled within her.

Louisa leaned back into the sofa cushions and sighed. "Charles never has anything of consequence to say, but now we are obligated to take the trouble of writing back."

"Do not trouble yourself," Caroline said as she broke the seal and unfolded the letter. "I shall make the necessary replies, for he likely has no interest in hearing of the seaside's improvements on your skin coloring."

Louisa regarded her with an icy expression. "You are in a fine temper tonight, Caroline. Perhaps you might take some fresh air…."

Louisa continued speaking, but Caroline did not hear a word of it, for as she began to decipher her brother's messy handwriting, the room around her fell away.

Several strategic words fairly leapt from the page: "pleased to announce my engagement to Miss Jane Bennet…other happy news of Mr. Darcy's proposal to Miss Elizabeth Bennet…double wedding in Hertfordshire."

No, it could not be, Caroline thought, as she reread the letter more slowly this time.

Each word stabbed at her heart and pricked at her soul. It was true. Mr. Darcy was to be married.

There, in that blasted inn at Scarborough as her sister's voice droned in the background, Caroline's heart had rent in two. All her dreams of Pemberley had been spoiled and all her hopes for her brother destroyed in one practically illegible epistle.

She quickly thrust the letter into her sister's hands and excused herself from the Hursts' company.

Behind her, she heard her sister say, "Ah, you take my advice after all and are seeking some night air. It will be a benefit surely…."

Caroline did not respond to her sister, but rushed to her chamber, determined to hide her feelings somewhere deep within her and do her duty. She would write to her brother immediately and assure him of her felicitations, for that was what a sister ought to do, even if she believed he had chosen to wed a fortune hunter.

And that is precisely what Caroline did, though she gripped the pen with such ferocity that it nearly shattered. She looked upon the paper with tears in her eyes, and the words came in fits and spurts as she struggled with her sentiments. She knew what she must say, but she certainly did not want to say it.

She must say how pleased she was to hear of both engagements, how eager she was to attend the double wedding, how everyone would surely be blissfully happy from now on. But she simply could not issue a statement of outright approval.

How could she?

It had been the brightest wish of her family, especially of her father, that Charles might marry a woman of standing, and to see him shackle himself to a lady of significantly lower rank was painful. Caroline could neither approve nor rejoice in his decision.

But truly, Charles did seem pleased with his choice. Of course, Charles was easily pleased by everything and everybody he met. This was precisely why Caroline had been forced to conspire with Mr. Darcy to remove him from Miss Bennet's sphere early in their acquaintance.

Their party had stolen away to London, but Miss Jane Bennet could not be so easily thwarted. Under the encouragement of her sister Elizabeth no doubt, Jane had also gone to London to stay with her relations in Cheapside, causing Caroline and Mr. Darcy the trouble of concealing her presence from Charles for the duration of their stay. Caroline had not enjoyed her deceit, but she had believed herself to be acting only in the best interests of her family.

She had hoped that such a separation from Miss Bennet would remind Charles of his duty to his family and allow him to meet another young lady, albeit one who boasted a large dowry or who hailed from a titled family, with whom he might be equally pleased.

Unfortunately, his attachment to Miss Bennet was complete, and his feelings for her were much more deeply felt than Caroline and Mr. Darcy had imagined.

Yes, she had misjudged her brother and the force of his sentiments and had taken actions that injured him, but she had done so with the best of intentions. Indeed, both she and Mr. Darcy had nothing but the very best of intentions.

But now Mr. Darcy was to be married as well.

And to Miss Elizabeth Bennet!

One of the wealthiest, worthiest gentlemen in all of England was to wed a mere country miss of no fortune or standing.

Each time this thought entered her mind, Caroline was forced to lay aside her pen and paper for fear that her tears might cause the ink to run, leaving evidence of her brittle emotions for her brother to observe.

Caroline did not care for such displays of her own fragility. She did not care for the appearance of weakness in anyone, especially herself.

She must remain aloof and practical.

She must find a method of coexisting peacefully with the Bennet sisters, and the most expedient method for that was to scribe a letter to Jane, for she had a softer heart and more forgiving temperament than her sister Elizabeth. Besides, Caroline had no wish to throw herself upon the mercy of Miss Elizabeth Bennet, the woman who had been the source of her greatest sorrow: the loss of Mr. Fitzwilliam Darcy's favor.

And so when she had finished her letter to Charles, she added a page to Jane:

My dearest Jane,

It is with true joy that I write to you this day, for I have just received my brother's letter, which informed me that I will soon be able to call you my sister. A happy thought indeed!

I hope you will not misinterpret my behavior to you in London, for I was acting based upon a misunderstanding of the true nature of my brother's fondness for you. Had I but comprehended the violence of his affection for you, my dearest friend, I would have never taken such pains to protect you from what I believed to be certain disappointment. My hesitancy to call upon you and your relations in Cheapside or to invite you to dine in Grosvenor Street issued from nothing more than my earnest desire to protect you from sorrow.

However, once I became aware of my brother's true feelings, which he had experienced from your first meeting at the Meryton assembly, I have been free to treat you in the manner in which I have always viewed you—as a most honored friend and, now, sister.

Please accept the most humble declarations of warmest emotion from

Your most devoted sister,
Caroline Bingley

Caroline remained determinedly practical until the moment she sealed the letter and rang for the servant, who came in short order with the promise that the missive would be posted on the morrow.

Then, upon the servant's departure, Caroline pushed away from the small escritoire, walked calmly to her bedchamber, and collapsed atop the bed linens as grief for the loss of her fondest dreams overwhelmed her. Pemberley, Georgiana, Mr. Darcy, a life of confidence and ease...they were all lost to her now.

Would Caroline never be able to exist without the fear that someone might discover her secret history? Would she always be forced to hide her lowly origins in trade? Would she be locked forever in an attempt to scrabble her way out of the middling classes toward the stability of polite society?

No matter how great her inheritance, society would always view her as a pariah, an unworthy outsider, unless she married well or managed to insinuate herself into the very best company. Now she had no hope of either.

It was utterly unfair that Miss Elizabeth Bennet had been chosen to rise in society while Caroline, who had worked to gain an education, to become well versed on any topic of conversation, and to excel at every worthy accomplishment, had been bypassed.

Caroline wept bitterly the night through, but in the morning she showed no hint of her true distress. If her eyes were a bit reddened, she would only claim that it must be the salty sea air that had irritated them.

ᴓᴓ ᴓᴓ

Having been so certain of her victory in assuaging the feelings of the entire Bennet clan with one simple letter, Caroline had been quite surprised when, upon returning to Netherfield Park in November to prepare for her brother's wedding, she discovered that Charles had not been as mollified as his fiancée.

And what, pray, had been Charles's response?

He had begun thus: "Caroline, that letter was abominable."

Caroline had laid aside the book of history she had been pretending to read and looked into her brother's usually docile blue eyes. They flashed cold with anger, but she remained calm, saying, "Whatever can you mean, Charles? To what letter do you refer?"

His blue eyes flashed again. "You know very well to which letter I refer: the one you wrote Miss Bennet."

"Oh, that!" Caroline said with as much innocence as she could muster. "It was a letter of congratulations to your betrothed."

"Congratulations, indeed!" Charles clasped his hands behind his back and came off looking very regal, his head of light brown curls held high, as he continued, "Yes, you may have touched the heart of my dear, forgiving Miss Bennet, but from a brother's perspective, it will not do."

"Will not do?" Caroline repeated. "If Miss Bennet has seen fit to accept my felicitations and explanations, then I can see no reason why you may not."

"Do you not, Caroline?" He paused for a moment, clearly pondering his next words, and then he took on an air of determination. It was rare for such an expression to grace Charles's open features, but when he wore it, his desires must be respected, for he was the head of the Bingley family. "I am aware that you and Darcy conspired to separate Miss Bennet and me, and I am deeply ashamed at my own spiritless decision to believe you both when you proclaimed that she had no true feelings for me. Miss Bennet is so modest and reserved that I can well believe you both thought your interpretation of her behavior was accurate and that your actions were for my own good."

"Yes, I was only—"

He held up a hand and his expression hardened further. "But Darcy confessed his part in the matter and the intentions behind it. He has apologized, admitted his wrong, and made amends."

Caroline could hardly believe her brother's words. "Have I not done as much in my letter to Jane?"

"No, Caroline, you have excused your actions and made no amends, and though Miss Bennet may allow the goodness of her heart to sway her opinion of you, I may not be so charitable. I cannot." He paused, seemingly in contemplation. "Perhaps...no, indeed, there are others to whom an apology may be given."

Caroline stood and turned away from her brother, for she could not bear the force of his gaze. "To whom should I apologize?"

"Well, to those you offended, naturally."

Over her shoulder Caroline said, "You refer to Miss Elizabeth Bennet."

"No," he said. Caroline's surprise at his denial caused her to face him as he continued to speak. "I refer to Mrs. Fitzwilliam Darcy, as she shall be in a few days' time."

There was a long silence during which Caroline pondered her choice of response while Charles paced the room with a grim set to his face.

"Miss Elizabeth was most upset by your actions toward her sister," he said, midstride.

Here, Caroline very nearly made an unladylike snort. She knew well that Miss Elizabeth Bennet's anger had its origins in more than

Caroline's actions toward her sister. She disliked Caroline for her attempt to gain Mr. Darcy as a husband and to become mistress of Pemberley.

And Caroline found she could not blame her, for she despised Miss Elizabeth Bennet for attempting to win him and succeeding.

Caroline's hands clenched the book she still held, its pages wrinkling a bit under her harsh grasp. No, the prospect of apologizing to Mr. Darcy's choice of bride was not to be borne.

"Even for you, Charles, I cannot do it," she said.

"But you must." Charles stopped pacing and turned to look full upon his sister. He appeared to be mustering his courage to continue, and Caroline knew that he was attempting to exert his own will and not allow her to influence him again. "Yes, you must. Mr. Darcy is my closest friend and is betrothed to Miss Bennet's sister. We shall all be permanently linked. A family! If you cannot find it within yourself to make amends, then our family will always be divided, and you, I fear, will always be…." He hesitated again. "You will always be the person cast aside."

Caroline sucked in a breath at the harshness of her brother's tone. He could not mean it. He simply could not cast her aside. But as she pondered his words, she realized their truth.

Jane and Elizabeth Bennet were close, and they would often keep company together.

Jane, of course, was easily swayed, and Caroline had thought to turn this to her advantage, but Jane was more influenced by her sister, and that had to be taken into consideration. If Elizabeth never accepted Caroline, then neither would Jane.

And if Jane never accepted Caroline, then Charles would not be free to make her a member of his household once again.

Mr. Darcy, of course, would not invite her to Pemberley if Elizabeth were against her.

And this was intolerable, for an invitation to Pemberley and social intercourse with her brother and the Darcy family were crucial to her status in society.

Alas, Miss Elizabeth Bennet was the key to Caroline's return to society.

Caroline studied Charles. What was to be said that might alter the course of his discussion? Could anything accomplish such a task? It was easy for Caroline—for anyone really—to believe that her agreeably inclined brother might be managed in every circumstance, but it was simply not true.

Why, she only had to recall his treatment of her when every Bennet in Hertfordshire had arrived at Netherfield to check on Miss Jane Bennet, who had remained there to nurse her little cold. Yes, his countenance had clearly told her that she had better remain polite. The expression on her brother's face then—when he required Caroline to be civil to the girls' dimwitted mother—bore a great resemblance to the one he currently wore.

Only now, his expression was even more resolute. This was the result of his romance with Miss Jane Bennet.

He had allowed his family and friends to influence him more than his own heart, and he had suffered greatly. Realizing the error he had committed in being overly agreeable, he had clearly become determined that he should never again let anyone influence him.

He was exercising that decision as he handed down judgment on Caroline.

But Caroline was in no mood to accept his decision so easily. "My letter was kindly meant, even if you believe it to have been so poorly written. I do hope you can find it within your heart to offer me your forgiveness."

At this, he turned away, leaving Caroline to look at the hands clasped resolutely behind his back and to face the following words: "I forgive you, for you are my sister, and I cannot believe that you would purposely attempt to ruin my future happiness."

Hoping he had softened toward her, Caroline stood and placed a hand on his shoulder. "No indeed, brother. I only wanted to save you from an unequal marriage."

He turned his head so that he could meet her eyes fully. His expression held a sincerity that surprised Caroline as he said, "But a marriage is not unequal where there is an equality of love."

Caroline could not conceal her disdain. "Can you name any unequal marriages that did not end in misery for one or the other?"

"Those were marriages of unequal minds."

"Unequal fortunes must have the same effect," Caroline reasoned, "for does not money provide the opportunity for the improvement of the mind? I can hardly believe that Miss Bennet is your equal if she spent her youth without the benefit of a governess. Why, she can probably barely embroider a cushion, much less play the pianoforte!"

A muscle worked in Charles's jaw, and Caroline feared an outburst of anger, but then he sighed. "And this is precisely why I must take bold action. You refuse to see the truth before you. I love Miss Bennet, no matter how much money she has, who her relations may be, or how talented she is with needle and thread. She will be my wife, and I am unwilling to begin my marriage by inviting one who harbors such unrepentant disapproval to share our home. I shall not allow myself to be persuaded against my own good judgment, Caroline. I must act."

Cold fear rushed over Caroline, and her legs seemed no longer capable of supporting her, so she returned to her seat. She looked up at Charles, whose face was resolute, and realized that her situation was worse than she had anticipated.

"I think it best if you removed for a time," Charles said. His tone held an alarming ring of finality. "You must go home to Kendal."

"Home?" Caroline could not withhold her protest. "I have no home in Kendal."

"You shall go to our mother's home, then, if you insist on grammatical precision."

"Yes," Caroline said as her hands balled into fists. "I do insist upon it, for Newton House is not my home and it never shall be."

His reference to Newton House as "home" wounded Caroline more deeply than he could have realized. There were few people who knew how greatly she despised the very notion of home. Though she was a woman of no little fortune—20,000 pounds could hardly be considered insignificant—she had been denied the benefit of such a place from her infancy. Her father—heaven bless him—had expired before he had been able to purchase the estate his family deserved, and the inheritance, the bulk of which had been left to her brother Charles, had not yet been invested in family lands.

No, instead, it had been spent on the lease of a country manor in Hertfordshire and would soon be spent further on her brother's marriage to a country maiden. Imagine. Charles had the fortitude to commit to a woman, but not to a piece of real estate.

These were great vexations indeed, for above all else, Caroline had always yearned for a home of her own. The ownership of such a place meant far more than the possession of a piece of property. It meant a husband: a landed gentleman or perhaps someone with a title. And it meant security and status that could not easily be wrested from her.

To all outward appearances, Caroline was a woman to be envied. She wore the latest fashions, attended the most lavish balls, and associated with the wealthy and titled—and she had always tried to reflect an attitude superior to the confidence she felt inside herself—but in reality, she was nothing more than the homeless daughter of a tradesman.

Yes, Caroline would own to it: she had hoped to gain a home of her own in the form of Pemberley, but instead of gaining the home and husband of her deepest desires, she had succeeded in angering her brother, losing the good opinion of his betrothed, and humiliating herself.

"No, indeed," Caroline repeated. "I shall not go to the north of England. Surely, a journey of that magnitude is not necessary. I shall stay with Louisa in London."

"Your destination is already decided. I have written to Mama of your coming."

Caroline would not allow the mention of her mother to dissuade her from objecting again. Yes, she loved her mother and yearned to see her, but not in this manner. "Mama will bear up under her disappointment, for I refuse to go such a distance for no purpose."

Charles's jaw clenched. "But it is required," he said, and then he walked from the room, leaving only hurtful words in his wake. "Caroline, you shall not be welcome in my household until you make proper amends, and I can assure you that your welcome at Pemberley has been suspended until such a time as well."

Caroline sighed. There must yet be something she might attempt to rectify her situation, for she would neither apologize nor go to the north.

✎ ✐✎

Louisa surely must have pity on her, Caroline reasoned, for her sister had been chief in both separating Charles from Miss Jane Bennet and advising her about how to proceed with Mr. Darcy. Having little experience with romance, Caroline had sought her sister's advice and followed it closely.

Yes, Louisa would understand and would save her from Charles's disastrous plan. She would not allow her beloved sister to suffer for committing the crimes in which she herself was an accomplice.

"But Mr. Hurst and I do not go to London, Caroline," Louisa said, "or else you should be most welcome, certainly."

Shocked at the lack of regret in her sister's tone, Caroline demanded, "Do not go to London? Whatever can you mean? Where do you go?"

"Mr. Hurst has engaged us for a large house party in Devonshire."

"In Devonshire?"

"Indeed," Louisa replied airily.

"But," Caroline protested, "Mr. Hurst may find just as much amusement in London, may he not?"

Louisa set aside the letter she had been composing and turned her attention to her younger sister. "Caroline, do not be obtuse. His schoolfellow has invited a house full, and we are to spend several months at cards and fine foods. It was the only inducement he could want."

"Cards and food are not exclusive to Devonshire," Caroline said as she slowly walked closer to her sister and slid her fingertips along the top of the escritoire. "Why must you stay with his friends?"

Louisa rolled her eyes. "Why, for the simple reason that we were invited. Can you not comprehend that?"

There must be a method of convincing her sister to alter her plans. Caroline thought for a moment and then said, "You have never before desired to be in the company of Mr. Hurst's friends. I recall you saying that they were a group of bloated fools, in fact."

Indeed, she could hardly imagine her sister willingly placing herself in such company. Mr. Hurst was a gentleman of fashion and fortune, but he was not known for good sense or impressive companions.

"I desire to socialize with them now." Louisa's expression clearly meant to convey more than her words made obvious. "And that is all that matters."

Caroline deliberately misunderstood.

"Then, though the company does not sound particularly educated or interesting, I shall be happy to attend."

Louisa looked up at her with surprise, and then her expression hardened. Her next words were spoken in the manipulative tone Caroline knew well. "Why, I believed you to be on your way to Cumbria to visit Mama. Charles has arranged it all, including a traveling companion, I believe. He said Mama's disappointment at missing his wedding could only be assuaged by his promise to deliver you to her door."

Caroline was affronted. Charles had arranged everything. He had consulted their mother and Louisa, and everyone, it seemed, was in agreement but her.

She chose to speak plainly. "So I am to be sent away."

Louisa blinked with feigned innocence. She was fully acquainted with Caroline's actions in London, and she was also privy to the workings of her heart where Mr. Darcy was concerned, so it surprised Caroline that not even the slightest expression of pity stole across her features.

She could pretend to misunderstand Louisa's intentions no longer. The simple fact was that her sister was removing herself entirely from the altercation. She, who had been of like mind when it came to Jane Bennet, was now more interested in staying out of matters than in supporting her own blood kin.

But Caroline's vexation and grief over her sister went far deeper.

She had divulged the full truth of her feelings to Louisa. To her, she had confessed her deepest longings. Louisa knew of her desire to marry Mr. Darcy and to gain her own home, to become mistress of Pemberley. Louisa had even offered her advice on how to influence a gentleman, and yet, when all her tactics had failed and Mr. Darcy had proposed to Miss Elizabeth Bennet, her sister had abandoned her.

"I am sorry for you, my dear sister," Louisa said, though she did not sound sorry at all. "But I cannot say I am surprised."

Caroline found herself overcome by shock at her sister's words. "Can you not?"

"No, for your intentions with Mr. Darcy were far too overt. It was, at times, painful to watch your interactions with him. You must learn, Caro, to employ a bit of artfulness if you should like to ensnare a gentleman such as my Mr. Hurst."

A feeling of betrayal settled upon Caroline at that moment. She was neither angry nor embarrassed, but her shock was utter and complete.

"What do you mean, Louisa?"

"Why, precisely what I said. You were ever trying to provoke Mr. Darcy by mentioning Miss Bennet and her connections. Though you believed yourself to be mocking her, you succeeded only in keeping the lady at the forefront of his mind." Here, Louisa paused in contemplation. "You may well be the most successful unintentional matchmaker in the country!"

Ire rose in Caroline at this suggestion, and her fingers gripped the edge of the writing table. "If that is true, Louisa, then you must also accept that you share that title, for it was chiefly your advice that I followed."

The sisters eyed each other for many long moments before Louisa said, "Do not you think it wise, sister, to retrench? To take some time away? Perhaps a fresh perspective will be good for everyone."

"Retrench?" Caroline could barely pronounce the word, so far from her nature was it to retreat from conflict. "I need no pause for perspective."

"Do you not perceive the benefits?"

"No, indeed. No good can come of such dissemination of our party."

"Can it not?" Louisa asked. "Our family is suddenly very different. We welcome a new sister to the fold, and naturally, we must all find our footing in the new order. In fact, I am anxious to be away so that I may return as if none of the unpleasantness in

London or at Pemberley ever occurred. You ought to do the same."

Caroline was so angry she could not utter a syllable.

"I perceive your anger, my dear sister," Louisa said, her eyes now full of false pity, "but you must understand that this decision is for the best. *Our* best." She offered Caroline another look that was all condescension. "You must weigh your choices. Is it more important to flatter your vanity or to preserve peace in the family? And I should think that you would like to retain your welcome at Pemberley."

With the latter, Caroline could not argue. She closed her eyes and allowed herself to contemplate Pemberley, the estate she had one day hoped to call home. In her mind, she could see the massive stone edifice, she could smell the roses that bloomed all summer in the manicured garden, and she could even feel the soft breeze that blew across the pond in the evenings. She could imagine herself ascending the massive staircase in the evenings after she indulged in a quick trip to the kitchen for a bedtime biscuit or glass of wine. She could feel the cool stone underfoot as she padded silently up to her chamber.

"I would never forfeit my rights to visit Pemberley," Caroline whispered.

"Then off you shall go to Mama."

"I suppose it is so," Caroline said.

✤ ✤

And here she was.

In Kendal.

Standing ankle deep in mud at a wretched coaching inn and endeavoring to conceal the full truth of what had taken place from her own mother, the woman she held most dear.

ༀ Three ༀ

Perhaps the long journey and the uncomfortable accommodations over the past six days had taxed Caroline beyond what she had expected, and now she was suffering from an excess of sentimentality. Yes, exhaustion was to blame for the warm sting of tears in her eyes and the heavy pull in her heart.

"Oh! How I have missed my youngest daughter." Mrs. Newton stepped back, holding Caroline at arm's length so she could better observe her. "But you have matured so much that you hardly resemble the little girl I sent to London all those years ago."

Caroline briefly lowered her eyes and smiled at her mother. "Mama, it has not been so long as that, for we have seen each other numerous times since I left the seminary."

"Yes, the seminary returned quite a changed young lady. Even your accent was different. You could have hailed from an aristocratic London family. But you were yet a little girl." Mrs. Newton caressed her daughter's cheek and then took both her hands. "Now, however, after a short two years in charge of your brother's household, I find a beautiful young woman before me."

Caroline forced a smile, but at that precise moment, she appreciated neither the benefits of her education nor her experience as mistress of her brother's household. Though outwardly she might appear to be a composed woman of sense and education, she felt more like a lost little girl than a woman of twenty years. She had no direction, no friends, no husband, no home, and—for the moment—no siblings.

Mrs. Newton squeezed Caroline's hands and then turned to Rosemary, who had also escaped the confines of the coach and was standing at a polite distance. "And will you introduce me to your friend, Caro?"

Caroline turned to regard the woman, her companion, whose full name she still could not recall. Covering her embarrassment, she said, "I should have thought Charles had supplied the name of his employee when he wrote of my arrival."

As Mrs. Newton's eyebrows raised and then drew down in confusion, Rosemary stepped closer and looked at Caroline with appraising eyes. Again, Caroline willed herself to remember the woman's surname, but it did not come.

Caroline's embarrassment only deepened when the woman supplied the name herself: "My name is Rosemary Pickersgill, and I find I am already most indebted to your family for its graciousness in seeing to the employment of a widow such as me."

Caroline gawped. Pickersgill! Her surname was far worse than her first name. Caroline cleared her throat, composed her expression, and continued by saying, as if she had been cognizant of the appellation all along, "Yes, Mama, this is Mrs. Pickersgill. And this is my mother, Mrs. Newton."

Her mother had shown no reaction to the horrid name. Instead, she said, "I am very happy to make your acquaintance, Mrs. Pickersgill, but I find I must correct you at the outset. *I* am already in *your* debt, for you have seen my daughter home to us safely."

At just that moment, Mr. Newton joined them and immediately took Caroline's hand and pressed it in his. To her consternation, she found he had neglected his gloves and was gripping her kid gloves with his bare hands. Not only was he without proper attire—either to be seen publicly or to combat the winter weather—but it reflected poorly on his wife for having allowed the circumstance in the first place, and Caroline did not like anything to reflect poorly on her mother. Besides, his hands must be quite cold.

Despite the temperature of his bare hands, he spoke with warmth, saying, "Caroline, you have been too long away from us. Your mother has missed you greatly."

Caroline concealed a wince. Mr. Newton was a kind man even though he had acquired the sum total of his fortune through the building trade. He purported to be an engineer, had been a visitor at the Royal Society in London, and claimed that the design of bridges was more complicated than it appeared, but Caroline harbored doubts. Was not a sturdy piece of timber and some supports all that was required to construct an adequate bridge? It seemed a task that required no special acumen, but he had traveled about the country assisting in their design and accumulating vast wealth.

Caroline forced a smile to her lips and said, "I hope I find you well, Mr. Newton."

He offered her a grin so wide that his graying sideburns seemed to shift their position upward. "Oh yes, I have a new bridge to design, and I cannot be unwell when my mind is so happily occupied."

"A new bridge?" Caroline asked quietly as she shot a look toward her mother. Here was Mr. Newton already discussing his trade and in public. "How quaint."

How unfortunate that his manners displayed no real improvement from his travels and his vocabulary showed no mental aptitude out of the common way. He was wealthy, to be sure, but had he allowed that circumstance to improve him?

Not that Caroline could discern.

In fact, Mr. Newton had always worn his wealth as if it were a newly starched shirt.

Uncomfortably.

Still, Caroline smiled at him, all the while thinking it was perhaps best that he and her mother remained tucked away so far north. Here, he could not cause as much of a scene, for there were few people of polite society to take offense.

He released Caroline's hand and smiled openly at Rosemary. "And who is your friend?"

Mr. Newton and Mrs. Pickersgill acknowledged each other with a bow and curtsey as the presentations were made.

"Mrs. Pickersgill," he said with a broad smile, "you are very welcome to the Lake District and, indeed, to our home as well. And now, let us be off to Newton House, for you must both be exhausted."

"Yes, my dears," Mrs. Newton said with a sweep of her arm, "do allow Mr. Newton to see to your belongings and come along to our carriage."

Caroline trudged behind her mother across the inn yard to the waiting conveyance, all the while taking care to keep her skirts lifted away from the mud. She did not relish yet another ride, but this trip would be mercifully brief.

The ladies settled themselves within the carriage, and Caroline watched with annoyance as Mr. Newton helped the postboys remove the trunks and boxes from the basket at the rear of the post chaise and carried them to the corresponding basket on the Newton's coach.

Caroline shook her head as her mother's husband heaved a large trunk across the inn yard. She had not approved of her mother's marriage to Mr. Newton for just this reason. Her own excellent father, though born to no social graces, had made certain that he fit into any society. Unfortunately, he had succumbed to fever before he could feel its full benefits. Mr. Newton's philosophy, however, dictated that he would practice only those manners that made others comfortable and not those that were designed to demonstrate his true position in society as a now-wealthy landowner.

What good was such a position if one did not take hold of all the benefits the status afforded? To Caroline, it was unfathomable. And worse, it kept her mother removed from most good society as well. They would be welcomed in no homes of worth in London.

"Oh Mama," Caroline said when she could bear it no longer, "can you not encourage Mr. Newton to behave himself?"

Mrs. Newton looked quickly to her husband. "Has he done something amiss?"

"Only look at how he carries his burden like a common plow horse. Why must he insist on undertaking such labors when there are servants about?"

Mrs. Newton turned back to her daughter with a vague look of disappointment on her face. That expression discomfited Caroline greatly, for she did not like to draw her mother's displeasure.

Mrs. Newton's lips drew into a cheerless smile as she said, "You must forgive Mr. Newton, my dear. He prefers being useful, and we must make certain allowances for those we love."

This had long been a point of contention. Her mother was always willing to make excuses whereas Caroline saw the world for what it was—a harsh and fearsome place—and endeavored to protect those she loved from its criticisms. Caroline sighed and said, "Can you and Charles not understand that reputations—and indeed marriages—are built on more than just feelings?" Her words had barely broken from her lips when regret impelled her to snatch them back. She had not meant to disagree with her mother so overtly, but could she not see that the fates of entire families rested on each action in society and on each matrimonial decision? That entire reputations could be destroyed so easily?

Mrs. Newton took both Caroline's hands in hers once more. "Oh, Caro, let us not begin with such a dismal subject. I am too pleased to have you back with us to spare a thought on a little difference of opinion."

Caroline answered her with only a tight smile and a heart full of regret.

✦

After three quarters of an hour on a lovely stretch of undulating terrain, Caroline had heard her fill of Mr. Newton's narrative on every winter-brown pasture, rock wall, and quaint cottage in sight and was relieved when they arrived at Newton House.

When the coach stopped before the main entrance, Mr. Newton exited and assisted the ladies to the ground, and for a moment, they all looked at the edifice before them.

Caroline was forced to admit, if only to herself, the beauty of the house despite the fact that it held no connection with an ancient family and was, unfortunately, newly built. No sprawling additions or wings of different architectural styles cluttered the building's façade. Newton House was of unified theme with little adornment. Large windows lined the exterior in perfect symmetry, and the double door placed precisely at its center was now opened in invitation. And though it was not of the imposing scale of Pemberley, it was one of the largest homes of the neighborhood and was well situated on a comfortable acreage.

In all, Newton House would make as serviceable a prison as any home in the countryside.

Still, Caroline could not help but wonder how long she would be confined within its walls. When would her banishment come to an end? How would she rectify matters with her brother and return to his society? She must conceive of a method for doing so soon, for though this home was pleasing to the eye, it was yet her jail.

Mrs. Newton was the first to speak. "Well, as you see, it is still standing, and you have at long last arrived. I am ever so pleased at the prospect of a house full of guests." She took Caroline's arm. "Now, do come in."

"Yes, indeed, you are most welcome," Mr. Newton said as he offered Rosemary his arm and escorted her up the stairs.

Caroline shook her head at Mr. Newton's undue attention to a servant and listened with displeasure as he made a great pretense of pointing out every feature of the house as they entered the foyer.

"You see, my dear Mrs. Pickersgill, I built Newton House myself."

"Did you, Mr. Newton?" Rosemary asked as she untied her cloak and bonnet and handed them to the maid who was awaiting them in the entryway. She looked about her with apparent interest, her eyes finally alighting on the towering ceiling, which had been painted to represent the sky. "It is lovely, and I must say how much I admire your high ceilings. Their ornamentation is quite pleasing."

"The painting was Mrs. Newton's idea," Mr. Newton said with a smile, obviously pleased that someone had noticed his wife's addition to the design. "I am far too practically minded to have thought of something as artistic as that. You see, high ceilings can make a room difficult to heat, but with proper hearth placement and design, it can be done quite effectively. Only come along and allow me to show you...."

They disappeared down the hallway, leaving Mr. Newton's voice in a trail behind him as he no doubt gave Rosemary an account and view of every room on the first floor, including the servant's quarters. The woman would likely be required to hear minute details of each chamber from the dining room to the music room.

"Come, Caro," Mrs. Newton said upon shedding her outerwear, "I have ordered some refreshments to be laid out in the sitting room, and your belongings will be placed in your chambers momentarily. Then you may spend the rest of the day in recovery from your journey."

Caroline felt true joy at the prospect of a proper buffet after often having to endure food of poor quality in the posting inns over the past six days, and she followed her mother eagerly in the direction Mr. Newton and Rosemary had walked.

"Mr. Newton," Mrs. Newton called toward the back of the house, "do stop explaining the nuances of engineering to our friend and allow her to join us in the sitting room for a cup of tea."

Mr. Newton's face emerged from around the corner. "I do become quite carried away, do I not, my dear? We shall join you at this moment."

He disappeared briefly and then reemerged with Rosemary in tow.

Mrs. Newton shook her head. "You must excuse my dear Mr. Newton," she said to Rosemary. "He forgets that not all people are as interested in brick and mortar as he is."

Caroline, for once, agreed with her mother's assessment, but she did not say so.

"Not at all, Mrs. Newton," Rosemary said. "His descriptions have been most instructive."

"Well, then you will certainly have your fill of instruction here," Mrs. Newton said. "Now, come along, for I have had the servants lay a tray of cold meats."

"That is very kind, Mrs. Newton," Rosemary said as she lagged a bit behind the others. "But shall I not oversee the trunks while you enjoy your time with your daughter?"

"Indeed, I shall not hear of it, Mrs. Pickersgill, though it is kind of you to offer." Mrs. Newton led the women along the hallway, turning to share her joyous smile with them. "I am in a mood to celebrate my daughter's arrival, and you must take part. Were it up to me, we would have killed the fatted calf and celebrated all night now that Caro is home, but I did try to be sensible. Though there is a bit of ham on the tray."

Mrs. Newton pushed open the sitting room door to discover a blond-haired gentleman standing over the selection of meats and bread. "I see that we are not the first to discover the refreshments," she said with a laugh.

The gentleman turned and smiled broadly. His blue eyes rested on Caroline before they returned to her mother. "Guilty. This elegant display was too tempting to resist."

Intrigued, Caroline studied the man. He was average in height or a little taller, but he had a breadth of shoulder and a depth of musculature that gave him the appearance of being larger. He seemed familiar, but she could not quite place him.

"Ah, Rushton," Mr. Newton said from the doorway. "Once you have filled your plate, join me in the study so that the ladies may not be bothered by business. I have some design ideas for the Fairmont Bridge."

Rushton.

Caroline narrowed her eyes as the gentleman acknowledged Mr. Newton's request with a nod and a wave of his plate. Yes, she remembered him now.

Patrick Rushton. He was the son of the unfortunate Mr. James Rushton of Keswick. While the Bingleys had been ascending in wealth and status, the Rushton family was in decline. Through several generations, they owned a large tract of land that included a graphite quarry, but the mine was yielding less graphite, and with each passing year the Rushton clan had fallen a little lower.

When Caroline was a young girl, she could remember her parents discussing the elder Mr. Rushton's decision to support his family by selling as much land as was permitted in the entail. By the time Mr. Rushton had died, he had already divested himself of much of his property in order to pay his debts, and still they were not satisfied. By now, their circumstances must be dire indeed, and their family home had likely fallen into hopeless disrepair.

How very pitiable to lose one's wealth and standing in such a way.

Based on her memories of Mr. Patrick Rushton, Caroline thought it was unlikely that he would be the one to rescue the family from their plight. She remembered him as an insolent sort of youth, and based on the fact that he was currently engaged in stealing food from her mother's sitting room, he was, in her estimation, unchanged in adulthood.

"Caroline, my dear," Mrs. Newton said, "you remember Mr. Rushton, do you not? Our families have been acquainted for generations, you know, though I do not believe you ever played together as children, for he was a bit older than you. He was at university, I think, when you went to the seminary in town."

"Yes, Mama, I do remember Mr. Rushton." Caroline strode forward and curtseyed with extreme decorum. "Mr. Rushton, how very…"—she chose the word carefully—"surprising it is to see you in my mother's home."

Mr. Rushton studied her for a moment before setting his plate aside and bowing in return. "Miss Bingley," said he in an ironical tone, his eyes mischievous, "the years have not altered you, I find."

Caroline blinked at his tone but was not distracted enough to neglect her duty. "You and your family are well, I hope," she said.

"Yes, my family is in good health, Miss Bingley. Thank you for inquiring. I shall not make the same inquiry of you, for I can see that your nearest relations are all well, and your mother has assured me that your siblings do well too." He looked at Rosemary. "And will you do me the honor of introducing your friend?"

Caroline gaped at him as he crossed to stand before Rosemary. Why did everyone persist in describing this horrid servant as her friend? Could they not tell that Rosemary Pickersgill was an old widow who was not of her social class and thus not suitable for an association—much less a friendship—with Caroline?

Mrs. Newton spoke for her, saying, "Mr. Rushton, allow me to present Mrs. Pickersgill, Caroline's companion from London. We are ever so pleased to have her in our home this winter."

He gave her a polite bow, they exchanged a few civil words, and then he turned to Mr. Newton, who had been lingering with some impatience at the chamber door. "Well, Newton, shall we see to those bridges?"

With a nod at the assembled ladies, Mr. Rushton picked up his plate and departed.

৵ে Four ঙ৹৶

Once the door was closed and the men's voices receded, Caroline turned to the buffet, wondering idly if Mr. Rushton had left any victuals for their intended recipients. Finding that there was a sufficient supply, she began to fill a plate.

"Mrs. Pickersgill, do join Caro in taking some nourishment, if Mr. Rushton has left anything. That young man certainly has an appetite."

Caroline restrained a laugh at Mr. Rushton's being called young, for he was quite a few years older than she was. "What does Mr. Rushton do here at Newton House, Mama?"

"Why, he is Mr. Newton's business partner."

"Business partner?" Caroline forgot the piece of ham she had been transporting to her plate, holding it aloft, and frowned at the question. "Why should Mr. Newton require a partner in throwing a few logs across a river?"

"Indeed, Caroline, I believe the construction of bridges is more complicated than that," Mrs. Newton said as she crossed to the buffet. "Poor Mr. Rushton is always welcome in our home, and you must not taunt him, for he has had quite a difficult time of late."

"Has he?" Caroline asked, not truly caring whether or not he had suffered. She suddenly had no taste for ham and dropped it back to the tray, taking a large piece of bread instead.

"Oh yes! If you apply to anyone in town, you will find that he has developed the unjust reputation of a confirmed fortune hunter." Mrs. Newton turned to Rosemary to explain. "His poor father lost a great deal of money, my dear, and their estate is only now recovering. He was to be married to a wealthy young heiress, but there was a dreadful split just before the union was to take place."

"Oh dear," Rosemary said, her eyes wide. "That must have been quite a scandal. A broken engagement always brings disgrace to one party or other."

"And so it did to Mr. Rushton. No one knows the full story—for Mr. Rushton has never volunteered his perspective—but everyone says that the lady jilted him when she discovered his true circumstances."

"I could well believe him a fortune hunter, Mama, and I do not like to see him in your household," Caroline said, truly concerned.

Mrs. Newton only laughed and said, "Oh, do not believe a word of it, my dear. I have always been an excellent judge of a person's true character, and so you must believe me when I say that he is no fortune hunter."

"How can you be certain?" Caroline asked, for though she had only become acquainted with the story a few moments ago, she was now greatly afraid that her mother had been duped by a cad. "You have just confessed that Mr. Rushton has not denied his part in the dissolution of his engagement."

"What reason can he have to deny anything? No one would believe him now. Besides, it is simply not in Mr. Rushton's nature to worry over such matters or to take the easy course. Why, after university, he came home, showed an interest in engineering, and that was all that was required for Mr. Newton to take him under his wing. He learned quickly, and the two have been partners for some years now."

How unfortunate, Caroline thought, though she could not decide whom she pitied more: Mr. Newton for having to put up with Mr. Rushton's wit or Mr. Rushton for having to contend with Mr. Newton's ramblings on inane subjects.

"Now, let us forget this business with dear Mr. Rushton. Settle yourselves by the fire, and I shall bring the tea," her mother said as she arranged the cups on their saucers and lifted the silver teapot. As she turned to deliver the full cups to her guests, she said, "Caro, you will also be pleased to find another old friend in the neighborhood."

"Shall I?" If this neighbor were anything like Mr. Rushton, she was certain she would take no pleasure in the hearing.

"The Honorable Miss Lavinia Charlton—Mrs. Ralph Winton now that she has married—has been at Oak Park for several months." Mrs. Newton turned to Rosemary and explained, "Lavinia and Caroline have been friends since their days at the seminary."

"Oh?" Caroline asked, ignoring Rosemary's part in the conversation as she scooted to the edge of her seat and leaned forward a bit. This was news of great consequence, for Lavinia was the only daughter of Lord Charlton, who held a large barony and retained great wealth and status in the county. "Lavinia is in Kendal?"

"Indeed, the whole county is well pleased to see her again. She has not returned since she was sent to London all those years ago." Mrs. Newton again turned to Rosemary. "After Lord Charlton's wife died, Lavinia was packed away to London to be educated, for her father was in no position to educate a female when he had two sons—Harold and William—for whom to account."

Rosemary, whom to Caroline's eye was trying to impress her new mistress's mother by behaving so politely, set aside her teacup and saucer. "Yes, Mrs. Newton, that often seems to occur among those of rank. Young ladies become rather disposable objects."

Caroline recalled how upset Lavinia had been over her removal from Oak Park, having been educated her whole life at home. "Come," Caroline said, "you must admit that if she had to be removed, it was at least to pleasing circumstances. She went to 'ladies' Eton' in Queen's Square, one of the most prestigious female seminaries in Town. I found it to be a first-rate seminary, and Lavinia soon came to share my opinion."

To Rosemary, Mrs. Newton said, "Caroline's father always intended to send his daughters to London for an education, so he elected to send them to Queen's Square also, and that is how their friendship grew."

Yes, Caroline's time in Queen's Square had been a great benefit to her, for she had finally been able to associate with Lavinia on the comparatively level footing the school provided.

They had indeed become fast friends, but distance had separated them when, upon leaving the seminary, Caroline had begun traveling with Charles and Mr. Darcy, and Lavinia had eventually married Mr. Ralph Winton, an excessively wealthy London gentleman.

They had exchanged a few polite letters over the intervening three years, and Caroline had been satisfied that their friendship was safe. She had not realized until just this moment how superficial the correspondence must have been, for she had not known her friend had returned to Kendal. Obviously, Lavinia had withheld some facts from her.

Almost to herself, she said, "Lavinia said nothing of a return to Kendal in her letters."

"Oh no?" Mrs. Newton asked as she joined the women by the fire with her cup and saucer balanced in her dimpled hand. "Mrs. Halstead—you recall her, do you not?—tells me that the Charlton household has been in quite an uproar. I imagine Lavinia has not had time to write of her current circumstances."

Caroline's eyes widened. "What are her current circumstances?"

"Oh my! You must not have heard." Mrs. Newton set her cup and saucer on the side table and reached for Caroline's arm and gave it a soft pat. "Her brother Harold has died."

At first, Caroline could only look at her mother to seek further confirmation, and then her mind began to process the information. "This is shocking news indeed," she said. A death in the family must certainly warrant a word or two from her friend on the subject. "Lavinia said nothing of this tragedy either."

"I am grieved to hear of the loss," Rosemary offered politely with a glance at Caroline, seemingly to gauge her reaction. "Was he a close acquaintance of your family?"

"How kind of you to offer condolences, my dear," Mrs. Newton said, "but our families were only a little acquainted, mostly due to Caroline's friendship with Lavinia. Mr. Harold Charlton was the eldest son and heir to the barony, so we associated little with him, but occasionally we were invited to Oak Park. Customs of rank are not so strictly adhered to in the country, you know."

"How did he die?" Caroline asked.

"Consumption," Mrs. Newton said with a shake of her head. "It happened last summer."

Caroline could not stifle her curiosity and asked, "Was he married? Did he leave an heir?"

"No, unfortunately, Mr. Charlton never married, and that leaves William to inherit the title."

"Oh, that is an interesting development." Caroline's eyebrows raised at the thought of William Charlton, the younger son, holding the barony. She recalled him as a pleasant but indulged young man. Beyond that, as a younger son, he was often forgotten, even by his own relations. "I admit I cannot imagine William Charlton sitting in Parliament. How has he taken to being trained for the title and its resulting duties?"

"Not well, I fear. I expect he planned to retain his carefree ways." Mrs. Newton leaned forward and whispered, "Mrs. Halstead told me in the strictest confidence of a conversation she had lately with Lord Charlton on this very subject. Young Mr. Charlton, it seems, has shown the greatest reluctance to rise to the peerage and run the estate."

"I cannot imagine any rational gentleman being so disinclined to ascend in society." Caroline shook her head. "I confess that I do not comprehend it."

Rosemary surprised Caroline by responding, "I have found, Miss Bingley, that not all people are so inclined to grasp for rank, though some will do anything to attain it."

"How very..."—Caroline considered her words again— "obvious a statement to make."

Mrs. Newton took a sip of tea and then resumed her conspiratorial posture. "You know, my dear, that I do not care to indulge in idle gossip, and I pride myself on only sharing news of a factual, verified nature. But," she said with a swirl of her teaspoon, "I must tell you that Mr. Charlton has developed an infamous reputation since you have been away, and unlike the gossip surrounding Mr. Rushton, I find I must believe it, for he has been linked quite reliably with a servant in his household."

Caroline leaned back to consider her mother's news. "I do recall," she said, "that as a child Mr. Charlton was fond of creating mischief, but to dally with a maid so openly? That is something one often sees in London, but in the country, it seems likely to be nothing more than tittle-tattle."

"You must take into account his circumstances. He is a member of the titled class and a younger son after all. If his reputation is based on truth, it should not surprise you," Mrs. Newton said with a glance at Rosemary. "Is that not so, Mrs. Pickersgill? Are not many of the titled classes, wherever their domicile, engaged in such behavior?"

"It is quite often so, I have found, Mrs. Newton."

Caroline shook her head at Rosemary's response. What did the opinion of a servant matter? "Come, Mrs. Pickersgill is hardly qualified to offer any wisdom on this subject."

"Caro! One must only glance at Mrs. Pickersgill to see that she is a woman of breeding and good sense."

Caroline glanced at Rosemary but saw neither breeding nor sense.

Rosemary set aside her teacup and crossed her hands in her lap. "It is true, Mrs. Newton. I am nothing more than your daughter's companion and ought not offer my opinions so openly." She met Caroline's eyes and added, "Accurate though they may be."

"But—" Mrs. Newton said, apparently on the verge of pursuing this line of conversation. Caroline was uninterested.

"But is there truth to these rumors?" Caroline demanded of her mother instead.

Both women looked abruptly at her.

"About Mr. Charlton. Has he been proven unworthy?"

"That I cannot say for certain," Mrs. Newton said slowly and then smiled. "I am pleased, however, to find that your time in London has not persuaded you to accept such behavior."

Caroline winced a bit. She wished to blend thoroughly with London society and accept the behavior they found suitable, but she could not deny her innate abhorrence for the practice of keeping mistresses or conducting affairs, accepted though they may be. She, who prided herself on being erudite and sophisticated, had never been able to shed her country upbringing so wholly as to approve of such affairs between gentlemen and women who were not their wives. But if that is what polite society demanded of her, then she would strive to alter her judgment.

Rather than opining on her own conflicting views of fornication, she chose to focus on the opinions of another. "Lord Charlton must be displeased, for the barony has always maintained the highest of reputations."

Mrs. Newton nodded. "Indeed, Lord Charlton must be quite concerned, for he has arranged for Lavinia to see to her brother's well-being. Lord Charlton has already departed for Town, I believe, though Parliament will not open until March. Lavinia runs the household now."

"I wonder that Lavinia's husband could spare her," Caroline said, setting aside her plate and focusing only on the conversation at hand.

"From what I hear, it is fortunate for the entire Charlton household that he could." Her mother paused a moment to sip her tea and continued, "Her six months of mourning for her brother have just ended, and certainly, she will call on you as soon as she hears you have come."

"I do not doubt that she will call, for Lavinia and I were fast friends at the seminary," Caroline said with more confidence than she felt.

Then she stood for no other reason than to expel some of the nervous energy that now coursed through her. She crossed to the buffet but did not look at its contents. Her mind was already at Oak Park, for within its walls lay her opportunity.

An association with Lavinia Winton could very much ease the damage of having been excluded from Charles and Mr. Darcy's company. To be connected with the family of a baron, though less wealthy than Mr. Darcy, would be a coup indeed!

Yes, Lavinia must come!

Caroline attempted to modulate her tone, which she knew must hold more than a hint of excitement. "Have you already shared the news of my return with Kendal society, Mama?"

Mrs. Newton nodded. "Why, yes, indeed I did, for I could hardly conceal my anticipation from my acquaintances, could I?"

Caroline smiled, pleased that her mother's easy manners for once had benefitted her. Word of her arrival would soon spread, and surely Lavinia would do her duty and call on her old friend.

She stood for a time at the buffet and imagined Charles's surprise at the turn in her circumstances. He would expect to find her contrite after her banishment, but she would greet him from a higher vantage point.

Her heart seized a bit with regret at the course of her thoughts. She did not relish the idea of Charles as her enemy and had no wish to consider their relationship as a struggle for power. She simply longed to be with him, to have his companionship once again. She wished he had never sent her away, but he had.

He had forced this disjointedness to enter their relationship, and she must deal with it as she saw fit, and she did not see fit to apologize to Miss Elizabeth Bennet.

No, she would simply have to show Charles how desirable her company was to prominent people. She would become the center of Kendal society, and when her brother returned for her, he would see his error. He would know that she was worthy to be in his society once again.

Caroline's thoughts of her brother so distracted her that she hardly heard as Mrs. Newton went on to the next topic and then the next. When finally there was a break in the conversation, she managed to say, "Mama, I beg your pardon, but fatigue suddenly overwhelms me."

Mrs. Newton's hand flew to her mouth. "Oh! Of course, of course, you are fatigued from your long journey, and here I sit nattering away." She leapt from the sofa, drawing Caroline and Rosemary with her. "Allow me to escort you both to your chambers."

They ascended the stairs in a tangle of skirts and apologies, and Mrs. Newton directed Rosemary to one of the house's finest bedchambers. "Mrs. Pickersgill," she said as she opened the door with a flourish, "I hope you will be quite comfortable here."

Rosemary sucked in a breath. The room was all plush linens and comfortable furnishings, and the large window looked upon a vast green meadow beyond. "I assure you I shall! It is a lovely room."

Caroline curbed her temptation to ask her mother why she should put a servant in such a fine room, for she truly was too exhausted to mention it.

"And it is adjacent to Caroline's room, so you two may stay up until all hours of the night chattering away as girls do," Mrs. Newton said.

Caroline grimaced. There would be little chattering with Rosemary, she felt certain.

With Rosemary shut securely in her room, Caroline walked alongside Mrs. Newton to her customary chamber, a lovely large corner room with both a view of the meadow and a delightful prospect of the pond.

"It is just as you recalled, is it not?" Mrs. Newton asked as they entered the chamber.

Caroline ventured to the window, her fingertips brushing across the bed linens as she passed. "Oh yes, Mama, the room is as lovely as it ever was," Caroline agreed.

Mrs. Newton took a seat on the bed and patted the space beside her. "Come sit with me."

Caroline was about to protest, reminding her mother of her fatigue, but one look at Mrs. Newton's hopeful face convinced her to obey.

"I am so pleased that you have come home to me, my girl, but you must tell me the truth. Has something happened between you and Charles?"

Caroline blinked at her, surprised at her mother's accuracy. Her mother may want to offer people the benefits of her trust and good opinion, but she always seemed to see straight to the heart of the matter when required. Still, Caroline could not confess the truth to her. Charles would not wish it, and neither did she. "No, why ever would you think such a thing?"

Mrs. Newton cocked her head skeptically. "Come, I know you have no wish to be here in Kendal. You aspire to a life in London and nothing less will do."

"I do love London." That was the half-truth, but she must yet conceal the unhappy portion from her mother.

As if her mother had read her thoughts, she said, "But you do not seem happy, Caro."

Caroline laughed to cover the correctness of her mother's assessment. It came out sounding bitter and sad. "Of course, I am happy. I am with you."

Mrs. Newton leaned forward, her eyes soft. "And I am happy too, my dear, but I cannot help but wonder why you left your brother and sister so suddenly."

"I missed you."

Her mother softened. "And I missed you, Caro, but I also know how well you enjoyed the benefits of Charles's household."

Caroline cleared her throat. "I found myself longing to see you again, and I knew you would be anxious to hear about Charles's marriage ceremony since you were unable to attend. It seemed the perfect opportunity to come away. Louisa and Mr. Hurst have gone to Devonshire, and of course, Charles has a wife capable of overseeing the running of Netherfield Park in my absence."

"And that is all?"

"Indeed, Mama, that is all."

Mrs. Newton did not appear truly satisfied, but she allowed the conversation to end.

⚙ Five ⚙

The onslaught of calls began promptly the next morning, and the complete rite—call and requisite return of call—endured full a week. Every member of polite society in Cumbria, it seemed, had been alerted to Caroline's arrival, and the ladies seemed all to desire to call at once.

All except the one lady whom Caroline most wanted to see.

Lavinia Charlton Winton.

She, most decidedly, did not come.

Still, from ten in the morning until after two in the afternoon, a parade of neighbors passed through the drawing room of Newton House, where Caroline sat with her mother and Mrs. Pickersgill to receive them. She responded to so many inquiries as to her health and that of her siblings that she began to wish she had been ill so that she might have avoided the morning call ritual altogether.

Were Caroline not as easily given to politeness, she fancied she might greet each caller at the door herself and say, "Good morning to you, Miss Nonesuch. How lovely to rekindle our acquaintance. Allow me to save time by telling you that my family is in good health, I am pleased to be in Cumbria—though the weather is indeed horrid—and I am pained at leaving my siblings but delighted to be with my mother. Leave your card, for I am required to return your call and hold this precise discussion with you once again within the next few days."

Alas, such a thing could not be done, and so Caroline remained in her chair and made the required chitchat with all who came. Rosemary behaved admirably, and though Caroline could not be proud of the woman, she was at least not embarrassed by her, for she sat correctly and behaved to all appearances as a well-bred lady.

In fact, she was quite sure that Rosemary had charmed more than one old widow with her stories of Town and its residents. Mrs. Halstead had quite fallen in love, Caroline thought.

Mrs. Newton was always perfectly civil and reserved with her country guests, and often, she followed the conversation as she took up a bit of sewing. On the second morning, Caroline had sneaked into the drawing room early to remove all items of underlinen from the work basket. She simply refused to allow her mother to darn stockings if there were a chance that her schoolfellow Lavinia Winton might pay a call at any moment.

That moment, however, did not come until a week later. When Lavinia finally called upon the ladies of Newton House, they were absent on another visit.

Caroline, Mrs. Newton, and Rosemary had returned home through a dull drizzle of cold rain after returning a call to Mrs. Halstead, which had lasted quite a bit longer than Caroline had anticipated, and now the whole day was wasted and her spirits much depressed. She had quite given up the idea that Lavinia might call and was sure she had been snubbed, and she had no wish to do anything besides sit before the fire with a tin of biscuits and a pot of tea.

She shed her cloak and bonnet, eyeing the silver salver full of calling cards without the least feeling of hope.

Mrs. Newton pounced on the cards, however, and with shining eyes, she turned to Caroline. "Look, my dear, and you will find that your mother is always right. I told you Lavinia would call, and here is the proof."

Caroline felt her eyes widen in disbelief, and suddenly her pulse began to pound. Was it true? Had Lavinia called?

She looked down at the card her mother had extended to her.

The elegant black script read simply, "Mrs. Ralph Winton."

Caroline had the most girlish impulse to squeal and bounce up and down with glee, but she only looked at her mother and said, "I am pleased."

In truth, Caroline's relief was nearly complete, but the emotion was tainted by fear that Lavinia might have purposefully called at an early hour to avoid an actual visit and instead simply leave her card.

At least, Caroline reminded herself, Lavinia had called. She had not been slighted.

Now, it was upon her to wait on Lavinia, which she would do with the utmost courtesy and speed.

"We shall call upon her tomorrow first thing," she declared with a quick glance at Rosemary, who was watching her with a quizzical eye. "You will want to wear your nicest morning dress, Mrs. Pickersgill, for we wait upon the sister of a baron tomorrow."

Mrs. Pickersgill smiled faintly. "Indeed, a baron! I shall do my utmost to comport myself correctly."

"Yes, tomorrow is an important call." Thinking to avert any disasters that might arise from being forced to travel with her companion, she said, "It would be best if you remained as quiet as possible while we are at Oak Park."

Again, a faint smile. "Thank you, Miss Bingley. I shall take your recommendations on the value of silence into consideration. Now, if you will excuse me, I think you have long been desiring my absence."

Mrs. Pickersgill disappeared upstairs, leaving Mrs. Newton and Caroline alone in the entry hall.

"Caro, do you think it necessary to caution Mrs. Pickersgill? I have heard little of her history, but she has behaved as a well-mannered lady the entire week through, do not you think?"

Caroline was unsurprised by her mother's gentle defense of Mrs. Pickersgill, for it was just the sort of thing she would do. However, Caroline was acquainted with the wider world, and she knew the power of the titled to inflict social wounds upon the unsuspecting and the unmannered, and she would do everything she could in order to prevent anyone from bringing shame upon her family. If that meant risking slight rudeness at cautioning Mrs. Pickersgill, then so be it.

"She has been adequate, certainly," Caroline admitted, "but one cannot be too careful when one associates with the titled class. One slip and shame could rain upon us."

"My dear, you are far too dramatic for your own good," said her mother, as if Caroline's words held no greater import than newspaper gossip. "Now, do come into the music room, for I have not heard you play a note since you arrived, and you know what great pleasure I take in music."

She allowed her mother to lead the way to the music room, even though she was not in the mood to perform at the moment. She had much rather think on tomorrow's call, her wardrobe, and topics of conversation that would display her in the best light. Instead, she asked, "Have you retained the old square pianoforte then, Mama?"

"No, I believe you will be surprised to find that we have a new instrument for you to enjoy."

Mrs. Newton opened the door to a large chamber off the main hallway. The room was surrounded by casement windows, which were wonderful for allowing in light but less conducive for the highest sound quality. Today, they only admitted a dull gray and amplified the sound of the rain as it struck the large glass panes.

Several intimate seating areas were spread about the perimeter, and the furniture was comfortably upholstered in rich fabrics, but Mrs. Newton had clearly arranged the room around the pianoforte that stood at its center.

It was a beautiful instrument.

Caroline circled it, not allowing even the fabric of her skirts to touch it, as if the slightest human contact might somehow sully its perfection. Made of polished rosewood and standing upon elegantly turned legs, the piano was beyond what Caroline had anticipated.

"A Broadwood," she breathed. "I did not expect you to have acquired one so fine as this."

"I know! It was indeed a lavish expense for a household with no musical occupants, but we often have musical guests, and of course, I had hoped one day you would return and play for us."

It was a great extravagance, but Caroline could not disapprove of it. It was a sign of her mother's wealth and status, and it was indeed a thing of beauty to behold.

And she longed to play it and hear if its intonations matched its exterior beauty.

Caroline pulled the stool away, seated herself with her customary ceremony, and placed her fingertips on the cool ivory keys. She nearly sighed aloud at that simple pleasure. Seemingly without conscious decision, she began to play, her fingers automatically beginning the piece she often chose in company. It sounded even more beautiful on the Broadwood. Yes, the pianoforte had a sound as deep and lush as the darkest of chocolates. The music glided about the room and wrapped its hearers in a spell of sound.

At the seminary in London, Caroline had practiced long hours, for her father paid a great deal for her to have lessons with the music master. She could hear him now, saying, "Caroline, you must learn to play the pianoforte very well indeed, for the ability to produce a great performance on the instrument is one hallmark of an accomplished young woman, and one day, it will win you a gentleman of great worth. Mark my words."

Indeed, she had taken to her lessons with great vigor, but she could not give her father the credit for having inspired her. She had loved to play, and soon she quite outshone the other girls at the seminary.

Now, Caroline played with singular focus on her task. She knew each piece from memory, and though she had played them many times at countless parties and dinners, she fancied they still served their purpose.

And her mother's applause confirmed it.

"Oh!" she said. "Now, Mr. Newton may never chide me again for having insisted on the pianoforte, may he, Mr. Rushton? Caroline has certainly made the purchase worthwhile."

Caroline looked away from the pianoforte to discover Mr. Rushton languishing on the periphery of the chamber.

He was giving her the oddest look, and she found she could not quite meet his eyes. She looked away, and inexplicably she found herself fighting not to blush.

Then the gentleman spoke. "It was a well-rehearsed performance and very pleasing to most listeners, I am certain."

At this, Caroline did meet his gaze, for she could not take his meaning, so she chose the most direct approach and simply asked him. "What does that signify, 'well-rehearsed'? It sounds as if it were a compliment, but your tone of voice implies some sort of hidden meaning."

He smiled. "I meant just what I said. Your performance was practiced. In fact, you are so well acquainted with every note and nuance of that piece that you hardly even need to hear the actual music anymore."

"Do you mean to insinuate, then, that practice is somehow to be discouraged? I have always found, Mr. Rushton, that no great accomplishment can be made without taking the opportunity of practicing. A lack of rehearsal results in mistakes, and those can never be to one's benefit, can they?"

"I would not argue with you, Miss Bingley. I may only say this: there is also something pleasing in the unbridled joy of making errors."

"Unlike you, sir, I take no pleasure in my blunders but seek to minimize their existence."

"How unfortunate, for I have found that my greatest mistakes can sometimes yield the greatest pleasures."

Caroline laughed at this outright. "I am certain you believe yourself to be clever by speaking in paradoxes, but it shows me only how very impractical and foolish you are."

"I would expect you to think nothing different." He spoke these words with an undeniable tone of irony.

But before Caroline could question him further, her mother spoke. "Oh, you must stop teasing my daughter so, Mr. Rushton. You know very well that she plays beautifully."

"Indeed, she does everything beautifully," he said as he bowed to Mrs. Newton. Then, he turned toward the pianoforte and bowed to the musician as well, and as he raised himself back to his full height, Caroline was surprised to see a smirk on his face.

It was as if he had just negated his compliment with his sarcastic expression. Caroline scowled back. "Sir, your countenance belies your accolades, and I feel sure you must be insulting me."

"I would never presume to insult you, Miss Bingley."

"I should think not," Caroline said with venom, "for I have heard of your actions since I have been away."

"Have you indeed?" he asked with a grin. "And what, pray tell, have you heard?"

Caroline studied him in silence for a long moment, deciding whether or not to mention his broken engagement. One look at her mother told her it would be wise to hold her tongue, but upon glancing back at Mr. Rushton, she found that his expression nearly begged her to continue.

He seemed to be having fun.

And that is what kept her from saying another word. She only smirked at him as if she harbored a secret about him that even he did not know.

"That smile intrigues me, Miss Bingley."

"Does it?"

"Yes, I wonder what stories you have heard and what you have been foolish enough to believe."

"I assure you, Mr. Rushton, that nothing I have heard is likely to be as dreadful as what you have actually done."

He gave a hearty laugh. "Indeed, Miss Bingley, that is probably the truth."

"Oh come," Mrs. Newton said in his defense, "you are as upstanding a young man as ever I have seen."

He smiled genuinely at her. "I am pleased you think so, Mrs. Newton, for I hold you in the highest regard." He glanced at Caroline. "But I must depart. I was drawn to the room only to hear the performance, and Mr. Newton has now been waiting many minutes for my return to the study and our bridge plans."

"Go on, then," Mrs. Newton said.

To which Caroline added, "We will not miss you here."

Mr. Rushton only smiled once more as he exited the music room.

Caroline rose from the stool and chose a seat next to her mother. "I do not comprehend why you allow him in the house. He is a most confounding man."

⚙ Six ⚙

Caroline awakened early the next morning to prepare for her call upon Lavinia, and her excitement over the prospect must have overflowed to the rest of the household, for her mother had arrived with Rosemary close behind to help her dress.

So full of anticipation was Caroline that she could not even chide her mother for foisting Rosemary upon her.

She only sat at her dressing table and watched as her maid brushed her long brown hair into smooth waves.

Mrs. Newton and Rosemary sat on the bed, already completely dressed for their morning call, and observed. "Mrs. Pickersgill, you will like Oak Park."

"Will I? If you say so, Mrs. Newton, then I truly look forward to seeing it."

"It is the finest in the neighborhood, excepting my beloved Newton House of course."

"Oak Park is a lovely property," Caroline said from across the room. She was surprised at the wistfulness of her tone as she spoke. "But I do so wish you might have seen Pemberley, for it will quite spoil your view of any other home in England."

"But I have seen Pemberley," Mrs. Newton assured her daughter, "through your description. You make it sound so lovely that the reality cannot possibly match it. Besides, you know how I abhor travel. I would not enjoy myself if I were to venture so far from home. Oak Park will be the finest house I shall ever enter."

Caroline met her mother's eyes in the mirror. "I have always marveled at how different you and Papa were in your opinions on the subject of travel."

Mrs. Newton laughed. "Oh yes, we were certainly disparate in many of our opinions. He loved to wander. It was no sacrifice to him to go all the way to the Indies to earn his fortune, and though he always said he wanted to purchase an estate, I do not think he would have ever settled down enough to undertake it."

Caroline smiled at the memories of her father that were evoked within her. "I think he would have, eventually, for he knew that land is crucial to rising in society. And he desired for all of us to rise."

"Yes, he did, and you have all done so. You have such fashionable friends and have been about such interesting entertainments. And you have brought one such friend to visit us." She patted Rosemary's hand. "But I have always thought, my dear, that even the largest of houses and the finest of properties could not ensure the happiness your father and I desired for you, Charles, and Louisa. I am pleased that my children have all found their own sort of happiness and even remained as friends. It warms a mother's heart."

Caroline could not continue to meet her mother's eyes, even in the mirror, and she made a great pretense of studying her comb instead. Not only had Caroline failed to accede to her father's wishes of raising the status of the Bingley family, but she had made herself and everyone else unhappy in the process.

But this morning she had the opportunity to remedy her mistake. Today she would solidify her place in Kendal society, and from there, well, from there she could not say.

But she would rise, and it would all begin with her call on Lavinia.

⚬⚬⚬ ⚬⚬⚬

As Mr. Newton's coach turned onto the long approach road to Oak Park, Caroline had the oddest inclination to leap from the conveyance, for it was traveling slower than normal, surely, and dash to the door. Instead, she clasped her hands in her lap and watched as the house began to rise upon the horizon. She experienced a moment of pure envy.

Oak Park was an elaborately constructed stone edifice that took up what appeared to be the equivalent of an entire city block. Unlike Newton House, Oak Park had grown over time, with one wing decidedly neo-classical and another of Gothic influence. Somehow, the dissimilar architectural styles melded together in the domed entryway that once had served as the entire main house.

It was nothing to Pemberley, of course; few properties could rival it. Still, Oak Park represented a particular stability of rank and standing within the community that could not easily be ignored or forgotten.

It was not possible for anyone to look down upon Lavinia or Mr. Charlton, no matter what missteps they might make, for they had been fortunate enough to be born to the life to which all people aspired. They had received the best education, had access to the finest society, and lived quite at their leisure. They could behave as they chose, and no one could oust them from their proper place. Their positions were as settled as the foundation upon which Oak Park itself rested.

It was vexing to Caroline to realize that she had no such advantage. Her family had money, certainly, and that was not something to be ignored. Money was important indeed, but she knew very well that it was only one component in the quest for happiness.

And she had indeed attended the finest London seminary, she did retain access to many people within polite society, and she did live at her leisure, but she was also acutely aware that one ill-placed word of her family's origins in trade could damage every advantage she possessed.

She had no ancestors of note and no ancient family lands to lend her credibility in the face of her potential detractors.

And worse, Caroline's inheritance of 20,000 pounds was controlled by her brother until her marriage, whereupon it would be controlled by her husband. Certainly, Charles was generous with her allowances, and she would admit to having occasionally spent more than she ought to have, but the truth of the matter was that she, like every other lady, would never have the opportunity of managing her own wealth without the interference of some man or other.

Oh, how she wished for the permanency and stability afforded by a house such as Pemberley or even Oak Park, for at the very least, a woman's place was in the management of the home. It would be her place.

"Did I not tell you, Mrs. Pickersgill?" Mrs. Newton said as they drew nearer to Oak Park. "It always has been the loveliest house in the neighborhood."

Looking upon it now, Caroline could not but agree. It was lovely, especially on such a day when the sun was bright and cast upon the structure a glow of warmth and welcome.

Rosemary, however, did not seem to agree, for she said, "It is the largest, certainly, but I cannot say it holds any beauty over Newton House."

Caroline shook her head. "You are not required to flatter my mother, Mrs. Pickersgill."

"It was not mere flattery, Miss Bingley, for I expressed my honest opinion of the matter. A large house is not necessarily more pleasing to the eye than a small one. It is simply, well, larger."

"Clearly, you have never experienced the pleasures of a large house. I am certain that once you enter one as grand as Oak Park, your opinion will change."

"Oh, Caro, not everyone has the same taste," Mrs. Newton said with a smile. "You may allow Mrs. Pickersgill to admire a small house if she wishes. Besides, it will please Mr. Newton greatly to hear that she does."

Caroline was on the verge of saying, "Oh, hang Mr. Newton," but she restrained herself, realizing that there was no point, for an opinion was difficult to change, even one's own.

Rosemary cocked her head to one side and studied her through narrowed eyes. Then, as if having come to a satisfactory conclusion, she said, "I will defer to your judgment, Miss Bingley, for I see you are in no mood for debate."

"I am always in the mood for debate, Mrs. Pickersgill, but on this subject, there can be none. A woman of sense cannot prefer a small house to a large one. It is utterly ridiculous."

"Indeed, Miss Bingley."

Rosemary's voice held a distinct note of irony, but Caroline did not comment on it. In fact, the ladies did not converse again until they had completed the ride along the approach road, were received into the grand house in question, and were announced at the sitting room door by a manservant of stern countenance.

"Mrs. Newton, Miss Bingley, and Mrs. Pickersgill, madam," he said. His voice sounded strangely ominous to Caroline's ears as his words rang into the vast room and echoed off the high ceilings and art-covered walls.

Indeed, the room was lavishly done. The furniture was of the highest quality and was arranged so that it could be shown to its best advantage and not for the comfort of the room's occupants. Matching sofas, upholstered in gold and white brocade, stood in front of each of the towering windows that flanked the carved stone fireplace, and the sheer span between the two seats would likely make conversation—and even visual contact—awkward. Two high-backed chairs completed the arrangement while floor-to-ceiling draperies of heavy gold material framed the whole scene. The drapes had been pulled aside, allowing light to stream into the cavernous chamber in bright beams. Even the sunlight, it seemed, had been arranged with purposeful formality, for it descended in a most appealing manner on various points in the room.

Even though the chamber was not conducive to intimate conversation, Lavinia had seen to every other comfort. The fire had obviously been laid with care, small enough not to cause overheating but large enough to take the chill out of the air. On the far wall stood a buffet covered with full decanters and carafes of wine, sherry, and port, and crystal glasses were lined up like soldiers at the ready, always prepared to receive libations. Books were fortuitously arranged on polished wooden side tables, and a writing table was settled along the far wall. Every detail had been seen to, every necessity provided. Lavinia was obviously adept at managing her father's household, and if true comfort was lacking, it could be forgiven in the face of sheer opulence.

And Caroline was ever in favor of opulence.

As the door closed behind them, Lavinia emerged from her place in a high-backed chair like a butterfly from a cocoon. The light behind her was so dazzling that Caroline was forced to blink often as she attempted to look at her friend.

At that precise moment, Caroline could have allowed herself to be intimidated by her friend's grand appearance, by her family's even grander estate, or even by the sheer scale of the room, but she would not permit herself to be susceptible to such a weakness of emotion.

Why, she herself had very nearly been the mistress of a great household. In any case, she had visited Lavinia's home numerous times in the past, and she had been acquainted with her long before she had made the transformation from awkward caterpillar to the beautiful winged creature that now stood before Caroline.

The perfectly styled woman converged upon their party forthwith and curtseyed in Mrs. Newton's general direction. Then she smiled at Caroline, saying, "My dear friend! How good it is to see you."

Lavinia leaned in as if to take both Caroline's hands, but she stopped short and only managed to touch one hand briefly.

Caroline straightened herself. "I am very pleased to be at Oak Park again. It holds so many pleasant memories, and I find it has not altered one bit, though the view from the drive, I find, is more stunning than ever."

"How very gracious of you to notice," Lavinia said and then turned to Mrs. Pickersgill. "Caroline, will you do me the honor of introducing your friend?"

Caroline did as she was bid, and upon the pronouncement of her companion's name, Lavinia cocked her head to the side. "Pickersgill," she said. "What an odd surname, but it is strangely familiar."

Rosemary glanced at Caroline, and her expression seemed to convey surprise and perhaps a hint of dread.

Caroline, wishing to divert the conversation away from her companion, said, "A unique surname such as Pickersgill is bound to attract undue notice, I am sure, even if it is not attached to a family of dignity."

"Yes, I suppose that is so." Lavinia gestured toward the grouping of furniture where she had previously reclined. "Now, do sit down, and I shall ring for tea."

The visiting party walked dutifully to select their seats while Lavinia strode across the large chamber and rang the bell. As she made the return trip across the space, she straightened her already perfectly arranged hair and then settled herself on the sofa across from Caroline and her mother.

Lavinia looked much as she had as a schoolgirl—a lithe figure, unblemished skin, and wavy dark hair that had been the envy of more than one young lady of their acquaintance. She gave all the appearance of a distant, untouchable aristocrat. Indeed, with the sun's rays and the distance between the furniture, this was far from the intimate reunion for which Caroline had hoped.

In short course, a maid arrived with a tray, poured the visitors' tea, and then crossed the room to deliver the beverage to her mistress. The maid was of diminutive stature, and her small steps made the trip from sofa to sofa seem as though it were a journey of a thousand miles.

"Will there be anything else, madam?" the maid asked.

Clearly annoyed, Lavinia looked to her servant, saying, "No, you may go."

The maid offered a slight curtsey and made the trip from the sitting area to the door with admirable endurance.

Caroline picked up her teacup and saucer. The china was so fine that it was nearly translucent, and the aroma of the tea was so heartening that she almost sighed.

"This tea is lovely, Lavinia."

"I am so glad it pleases you," Lavinia said. "And now tell me; is your family in good health?"

And though Caroline despised repeating these bothersome social conventions, she reminded herself that this was the most important call they had paid since her arrival in Kendal and went to the trouble of responding to each inquiry and of asking the proper questions in return. When the requisite dialogue was complete, she searched for a subtle way to steer the discussion in a direction that would result ultimately in an invitation to continue their acquaintance now that they were living within so easy a distance of each other.

Perhaps, Caroline thought, it would be best to remind Lavinia of their former association, their many hours of girlish chitchat while at the seminary, or of their—admittedly sparse—written correspondence over the past years. Such memories might incite feelings of nostalgia, which naturally would lead to a renewal of their friendship.

And this was essential, for Caroline would not allow herself to languish in her exiled state.

Yes, nostalgia was the proper tool.

Caroline lifted her chin and had just resolved to speak of their shared history when the door to the chamber jerked open and in strode William Charlton.

The ladies all rose with alacrity, and Lavinia, with a hand to her breast, said, "Oh! William, you startled me!"

The Honorable Mr. William Charlton, the second son of Lord Charlton and now his heir, appeared equally surprised to have discovered the room to be occupied, and he bowed awkwardly to the gathered ladies. "I do apologize, Lavinia, but I did not realize morning calls were still taking place."

Lavinia's brow furrowed. "It is yet morning, as you see by the position of the sun through the window."

As the rest of the party turned to observe the sun's placement in the sky, Caroline studied Mr. Charlton. She had not seen him in the past few years, but time had been beneficial to him. He had filled out in both height and breadth, but he was still rather thin, and Caroline could not complain about his choice of clothing or coiffure. Yes, he had gone from having all appearances of youth and irresponsibility to improving in manliness, though perhaps not in responsibility.

Or so she had heard.

Mr. Charlton turned away from the window and adjusted the sleeves of his coat, his dark head angled down in concentration. "Yes, yes, apologies again. I have been at the accounts for so long I assumed it must be nearly sunset! But that is neither here nor there, for no matter the hour, I must not neglect our guests." He lifted his eyes and surveyed the women, his gaze stopping briefly at each one. "Mrs. Newton, a pleasure to see you. And will you not introduce me to your companions?"

"This, sir," Mrs. Newton began as she gestured to Caroline, "is my youngest daughter Caroline. Surely, you must remember her from your youth."

"Ah!" he said with a bow. Caroline curtseyed deeply and then raised her eyes with practiced allure to find that his expression had brightened considerably. "I do remember you. Did you not attend the seminary with Lavinia?"

"Indeed, I was most fortunate to spend a great deal of time with your excellent sister while we were both in London as girls."

Mr. Charlton smiled at her, and his polished air and appearance struck Caroline. He certainly had changed.

"And this," continued Mrs. Newton, "is Caroline's companion, Mrs. Pickersgill."

Bow and curtsey were exchanged, and then the ladies returned to their seats. Mr. Charlton took one of the high-backed chairs for himself and smiled broadly at Caroline, saying, "I am very pleased to see you back in the Lake District, Miss Bingley. I do hope you and Mrs. Pickersgill intend a long visit, though I myself would much rather be in Town for the season."

"I could not be in better agreement, Mr. Charlton. I have the greatest fondness for Town and will be very pleased to return there as soon as my visit here is through."

"I do not know, my dear," Mrs. Newton said. A small frown tugged at the corners of her mouth. "I have always had a certain fondness for the countryside. I hope you will not rush back to your brother and his friends in London before regaining some appreciation for the county in which you were born."

"Indeed, Mama, I do not mean any insult to Kendal. I only wanted to convey my preference for a different sort of life, one that contains more variety than may be found in a less populated region. Do not you agree, Lavinia?"

Lavinia seemed momentarily at odds with herself, and Caroline found that rather surprising. But perhaps she had imagined the confusion, for her friend's next words were rather definite. "I prefer Town. The company here is unvaried and tedious, but I will remain as long as I am required, for it is my duty to our family."

Mr. Charlton smiled, tight-lipped and rueful. "I do so wish that such duty had fallen upon neither of us. When Harold departed this mortal coil, he left us quite ensnared. He was so much better suited to the barony, its seat in Parliament, and the overseeing of this estate than I shall ever hope to be. I regret every facet of the situation."

Caroline could not believe that he was foolish enough to value his title so cheaply. "While I certainly feel deep sorrow at your brother's untimely death, I cannot imagine viewing the inheritance of a barony as a thing to be regretted."

"Can you not, Miss Bingley?" asked Mr. Charlton.

"My brother has always been perfectly at ease with his station as second son," Lavinia added.

"I do not deny it! I have no wish to."

Caroline nearly followed her impulse to snort at Mr. Charlton's naïveté and then corrected herself. Less than a month in the country and she was already losing the polish of Town. When she spoke, she made certain that she did so with the highly cultured tone she had affected over the years. "Your beloved brother was a gentleman of the highest order, respected by all who knew him. But it is human nature to improve one's mind and position, is it not?"

Brother and sister remained silent, and sensing a dark turn in their countenances, Caroline struggled to speak, but Rosemary's cultured voice next filled the room. "My friends tell me, Mr. Charlton, that you will be adequate to the title once it becomes yours."

He smiled. "It is clear that Mrs. Newton and Miss Bingley are much too generous in their opinion of me, for I intend to make at best a mediocre member of Parliament. It is only through my sister's good graces that Oak Park remains running at all, for given to my control, it would surely have disintegrated by now."

Caroline nodded. "Mrs. Winton is well suited to running a large household."

Mrs. Newton's large brown eyes studied Lavinia, but she smiled as she said, "It was kind of Mr. Winton to spare you, but it must be difficult for you to endure the separation. I do not like being parted from Mr. Newton when he is required to travel."

"I bear the distance as best I can, Mrs. Newton." Lavinia looked pointedly at her brother before continuing. "And indeed, Mr. Winton has been very generous in sparing me."

Conversation paused as brother and sister exchanged another look, and then Mr. Charlton said brightly, "Shall we all not walk about? I would greatly love an excuse not to return to my papers."

He stood and offered Lavinia his arm, which she ignored. "I believe I shall stay here if Miss Bingley will remain with me," she said, glancing now at Caroline. "I would cherish time to hear what she has been doing these past years."

"I would be honored," Mr. Charlton said as he transferred the offer of his arm to Caroline's mother, "if you would join me, Mrs. Newton. Do give me an excuse not to be about my labors."

Mrs. Newton looked between Lavinia and Caroline before nodding her assent and taking his arm. "I would not wish to hamper your business, Mr. Charlton, but I do hope my daughter will be able to rekindle her friendship with Mrs. Winton, and so I cannot deny you."

"I do so appreciate a woman who cannot deny me," he said with an innocent smile. "And you, Mrs. Pickersgill, can you deny me?"

Mrs. Pickersgill stood. "I am certain I could deny you under the correct circumstances, sir, but I find this is not one of them. I will walk with you and Mrs. Newton."

With that, they disappeared from the room, leaving Lavinia and Caroline to stare at each other across the vast physical distance that separated them.

Caroline had the oddest impression that the divide was composed of more than mere space, but she could not say why she thought that. It must be a fleeting feeling brought on by the sudden silence in the room.

"Do take the seat beside me, my dear, so we can speak more freely." Lavinia gestured toward the space beside her.

Gratefully, Caroline covered the distance, keeping in mind to move without haste, and lowered herself onto the stiff cushions. She gestured about the chamber. "I can see very well that you are suited to keeping your father's household, though I am certain you dislike being away from Mr. Winton so long."

"Yes, Mr. Winton…." Lavinia tapered off and then studied the room as though she were looking for the minutest imperfection in her decor. "I quite fancy myself the queen of the castle here. I take great pride in the daily running of the household, planning meals and such for my brother, but I had much rather not have had reason to come. I dearly miss Harold."

"I have no doubt that you still grieve his loss."

A shadow crossed Lavinia's face, and then the weather seemed to clear. "Harold is very much missed by us all. It was such a disappointment to lose him just when he had come into his own. William, especially, feels the loss, for he must face the prospect of the barony without adequate preparation. Harold would have been a credit to the title."

Caroline recognized what was unspoken. William, of course, was not a credit. He was more like a debt that would never be paid.

"It is a shame, then," she said, "that your eldest brother did not leave an heir."

Lavinia's eyebrows knit together briefly. "Indeed, that was a great loss, but at the very least, the barony is in no danger of being displaced by entail."

"Oh, that is good news indeed. But who is to inherit it? I believed your younger brother to be unwed." A bit of errant disappointment crept into Caroline at the thought of an eligible gentleman of title being taken from the marriage mart.

Why, she had never thought of the younger Mr. Charlton as anyone of significance, but now that he was to be a baron, he was ever so much more attractive.

"Good heavens, no, William is not married," Lavinia said on a laugh, and then she sobered. "Do not misunderstand. I have no intention of speaking ill of my dear brother, but he has a bit of a rakish tendency. He has shown no inclination to marry."

Caroline wondered how true Lavinia's words were. Was there any inducement that might cause Mr. Charlton to marry?

"It is of little consequence, for the title is safe," Lavinia continued. "My own son Samuel is already being groomed for the position. He is set to inherit the title and land, so, you see, it has all fallen to me. I must preserve the house and land and see to providing an heir. The only thing I may not do is sit in Parliament."

She laughed, but it sounded hollow to Caroline's ears.

"Women are, more often than not, left to pick up where their masculine counterparts have fallen short," Caroline said. "Of course, we do not receive credit for our actions. But by all accounts, you have succeeded, Lavinia. I am certain your son will do the title credit."

Then, only because it was the polite conversation topic, she inquired after Samuel. It was Caroline's experience that mothers found no greater pleasure than discussing their children, and opening the subject resulted in long discussions of such things as spittle, babble, and random excreta that, relating to an adult, would have been highly improper.

Apparently, Lavinia was not like other mothers, for she quickly looked around as though Caroline's mention of her young son would cause him to appear. "He is well and with his nurse, I should hope."

"Is he very much grown?"

"Oh, indeed he is. It seemed that he crawled for no longer than a week before he began to walk, and from there, he started running all about Oak Park. I do so love the boy." Lavinia sighed. "But I confess that I much preferred him when I could hold him in my arms like a little doll. But now he is up and dashing about the house. I quite fear for my upholstery."

Caroline felt that perhaps Lavinia wished to discuss another subject, and she did not mind a change in conversation. Children in general were lovely, and they ensured the survival of the family name and property, but one could not speak of them everlastingly.

Caroline caressed the arm of the sofa. "It is lovely fabric."

"Do you like it? I ordered it from the continent, and William did not approve of the expenditure. He ranted for days that the pattern was hideous enough to be hanging in the windows of a squalid coaching inn, but I believe it has quite grown on him now. Why just yesterday, he commented...."

Lavinia spoke on about the fabric for some minutes before a pause came into the conversation. Caroline was preparing to inquire again after Mr. Winton, Lavinia's absent husband, but instead, her friend turned to the topic Caroline had wished to avoid: "I must tell you that when you wrote of your..."—here,

Lavinia paused as if searching for the correct noun—
"…circumstances, I was incensed on your behalf."

"I thank you." Caroline lowered her eyes and began to wonder
if her hastily dashed missive to her old friend had been a wise idea.
She had been desperate to find someone who might share her
outrage over her expulsion from Netherfield, but perhaps she had
shared too much.

No, that could not be the case, for it was right and proper to
have divulged her anger and distress to a friend as dear as Lavinia.
And it was not as if she had shared her full humiliation regarding
Mr. Darcy. No, she had perhaps hinted that she had once had
hopes in his direction, but she was certain that her friend was
unaware of her true feelings on that subject.

"Abominable the way your siblings have treated you," Lavinia
continued. Her voice seemed inordinately loud, and Caroline
looked about her. She had no desire to discuss her situation so
openly with her mother in the house.

Had she happened to hear? Had anyone in the household not
heard?

"Quite so," Caroline agreed more quietly.

"Now, I must know all the details of the situation that brought
you to us, for your last letter was too vague for my tastes. What
occurred to cause your family to behave so abusively?"

Caroline attempted to meet Lavinia's gaze steadily, but she
could not manage it and looked away. The story was far too
embarrassing to be shared. "It is hardly even worth a sentence or
two, much less an entire discussion."

"I can see very well that you have been injured over the
matter."

"Injured! No, indeed. I am outraged." Caroline knew very well
that Lavinia was baiting her into divulging her secrets, but she did
not care. She suddenly needed to commiserate with someone. "I
have done nothing except that which any well-bred woman would
do to protect those she loves. And that is all there is to the matter:
I rightly opposed Charles's marriage to Jane Bennet and attempted
to separate them, and now they are angry with me."

Lavinia sat up straighter, giving the appearance of being
incensed for her friend. "You did only what you believed to be

right. I would have done nothing less had I believed an unsuitable woman cast her eye on Harold. Or even William. They really ought to forgive you."

"But there is nothing that requires their forgiveness! I was protecting my brother from a social climber."

"Of course you were, my dear. We must be careful of our brothers, must we not? Else they would all marry inappropriate women."

Caroline was about to make a suitable reply when she heard her mother's voice in the hallway. "We are grateful for the turn about your sculpture gallery, Mr. Charlton, but I fear we have intruded upon your time long enough."

As the party entered the sitting room, Lavinia asked with a rather blasé tone, "Oh dear, must you go?"

"I fear we must."

"I am sorry to hear that," Mr. Charlton said. "Lavinia, shall we not escort our guests to their conveyance?"

"Indeed." The response came with little energy, but Lavinia stood, and when Caroline did the same, she interlaced their arms together.

As they walked through the marble entry and toward the door, Caroline looked at Lavinia with some trepidation, which she hoped was well concealed. Would Lavinia issue an invitation? To dine? To drive? To do anything? Caroline would accept any of them.

Certainly, Lavinia would not snub her, for they were schoolfellows and friends and had just shared intimate conversation.

But now, as Mr. Charlton assisted her mother into the coach, it was almost too late. She was right behind and would soon be trapped within and back on her way to Newton House.

Finally, the words of salvation came from the lips of Mr. Charlton. "My sister and I would be delighted if you would join our dinner party on Thursday. Everyone in the county is to be present."

Only then did he look to his sister for approval.

From her vantage point on the stairs, Lavinia looked down upon them all. Her features were schooled into elegant perfection, and only the barest hint of a smile appeared on her face as she said, "Yes, indeed, you are most welcome."

"And do bring Mr. Newton and Mr. Rushton along. Would that suit you, ladies?" Mr. Charlton added as he took Caroline's hand and assisted her into the coach.

"We are honored, sir," Caroline said, looking upon Mr. Charlton with new eyes.

The idea that had begun to edge its way into her mind earlier struck her with full force. Yes, here, right before her, was a most tempting situation.

Here was an unwed gentleman who would one day inherit a barony, and he was ripe for the taking. Indeed, he possessed all to which any woman might aspire: land, an ancient family, and a title.

A smile spread across Caroline's face, and she studied him from underneath her eyelashes. Certainly, he was a well-looking man: clean, properly attired, and unspoiled by the stench of trade.

She must admit to having never thought upon him with such designs when he was but the second son, scampering about England and leaving his reputation in tatters. Of course, in the eyes of the elite, a bit of a sullied character was perfectly acceptable.

As if sensing the course of her contemplation, Mr. Charlton turned his dark eyes upon her. Caroline leaned her head away with as much coyness as she could muster given her current turn of thought.

Yes, this would solve all her problems. A union with Mr. Charlton would accomplish so much. She would no longer be required to humiliate herself by groveling before Miss Elizabeth Bennet in order to return to her former life. Her welcome at Pemberley would be renewed simply by virtue of the fact that she would one day be Lady Charlton, and who would not want the wife of a baron in their household? Her brother and sister would again invite her into their company, and finally, finally, she would be able to rest comfortably in the fact that all her education, improvements, and accomplishments would prove her worthy. She would be shed of the yoke of the middling classes, and her family's legacy would be secure.

Seven

"What an unfortunate evening for Mrs. Winton's dinner party," Caroline said more to herself than to the other occupants of Mr. Newton's coach. "The weather has ruined everything, and we shall arrive quite soaked through."

Showers had been threatening all day, and by the time the good people of Newton House pointed their carriage in the direction of Oak Park, rain was descending from the sky in cords.

Foul weather was quite a vexing prospect, for Caroline had been many hours at her dressing table and had used the service of more than one of her mother's maids in preparing her clothing and coiffure for the evening. She wanted to be certain that every nuance of her appearance was perfect, and as near as she could tell in the smallish looking glass in her bedchamber, she had accomplished her goal.

She had chosen every article of clothing to accentuate the fact that she was no longer a little girl. She could not afford to be viewed as nothing more than the youngest child of a neighboring family. She must be seen as a woman, capable and accomplished.

Yet she must also be seen as fresh and youthful, and so she had chosen to arrange her hair in ringlets, which she had always fancied as the most becoming option. Instead of the ostentatious hair adornments she had chosen in London, Caroline opted for three strings of pearls to be woven through her tresses. The effect was most pleasing. She appeared both mature enough to be considered for marriage to a baron and young enough not to be perceived as being in danger of imminent old-maidenhood.

It had been a delicate balance to achieve.

And now it was raining, and all her preparation would be for naught if her hair were to be ruined.

Across from her in the carriage, Mr. Rushton glanced at her with a sardonic eye and responded to her complaint about the weather, saying, "Yes, Miss Bingley, we shall all catch our deaths from mild discomfort."

Caroline narrowed her eyes at him. "You deliberately misunderstand me. I meant only that Mrs. Winton has chosen an ill night for a party."

"I misunderstand nothing." His blue eyes held a knowing quality that vexed her greatly. "I understand very well to what you were referring. You feared for your silken slippers in all this mud, did you not?"

"Indeed, I did not," she said truthfully, for she had feared for her hair.

His gaze had traveled to the slippers in question, and Caroline pulled her feet into a position that she hoped was out of his view, for she did not relish the idea of his looking at so intimate a detail of her person.

He did not respond, but only looked at her with a hint of a smile playing about his lips.

"I meant, Mr. Rushton," she said, adopting her most superior tone, "that weather of this sort does nothing for one's demeanor or digestion."

"I am sure that the rain may also be blamed if the evening's selection of meats should turn out to be overcooked."

"Do not be absurd, Mr. Rushton. Poorly prepared food has nothing to do with climatic issues. Surely, that may be blamed on the servants."

"Surely." He then lapsed into silence, but he continued to look at her with the hint of a smile. Caroline met his stare for as long as she thought proper and then glanced away, returning again to her previous musings.

Worse than weather and the possibility of overcooked meat was Caroline's trepidation of meeting again with Mr. Charlton and his guests in the presence of her less-than-socially-apt party. Would her tenuous association with the foremost family in the neighborhood survive the combination of Mr. Newton and Mr. Rushton? Would Mrs. Pickersgill behave as a proper companion and remain pleasantly silent for the duration of the evening?

One glance at Mrs. Pickersgill in her evening ensemble told her that she made a refined, if somewhat uncooperative, picture. She sat with her hands folded in her lap, but her smirk showed how much she had relished the exchange between Caroline and Mr. Rushton. It could be a bad omen if one's companion took so much pleasure in seeing her mistress thus challenged by a gentleman of the middling classes.

Caroline then looked to Mr. Newton, who was as he ever was: largely untouched by any social graces. He sat with a broad smile on his face as he looped an arm around Mrs. Newton and whispered something to her.

Caroline wished very much that he would behave like a gentleman, and she was tempted to say just that. But her mother appeared so happy and at ease that she could not bring herself to disturb her.

Mr. Rushton was not her responsibility, and she would do her best to dissociate from him as soon as was prudent.

When their party arrived at Oak Park, servants greeted them at the coach with umbrellas. Caroline found the entire disembarkation process to be rather untoward as she endeavored to stay out of the blowing rain, all the while dodging puddles, which would certainly ruin several pairs of ladies' silk slippers before the night was through, just as Mr. Rushton had suggested.

Caroline felt a presence at her elbow and found Mr. Rushton there. She narrowed her eyes at him.

"Allow me to help protect your slippers, Miss Bingley, for we simply cannot have them ruined."

Before she gave him leave to assist her physically, his hands grasped her elbow and helped her navigate the path to the door.

Once they had gained footing on the stone staircase of Oak Park, Mr. Rushton shifted slightly, and Caroline found her hand resting demurely on his forearm. Unaware of precisely how she had come to be in that position, Caroline began to experience growing horror at the prospect of entering the house on Mr. Rushton's arm. It would be better to enter unescorted than to be seen on the arm of a gentleman who was a known fortune hunter.

As they ascended the steps, she fought the temptation to shake herself free of him, but it would not do to behave in such a way in so close a proximity to Lavinia and Mr. Charlton or their guests.

She glanced at Mr. Rushton and was even more appalled to find that he was watching her with an expression of amusement. He knew precisely what he was about by putting her in this position, and he was relishing her reaction.

Well!

She tightened her fingers on his arm, feeling the rasp of the fabric of his coat against her kid gloves. "Your assistance is no longer required, Mr. Rushton, and I should thank you to concern yourself with Mrs. Pickersgill's slippers if you are so intent upon being the savior of ladies' footwear, for owning only one good pair, I am certain she would appreciate having them protected from the elements."

Mr. Rushton did not appear to be influenced by her command in the least and only smirked at her. He was clearly aware of her intentions to remove him from her presence, but he was not offended at all. In fact, he seemed to find the situation rather droll, and that mystified Caroline. He ought to be a great deal angrier or perhaps embarrassed at her desire not to enter Oak Park on his arm.

Caroline shook her head slightly at him and continued toward the comparatively arid environment of the entrance hall. She attempted to retain as much dignity as possible as she slipped and slid across the polished stone floors and toward the receiving line.

Mr. Rushton steadied her with a hand to her elbow and laughter in his eyes. "You see, Miss Bingley, if I had acceded to your demands, you would have ended in a puddle on the floor. Now, are you not pleased that I ignored your foolishness?"

Curse Mr. Rushton!

"Indeed, I am not thankful," she said quietly as she pulled herself away from him. Then, louder, she added, "Your services are no longer required as I am on dry ground now, Mr. Rushton."

Based on his jovial countenance as he looked upon her unsteadiness, he could not have been more unconcerned about her treatment of him. He only looked at her with bright blue eyes.

It was unnerving.

Well, she would not look upon him any longer!

Instead, she concentrated on the receiving line.

In total, four and twenty guests had arrived at Oak Park, and to her consternation, Caroline discovered that the number of ladies and gentlemen was unequal, which would make the seating arrangements at dinner a tedious affair, for no female guest had the least desire of being seated beside another lady.

Caroline put the dining dilemma from her mind, trusting that Lavinia would see that she was adequately seated. Instead, she tried her utmost to remember the names and ranks of each person to whom she was introduced, be they lady or gentleman. She had learned that it was to one's best interest to remember as much as possible, for one never knew who might become important in the future.

Of highest consequence, of course, was the Dowager Lady Kentworth, who was adorned in a bulbous gown of copper-colored silk. Caroline found her an awfully small woman to be able to carry such a dress, not to mention such a lofty title, but she seemed to have a keen eye. The older lady appeared to approve of Caroline based upon their introduction alone. After studying her entire appearance from the tips of her slippers to the ringlets in her hair, the Dowager Lady Kentworth had given her a nod accompanied with the words "Very nice, my dear."

Most of the other guests were distinguished in their own ways. They seemed either to be wealthy, from a titled family of an adjacent county, or both. At the very least, most stood to inherit or marry into fortunes or titles. It was the finest society the country could offer.

Caroline wondered again how her little party would fare among such company. It was a testament to her long-standing friendship with Lavinia that they had been invited at all, for though Mr.

Newton was quite one of the wealthiest men in the county, his money was incorrectly gained.

Though Caroline herself was used to moving in the finest circles in Town, her family party certainly was not. When seen in the company of the gathered assembly, they seemed slightly out of sorts. As she surveyed those who were sequestered in the large drawing room for aperitifs and conversation before dinner, it was obvious that her family's clothing was not quite correct and their manners were altogether too relaxed. Mrs. Pickersgill and Mr. Rushton blended somewhat more convincingly, perhaps because they were both youthful and therefore more easily adaptable. That must be the case, for Mrs. Pickersgill's dress was rather plain and Mr. Rushton, well, he was a great nuisance.

Her mother and Mr. Newton, however, had drawn no small amount of attention to themselves already.

They appeared to be conversing with the Dowager Lady Kentworth, and a group of onlookers had gathered around them.

Oh dear.

That could not bode well.

Before Caroline could cross the room to smooth the situation, Mr. Charlton appeared beside her.

"Good evening, Miss Bingley," he said with a bow.

Caroline returned his greeting with a curtsey.

"I observed you here alone, and I had the greatest desire to escape my duties for a few moments." He leaned in closer and whispered, "I am required to dine with the Dowager Lady Kentworth this evening, and I can think of nothing duller than listening to the old lady drone about the past."

Caroline smiled. Mr. Charlton's face was still rather near to hers, and she was able to study him at close proximity. He was a well-looking gentleman indeed, even at such a short distance, which often revealed flaws that could remain unobserved in more distant circumstances. His skin was clear and glowed with health and vigor, and his eyes were framed by the longest eyelashes she had ever seen. Overall, he exuded a charm that was not wholly unappealing to her. "It is impolitic to say such a thing about a woman of such high rank, but," she said as she leaned closer still and inhaled his cologne, "having said that, I do not envy your position."

His grin turned conspiratorial. "Ah! I knew you would agree with me. And now, allow me to ensure for you a slightly more appetizing meal. An aperitif? A glass of sherry?"

She would not have turned down any suggestion he made, and he returned with two small glasses of sherry and his open smile. "Now we can be assured of a truly appetizing meal, for we have had the correct beginning."

"Have we?" Caroline asked as she raised the glass to her lips.

"At the very least, we shall now be slightly more immune to dull conversation, shall we not?"

Caroline sipped her sherry again. "One can only hope it is so."

He laughed and then winced as Lavinia appeared at his arm.

"Oh dear, my keeper has arrived," he said to Caroline, and then he turned to Lavinia. "Have you come to ensure that I do not slip out the rear door before the meal begins?"

Lavinia did a poor job of concealing her annoyance.

"Mrs. Winton," Caroline said as a means of distraction, "I must compliment you on this lovely assembly. It is a great testament to you and your family to have such faithful friends with whom to dine."

Lavinia smiled. "And now you are counted among their number."

Caroline dipped her head, as if embarrassed by her friend's words, but truly, she was concealing her pleasure at having reinstalled herself amongst the acquaintances of the first family of the neighborhood. "I thank you for it."

"You will perform a small favor for me, will you not, Miss Bingley?"

Caroline could not but agree as Lavinia wrapped her silk-clad arm around Caroline's and led her gently from the center of the room, where she had purposefully positioned herself to be seen to the best advantage, toward the doorway through which she had originally entered.

"Certainly, I will perform any service you require of me." Caroline was pleased to assist her friend, for it spoke of their close relationship and would make her appear indispensible.

"William has insisted that I invite several guests of the lower social orders," Lavinia said softly so that her brother could not hear, and she looked around the room as if seeking out each lower-class offender. "And I do have some concern regarding their behavior tonight."

Caroline nodded and also looked about the room. "That is an understandable fear."

"If you, my dear, would be so kind as to occupy Miss Brodrick until dinner?"

"Which is Miss Brodrick?"

Lavinia pointed out a pale, slight creature who was sitting alone at the back of the room.

"Come, I shall introduce you."

The trio crossed the room to the young lady in question, and when they had drawn close enough, Lavinia said, "Miss Brodrick, I have the greatest desire to introduce you to our dear Miss Bingley."

Lavinia made the introductions, the ladies curtseyed to one another, and as she straightened again, Caroline took her first notice of the young lady.

Miss Brodrick appeared to be of no more than seventeen years, and she was everything that was fragile and slight. Even her face seemed small and was composed of delicate features and porcelain skin. Her hair was of the finest blonde coloration and decorated with a small white feathered ornament.

"Miss Bingley, it is an honor," said Miss Brodrick in a soft voice, and Caroline had to lean closer to hear her properly.

"It is equally my honor, I assure you," Caroline lied. She could not have cared less to have made her acquaintance, but it had proved her value to Lavinia, and that was all that was necessary to make her amenable.

"Miss Brodrick is recently returned from one of our old haunts, Miss Bingley," Mrs. Winton said.

"Oh?" Caroline asked, though she was quite uninterested.

"She was also a student at ladies' Eton."

"Ah, yes? Such a beneficial education for a young lady to receive," Caroline said with a glance at Mr. Charlton. "And you have certainly been admitted to society that will only serve to improve upon it."

"Yes," Miss Brodrick said in her whispered voice, "Mr. Charlton and Mrs. Winton have been very gracious in inviting me to attend."

"I do hope you will continue to think me gracious after I steal my brother away for a few moments," Lavinia said as she transferred her arm from Caroline's to her brother's. "A host's duties are never complete, it seems."

"Oh dear," Mr. Charlton said, "I must be away."

"Yes, the Dowager Lady Kentworth requires your presence." He rolled his eyes, and Lavinia sighed. "Do not be difficult, William."

Mr. Charlton bowed first to Miss Bingley and then to Miss Brodrick. "You will excuse me. It seems I must see to my duty, but you, Miss Brodrick, are in excellent care. Miss Bingley will ensure that you are not without amusing conversation."

"Excellent," Lavinia said as she held to her brother's arm and walked with him through the crowd toward the far end of the room, which held the entrance to the dining room.

Though she had the impression that he would like to slink away like a chastised child, Caroline watched as Mr. Charlton straightened his back and walked with dignity toward the opposite end of the room.

Caroline turned to Miss Brodrick. "Indeed, we shall enjoy becoming further acquainted, shall we not, Miss Brodrick?" Despite her disappointment in Mr. Charlton's departure, her pleasure in his kind words made her more able to bear it. "And so, tell me, who is your family?"

Miss Brodrick stepped back slightly, but responded with little hesitation. "My father owns a graphite mill."

"Graphite?" Caroline attempted to conceal her distaste. "I was unaware that the product was still being mined."

"Not mined, Miss Bingley. Milled."

"I see," she said, although she did not really know or care to know the difference.

"My father imports raw graphite from France and processes it so that it can be formed into proper English pencils."

"He sounds a very industrious man, though"—Caroline lowered her voice—"I would caution you, Miss Brodrick, not to make your family's dealings in trade so very public."

Miss Brodrick looked at her with pale blue eyes full of questions. "Why ever not?"

"Darling, have you learned nothing in Queen's Square?"

"I learned a great many things, Miss Bingley, among which was to value the livelihood that allowed me to be sent there."

"You may be grateful, but not quite so vocally, certainly."

"I shall not dissemble, Miss Bingley," said the pale creature. "I feel no shame; neither shall I pretend to."

"Then it shall be to your detriment," Caroline warned. "For you must realize how lowly the better classes regard such a history."

Miss Brodrick did not appear to give adequate weight to Caroline's words before she said with quiet confidence, "Then I suppose I shall just have to risk being seen as an oddity. It does not bother me, and neither should it trouble you."

"I assure you it does not. It was advice kindly meant."

"And it is kindly rejected, Miss Bingley, but I trust it will not damage our acquaintance."

Caroline smiled. Silly girl. They had no such acquaintance.

But she said, "Certainly not."

The conversation lulled, and Caroline turned to discover that Lavinia had begun the subtle organization of guests that preceded their entry into the dining area. The Dowager Lady Kentworth was already on Mr. Charlton's arm, and they were proceeding out of the drawing room. The rest of the assembly followed suit.

Caroline looked around as a feeling of panic descended over her. Everyone, it seemed, had found their escort—all except her and Miss Brodrick.

In a party composed of an uneven number of ladies and gentlemen, it was vital to secure a male dining companion early, but now it was almost too late. Caroline found herself in the company of a female and quite at the back of the party.

If she did not act quickly indeed, she would be doomed to dine in the company of Miss Brodrick.

Disaster!

She had hoped to wrangle the arm of an unattached gentleman and then select a seat as near to Mr. Charlton as possible. She would then ensure that she was well within his line of sight as she charmed her dinner partner, whomever he should be, with elegant conversation and wit.

Mr. Charlton would see what a desirable partner she was and seek her out for conversation after dinner.

A marriage proposal would be the next logical step, of course.

But now, her plan was spoiled, and she must reverse the damage if she possibly could. And quickly.

First, her eyes sought her mother and Mr. Newton. Perhaps they had been chatting with a gentleman on whose arm she could enter. She caught sight of their backs as they left the drawing room. She was already too late.

Next, she searched out Lavinia. Perhaps her friend had thought to hold aside a gentleman for her. Lavinia would prove a strong ally, certainly.

No, as Caroline looked about the chamber, she could not locate Lavinia. Likely, she was already in the dining room to see everyone comfortably settled.

Last, she looked, and not without a certain amount of desperation, for Rosemary and Mr. Rushton. Perhaps they had managed to enter a conversation with a gentleman with whom she might dine. Or, at the very least, perhaps she could enter on Mr. Rushton's arm.

If she must.

She spotted them sauntering along as if they had all the time in the world while the room emptied as guests were lured toward the scents of the meal that had been tempting them. Caroline hurried across the large drawing room toward the stragglers.

She had traversed half of the cavernous chamber when Lavinia emerged from the dining room and looked about the drawing room.

"Oh dear, Miss Bingley, I had thought you were already seated," she said. "What do you do all the way over there?"

"I…" Caroline paused as she studied Lavinia, who must have recalled leaving her at the back of the room to entertain Miss Brodrick not a quarter hour before. "I was detained."

"Ah, well, that is unfortunate indeed. And Miss Brodrick too has dawdled, I see." She ushered Mr. Rushton and Rosemary toward the door and then motioned for the young ladies. "Miss Bingley, do follow the example of your friends and come along, would you?"

Rosemary turned, her eyes seeking her mistress's. Caroline expected to find a haughty expression on the woman's face, but instead, she had the decency to appear embarrassed at entering before her mistress and on the arm of a gentleman when they were so very scarce that evening. Indeed, she was flushed red to the roots of her strawberry blond hair.

Good.

She may have the distinguishment of entering on Mr. Rushton's arm, but she would do so looking as red as a poppy.

Caroline attempted a look of nonchalance, but inwardly she seethed. To be forced to walk behind her companion. Her servant!

"Come, come!" Lavinia called to her again though they were practically side by side now. "Let us join the others. I fear, however, that you will not like your seat."

As soon as they crossed the threshold into the dining room, Caroline was escorted in the opposite direction whence Mr. Rushton and Rosemary had traveled to the other end of the long table, and Caroline did not mind being separated from them. Adequate distance was of the highest import, for she feared what she might say.

The evening was not going at all according to her plan. Mr. Rushton may have thought it appropriate to joke about it, but clearly, the rain had been an indication of the unfortunate course the evening would follow.

The dining table was so long that it would be well nigh impossible for conversation to flow between those seated at the head and those at its foot. Mr. Charlton was, of course, at its head, and Caroline found herself being directed to the midsection of the table, closer to the foot. She had no hope even of overhearing conversation that might prove useful later. All she could hear at the moment was the scrape of chairs' legs across the floor as servants assisted the guests to be seated.

Though she attempted to prevent it, her eyes sought Mr. Rushton and Rosemary. She watched him escort her to a pair of empty chairs near the head of the table—talking to a lady here, laughing with a gentleman there—and she felt her face flush with anger.

Still, Caroline would comport herself with dignity. She must do so, she reminded herself, in order to carry her plan to satisfactory completion. And though her first attempt at drawing nearer to Mr. Charlton had been thwarted, she would not give up.

It mattered not that the evening had begun in a manner so far at odds with her original design; it could be salvaged yet.

She must focus on the benefits she might glean from her current position.

She glanced at her dinner companion and discovered Miss Brodrick to be eyeing her.

Caroline already knew she would gain nothing from an association with her, so she looked across the low candle flames to those on the opposite side of the table.

There, she found a gentleman of middling age with a woman entirely too young to be his wife seated beside him. She could not remember having met either of them.

The room grew quiet, and Mr. Charlton stood and offered a few words of welcome before the servants began ladling soup for each guest.

While the servants went about their tasks, Caroline looked to her family party.

Neither her mother nor Mr. Newton seemed to notice her consternation over the order of entrance, but Mr. Rushton, it seemed, was not so dense. He was watching her, his roguish blue eyes shining.

Yes, oblivious though he seemed, she knew that he comprehended her dilemma perfectly and was reveling in it. He took pleasure in her awkwardness. It likely made him feel better about his own ineptitude and gracelessness. He appeared on the verge of smirking at her, but then he offered her a small half smile. It conveyed, well, a sort of camaraderie. That made little sense.

Perhaps Caroline was misreading him. She was looking at him from across the vast expanse of the dining table after all.

Caroline raised her chin and looked purposefully away.

ꙮ Eight ꙮ

Caroline was concentrating on arranging her skirts under the dining table to prevent as many wrinkles as possible when she felt a small tap on her arm. She looked down at the appendage, almost expecting to find that an insect of some sort had landed on her.

It was very nearly an insect. It was Rosemary Pickersgill. She was leaning close, her fingers resting on Caroline's arm.

Caroline concealed her surprise with irritation, narrowing her eyes at the woman.

"Miss Bingley?" Rosemary voice came quietly, but it arrested Caroline's movements almost as if it had been a shout. She looked at her companion, who seemed to be considering her words with extreme care. "I know this is very untoward, but something of great urgency has occurred to me and I must speak with you privately."

Caroline gaped at Rosemary. "What? Now?"

The soup had been served, and, in near unison, the members of the party had appropriated the proper utensil and were dipping delicately at their fare.

"If you please."

Could any more social faux pas occur this evening? Caroline hardly thought it was possible. It appeared that she had little choice but to leave the table and exit the room. She followed her companion into the drawing room and turned to face her. "What is it?" she whispered with as much harshness as she could muster. "Can you not see that dinner has begun?"

Rosemary hesitated, gave her a considering look, and then studied the floor.

"Stop looking at your toes, and tell me why you have dragged me out here!" Caroline demanded.

Another hesitation. Then, Rosemary spoke. "I could not sit down to a meal with you staring at me as if I had done you a desperate wrong."

"I hardly think this is the time for a discussion on all the ways in which I have been wronged by you," Caroline said. "We ought not to have left the table, and our absence will undoubtedly cause vexation to Mr. Charlton and Mrs. Winton. If their dinner party is ruined, I shall not shelter you from their wrath."

Caroline was intent on returning, but Rosemary's hand stopped her. "As your companion, Miss Bingley, I must explain." Her eyes appeared weary, as if she were the one who had become frustrated with their conversation. "Mr. Rushton would not allow me to leave his side."

"Lovely," Caroline said. "You make a very nice pair indeed."

Yes, they were well suited—insolent both of them.

"I attempted to decline, to take your place at the table amidst the unpaired women, but it is impossible to thwart him."

Caroline could hardly argue with that, for it seemed that Mr. Rushton often contrived to gain exactly what he desired, but she would not concede the point to Rosemary.

Instead, she looked down at the woman with as much pride as possible and said, "Well now, you have told me. Let us return."

Expecting Rosemary to tromp ahead of her, Caroline hesitated, but upon finding that the woman remained unmoving, she swept back into the dining room ahead of her.

The room was now filled with the low murmur of conversation and the clinking of glassware as liveried servants poured wine. Upon her reentry, one of the servants pulled out the chair beside Mr. Rushton, the very one that Rosemary had vacated, and waited expectantly for Caroline to take it.

And so she did.

What good fortune, Caroline thought as she took her rightful place. She watched as Rosemary was seated beside Miss Brodrick, who smiled at her new dining partner. Yes, they would do nicely now that their places were reversed.

She glanced about her to see if anyone had noticed the shift. Aside from the somewhat confused nods of her new dining companions, no one acknowledged the change.

Caroline smiled. Her situation had improved undeniably, for she was seated far nearer to her object, Mr. Charlton. Though she could not converse comfortably with him, she was now settled within a distance that would allow him to admire her without obstruction, and if she were diligent, she might overhear his conversations.

She might hear them if she could manage to ignore Mr. Rushton, with whom she was partnered.

From her left, Mr. Rushton spoke without so much as looking at her. "Mrs. Pickersgill, I find, has abandoned me to your company."

"Yes, she confessed she could not bear you a moment longer and would rather sit alone all evening than be made to suffer another minute with you," Caroline said with satisfaction. "As her superior, I felt it my duty to relieve her of such pain by sacrificing myself to your conversation for the duration of the meal."

Caroline glanced at Mr. Rushton, hoping to find him affronted, but he did not appear to be considering her speech at all. Instead, he was looking at Rosemary. And inconceivably, he was smiling. Rosemary returned it.

Why?

Then Mr. Rushton's eyes turned to Caroline's, his expression knowing and somewhat superior.

And she understood.

Rosemary had pulled her from the room in order to exchange seats, to give Caroline the place of higher honor.

Caroline did not know whether to be angry, embarrassed, or thankful. Anger came the easiest, so she scowled at her companion across the vast expanse of table and candles that separated them.

She refused to be indebted to that woman. After all, Rosemary had only surrendered to Caroline her rightful place at the table. She would not allow one act to change her opinion of this enforced companionship.

But Caroline was no longer doomed to be partnered with a lady for the evening, and against her will, something inside her—a very small portion—softened toward Rosemary Pickersgill. She glanced at her out of the corner of her eye, and Rosemary offered her a small smile.

Caroline frowned again in return.

"That was rather kind of your Mrs. Pickersgill, do not you agree?" Mr. Rushton asked with a deceptively companionable tone.

"Kind?" Caroline would never admit it.

"Yes, kind. She observed you seething down there at the foot of the table beside sweet Miss Brodrick, and she had mercy on you."

"Mercy was not her motivation. I am certain she was more interested in retaining her position within my household than anything else."

"Yes, I find I quite like Mrs. Pickersgill," Mr. Rushton said as if he had not heard a word Caroline spoke. "I am surprised that you would find such a charming companion who would remain so faithful."

To suggest that some flaw existed in Caroline that would prevent her from gathering faithful friends was ridiculous. She was preparing to chastise him severely for his audacity when she found him smirking at her openly.

He was baiting her and quite enjoying himself in the process.

Well!

Caroline would not give him the satisfaction of a fight. Instead, she said simply, "I find I do not like you, Mr. Rushton."

Then she cut her eyes demurely toward the head of the table, foregoing any further attempts at conversation with Mr. Rushton in exchange for observing Mr. Charlton as discreetly as possible through the soup course.

ஆ௸ ௸ஆ

Dinner proceeded as dinners invariably do. Servants deposited food before the diners, removed the soiled dishware, and replaced it with another course. Soon, the soup bowls were gone in favor of Lavinia's finest china plates, which had been arranged artfully with beef, quail, boiled potatoes, and assorted vegetables.

Caroline and Mr. Rushton ignored each other quite charmingly through the early courses, but soon, as other dinner partners spoke, their silence grew more noticeable.

"We must hold some discourse, Mr. Rushton," Caroline said.

"Ah," he replied. "So you have decided I am a worthy companion after all."

"I would not say you were worthy, but you are my evening's companion nonetheless. We must make the best of it."

Mr. Rushton smiled, and candlelight seemed to shimmer in his eyes. "I am surprised to find that you have such a practical bent, Miss Bingley."

"Indeed, I am quite practical when it is required. I have run my brother's household for several years, and my reputation as a hostess is impeccable, I assure you, though I always maintained the strictest of budgets. My management was unimpeachable."

"I see," he said, leaning back and pretending to look under the table, "that you are not one for frivolous purchases, such as silken slippers and pearls for your hair."

Caroline met his challenge fully. "There are moments, Mr. Rushton, when even the most austere woman splurges. I enjoy the finer things, and I always will, but I am not a squanderer of fortune."

She eyed his fine suit. "And you, sir, are finely attired this evening," she said, only mildly shocked at herself for commenting on someone's attire in public. "You are not moderate in all your purchases, I see."

"You have me there, Miss Bingley. I am not always moderate. At times, my passion quite gets away from me. We may not be so different after all."

"Perhaps not," Caroline said, though she was not convinced.

He lapsed into neutral topics, which required of her little by way of response, and thus their pleasant truce endured straight through dessert.

But no longer.

After the meal, Caroline retired dutifully into the drawing room with the other ladies, while the gentlemen remained behind to smoke, consume port, and carry on without them. She hoped to catch Lavinia alone so that she might be in her presence when the gentlemen—most especially her brother—joined them. Then, perhaps, she might find the opportunity to charm Mr. Charlton a bit since dinner had proven an impractical venue for flirtation.

However, this did not come to pass in quite the way she had hoped.

Rosemary entered the room after the other ladies had already assembled, and Caroline wondered vaguely where she had gotten herself, but she decided not to take the trouble of asking. It mattered not where she had been. She could not make any mischief if the gentlemen were busy smoking and the ladies were all in the drawing room.

Rosemary looked about the room, and upon seeing her mistress quite alone, she approached. Their conversation would have seemed benign to any eavesdroppers, but in actuality it was a cryptic treaty.

"Had you a pleasant meal, Miss Bingley?" *Can we make peace?*

"Tolerable." *I suppose it may not be necessary to be enemies.*

"May I join you?" *I am here at your brother's request, but that does not mean I must be a hindrance to you. Did I not see that you were settled more happily in the dining room?*

"I suppose there is room on the sofa, but take care not to crush my gown." *I understand your gesture of kindness earlier this evening, but do not allow yourself to believe that we are now friends. We are simply not enemies. And do take care not to crush my gown.*

"I will take care." *I understand.*

Rosemary sat carefully beside Caroline, and the two women remained for a time without speaking. The silence could have been awkward, but Caroline found the quiet companionship rather pleasant. Groups chattered around them, and the gentlemen soon returned.

Mr. Charlton entered, and after speaking briefly with Lavinia, Caroline was pleased to see him pour himself a glass of sherry and meander toward the sofa where she and Rosemary were seated.

Though she was tempted to shoo her companion, Caroline held her tongue. Instead, she smiled at Mr. Charlton and asked, "I thought you believed sherry to be the ideal aperitif, but is it also your choice for digestif as well?"

"Sherry was the first decanter available, and I do so despise waiting." He leaned forward, his dark hair falling in his eyes, and continued. "Generally, I prefer brandy, which has a much more calming effect on the stomach, especially after a questionable meal."

"You found the meal questionable?" Rosemary inquired.

"No indeed, and that is why I found it perfectly acceptable to have sherry in the place of brandy. My stomach did not require calming." As though to demonstrate proof of the quality of the meal, he finished the sherry in one long sip and then placed the glass on the side table. Then he glanced at Caroline with meaning. "My mind, however, did require a little soothing."

He was referring to his tedious conversation with the Dowager Lady Kentworth no doubt.

"I quite know how you must be feeling," Caroline said with a quick glance at Miss Brodrick and Mr. Rushton, who were engaged in conversation nearby.

He followed her gaze and then smiled. "Ah," he said. "Yes, we are not always free to associate with those of our choosing, are we?"

Mr. Charlton paused as he seemed to contemplate Miss Brodrick or perhaps his lack of freedom; Caroline could not be certain. Then, without preamble, he turned his lean body back to them and said, "And now, ladies, shall we not discuss a socially acceptable subject of great import and dreadful dullness?" He grinned, clasped his hands behind his back, and rose briefly to his toes. "What topics are of interest to you? Politics? War with France? Travel? Farming? Literature? What is your pleasure?"

"I am certain that you shall find Miss Bingley is well versed on any subject," Lavinia said, having descended unseen upon them. Apparently, they had left their flank unguarded. "But she is much in demand at the pianoforte."

Though Caroline was ordinarily appreciative when her friends offered her the opportunity of exhibiting at the pianoforte, she could not have been more displeased at Lavinia's timing. She wished for nothing more than to continue conversing uninterrupted with Mr. Charlton. "Oh, it is very kind of you to ask, Lavinia. But I beg you not to require it of me, for I am not in the humor for music tonight."

"But you must play for us, my dear. I shall appeal to your mother to persuade you if you will not agree."

And upon those words Lavinia called Mrs. Newton to join them, saying, "Caroline says she shall not play tonight. Do convince her."

Mrs. Newton appeared surprised. Her eyebrows were raised upon her plump face. "Oh, I would be so disappointed not to hear you this evening."

"You are both very kind," Caroline said as she glanced toward the pianoforte, which was settled far to one side of the room. She happened to glance at Mr. Rushton, and after recalling his vague insults regarding the rehearsed nature of her playing, she felt even less inclined to exhibit. "I had not the least intention of playing tonight."

"Nonsense," Lavinia said, as she pulled Caroline from her place beside Rosemary and led her toward the instrument. She leaned in close and whispered, "Do not be cross, my dear. Not only will this show your talents to their best advantage, but it will ease some tensions that are developing between Mr. and Mrs. Palmer."

She nodded in the general direction of the hearth, and Caroline observed a couple, the Palmers, obviously in the throes of some sort of heated debate.

"That," Lavinia continued with a sniff, "is why I am so thankful that Mr. Winton is so often away. We have no time to develop tensions."

Though she doubted that a few musical notes would do a thing to improve the course of the Palmers' marriage, Caroline relented. "If you insist, I shall play."

Lavinia did insist. In fact, she practically shoved Caroline onto the stool and then called out to the room in general, "Miss Bingley, my oldest friend, will now delight us all with a song."

All eyes in the room were now upon her, and Caroline began to feel a prickly, heated sensation radiate across her body. It felt strangely akin to nervousness, which was ridiculous, for she knew several appropriate pieces by heart.

Nervous? No. It was Mr. Rushton.

His oblique insult to her playing had shaken her confidence. That was all.

Caroline closed her eyes and took a moment to compose herself. Then, with purposeful hands, she arranged her skirts, which had wrinkled when Lavinia pushed her onto the stool, and finally made a great pretense of riffling through the music books before her.

She selected a volume of Italian airs. This particular collection was unknown to her, but as she studied the tiny black notes that danced across the page, she felt a little thrill of delight.

If Mr. Rushton believed her former performance had been too studied, then she would unleash upon him her talent for sight-reading. He would soon see that her accomplishments went far beyond simply memorizing a few show pieces.

No, she was truly a musician.

As she placed her fingers on the keys, her vision seemed to contract, and the music became her whole world. Gone were the arguing Palmers. Forgotten were Mr. Charlton and Lavinia. Even Mr. Rushton and his snide remarks receded.

Energy washed through her, and she began to play.

Perhaps her performance lacked a bit of polish and—though she was unwilling to admit it—her fingers did misplace themselves on occasion, but her listeners did not seem displeased. When she chanced a glance away from the page, she noticed several toes tapping.

She played three tunes and decided to stop, for it seemed an appropriate number. It was always best to leave one's audience desiring to hear more.

As Caroline sounded the final notes, she happened to glance at Mr. Rushton, who was looking at her with an odd expression. He was leaning against the far wall, arms crossed in front of his chest, feet crossed below him. He was studying her, but she could not discern any criticism in his expression.

Excellent.

A smile of victory spread across Caroline's lips.

Yes, her proficiency had impressed Mr. Rushton, and that gave her great pleasure indeed.

The rest of the room's occupants looked upon her with admiration, except for the Palmers, who were glaring at each other across the mantelpiece. At least they were no longer arguing.

"Shall you not delight us again, Caroline?" Lavinia asked.

Caroline knew that this was a query born more from politeness than a true desire for her to continue, so she declined. The interlude had served its purpose. The Palmers were silent, and it was time for her to relinquish the stage, which she did.

Caroline had many flaws—indeed, she admitted it—but the propensity of exhibiting too long was not among them. As she lifted herself from the stool, she looked over her shoulder at Mr. Rushton. He was yet watching her, and though she could not explain it, she felt herself blushing under his gaze.

∽ Nine ∾

Mr. Rushton should not be Caroline's concern. Her hopes lay in an altogether more superior object, and as she made her way back to the sofa, she discovered that her object, Mr. Charlton, awaited her there.

Mr. Charlton had engaged Rosemary in conversation. Much to her surprise, he seemed more than willing to condescend to her, waiving the privileges of his rank to hold what appeared to be a pleasant conversation with a paid companion.

As Caroline walked as gracefully as she could across the room, hoping to offer just the right amount of sway to her hips and allure to her gaze, Mr. Charlton stopped mid-word. He smiled overtly at her, and she knew she had accomplished her aim. Perhaps Mr. Darcy did not discern the merits of her movement, but Mr. Charlton apparently did.

Strangely, the thrill she had hoped to feel at catching the gentleman's interest did not spark within her.

But she smiled at him anyway as he stood to make room for her to sit.

"Ah! Miss Bingley, I had forgotten how well you played. The years have only served to improve your abilities, I think."

"I thank you, sir," she said as she lowered herself to the sofa, made great pretense of arranging her skirts, and met his eyes. "I do find much enjoyment in music."

"And it certainly was evident in your performance this evening. I do not believe my sister's pianoforte has ever sounded quite that lively."

Caroline lowered her gaze. "I thank you."

She smiled to herself. Mr. Charlton, thank heaven, seemed much more easily impressed than the dreadful Mr. Rushton.

"And I was just saying as much to Mrs. Pickersgill." He turned toward her. "Do you play as well?"

"I play a bit, sir, but very ill," she replied.

"Yes," Caroline interjected, "I am certain Mrs. Pickersgill would do well to avail herself of my mother's instrument while we are in Kendal."

Mrs. Pickersgill gave Caroline a bland look. "I do not believe any level of practice could improve my playing. I was not born to it, but I thank you for your kind offer."

The party was silent for a moment, and then Mr. Charlton spoke to Mrs. Pickersgill. "I do not believe you have yet had the opportunity to see much of Cumbria."

"Indeed, I have yet to see much of the area, sir." Her face had returned to a somewhat distant expression, and Caroline noted her well-moderated tone of voice and the manner in which she held herself. She sat like a lady, ankles crossed, hands in her lap, back erect. She did possess a certain amount of grace. She appeared to be any genteel young lady and not the unwanted companion that she was. "But it is a vast deal different from my home county."

"And from what exotic, mysterious land have you come?" Mr. Charlton asked. "I do not believe I had a chance to inquire when last we spoke."

"No, I do not believe so, sir." Rosemary laughed politely then, and said, "My family hails from the exotic county of Shropshire."

Mr. Charlton threw his head back, exposing a smooth, strong throat, and laughed loud and long. Then he turned his smile again to Rosemary. "I had no idea that Shropshire was so exotic and mysterious."

"One would not think that Shropshire holds many beauties," she said seriously, "but I have found that each county has unique charms of its own."

"Yes," Mr. Charlton said, giving her what appeared to Caroline to be an ironic look. His face was appraising and his eyebrows were raised, but a smile lingered. "Unique charms indeed."

Rosemary did not respond, and Mr. Charlton continued, "And how did you become acquainted with the family? Miss Bingley, I do not recall hearing that your family was connected with that part of the country."

"No indeed, we have no connections there," Caroline said. She was preparing to respond to his question regarding the nature of their first acquaintance, but she realized abruptly that she did not know how her brother had met this woman.

Mrs. Pickersgill said, "I became acquainted with Miss Bingley's brother in London."

"Ah! How very vague an explanation you offer, Mrs. Pickersgill. But of course, I must excuse you, for it is clear why Miss Bingley, who has exquisite taste, opted to make you her companion."

"And why might that be, Mr. Charlton?" Caroline asked. "Do enlighten us."

"Why, because she gives the appearance of a lady of worth, and you would choose nothing less for your companion, would you not?"

Caroline acknowledged his words with a nod, but she greatly wished the conversation might turn in another direction. "I do prefer to surround myself with the best company, and my family holds Mrs. Pickersgill in high regard."

"And well they should," said Mr. Charlton, "for she seems an amiable creature."

The amiable creature in question only offered a small smile.

❧ ❧

The dinner party at Oak Park concluded well after midnight, and the Newtons, Mr. Rushton, Rosemary, and Caroline departed for Newton House through cold and wet darkness. She undressed quickly with the help of a servant, and soon she lay down on the cold sheets and closed her eyes, but she found that sleep would not come.

Having kept these wretched country hours for so many weeks, Caroline ought to have slumbered easily, for early hours, morning calls, and polite conversation with one's neighbors was often more taxing than it sounded.

Caroline rolled to her side and looked out the rain-streaked window. The landscape was barely visible in the semi-dark, but she could see the silhouettes of the trees as they blew in the cold wind.

It was most beautiful, and yet somehow also it caused an ache within her breast.

How she missed Town. How she ached to be returned to those golden days when she had traveled with her brother and Mr. Darcy before the discovery of the Bennet sisters.

But now, she had fallen.

Hers, at least, was a quiet descent. Her family and friends had silently set her aside, but that was enough.

She had once again become Miss Caroline Bingley, the daughter of no one in particular.

By discovering the presence of Lavinia and the advent of a new gentleman to inherit the barony, Caroline's despair at her future prospects had been reversed.

This was her only opportunity.

Certainly, Mr. Charlton and Lavinia knew of her past. They knew precisely from whence her family's fortune came. They were acquainted with Mr. Newton, the bridge builder. And though she had been much frightened by Lavinia's laxity in paying a call and her apparent hesitation to invite her to dine at Oak Park, she was now certain of her acceptance there.

That family represented Caroline's salvation.

She had planned to pursue Mr. Charlton at a leisurely pace, allowing him to fall in love with her and propose just in time for her to join him as his wife for the London season, but after having been at Oak Park that evening and in his company, she was suddenly reinvigorated. She simply did not want to wait.

Her failures at the dinner party were the results of chance. Circumstances had hardly allowed her to converse with Mr. Charlton. She had been pulled away by Miss Brodrick, shackled to Mr. Rushton at dinner, and required to play the pianoforte. She had not a moment alone with her object, and that was required to win a gentleman, was it not? She must contrive to find him alone.

Caroline smiled at the thought of being alone with Mr. Charlton. Yes, she would undertake any task, bear any burden, and overcome any obstacle to entice Mr. Charlton.

She sat up in bed at that thought. She felt animated, ready to enact the next phase of her plan, but she could do nothing in the middle of the night.

She lay back down.

She fidgeted with the covers and adjusted her position, but sleep did not come.

Resigning herself to the fact that she was not going to drift easily into pleasant oblivion, Caroline sat up again and struggled to light her candle.

The small flame hardly lit the room, but she could see well enough to move about without crashing into the furniture. In her youth, she had sneaked below stairs to indulge in a bit of biscuit or chocolate and sit by a banked fire alone for a few moments. She longed to do so now.

And so that is precisely what she did.

After donning her wrap and a pair of slippers, she padded to the door, opened it, and peeked down the hall. She saw no one, heard no sound. She could certainly make the trip unnoticed. Of course, she was adequately covered should she come into contact with a male servant, Mr. Newton, or Mr. Rushton.

She did not want to encounter the latter, but she also did not want to remain trapped in her room, unable to sleep.

So Caroline crept down the corridor, feeling like a child in the midst of mischief, and managed to sneak into the kitchen without attracting notice. Caroline did not often enter the kitchen. As a very young child, before her father had made his fortune, she could remember helping her mother with food preparation. She knew that refined young ladies did not undertake such menial tasks. So now, Caroline generally kept as far from that room as possible.

When she had run Netherfield Park, she had consulted with the cook in the library, not the kitchen.

But occasionally, she needed to indulge in a small delicacy, so she would venture in when no one was about to notice, just as she was now.

Newton House's kitchen was designed in much the same manner as the rest of the house. It was arranged for maximum efficiency and comfort, but had little ostentation. Unlike in many of the finer houses, the room was adjacent to the dining room for the convenience of the servants. Mr. Newton obviously gave no thought to the lingering odors a kitchen was wont to produce and their effects on a lady's furniture. But her mother did not complain.

Caroline entered the pantry, rummaged a bit, and produced a tin of biscuits, which she carried to the large pine worktable that stood at the room's center. Placing the candle at a safe distance on the scrubbed wooden surface, she pulled out a heavy chair and turned it so that it was facing the banked fire that smoldered in the grate beside the stove.

She sat down and pulled the lid from the tin, and as she ate, the room seemed to cocoon her in its intimacy. Caroline smiled at the delicious feeling of warmth that spread through her and even stretched her legs toward the fire.

It was in that exact posture that Mr. Rushton found her when he entered the room with a brusque swing of the door.

Caroline looked down at the biscuit in her hand and panicked. She did not want to be caught in the throes of something as uncultured as reclining in a kitchen and eating biscuits. A lady ought to be seen at edifying tasks.

But it was too late now, for Mr. Rushton was already regarding her with a quizzical eye. "Good evening, Miss Bingley."

She returned his greeting, pretending to be absorbed by the play of the fire in the grate, but she allowed her displeasure to show on her face in the hopes that he might behave politely and leave her to herself.

That, of course, was too much to expect.

"What do you do about at this late hour?" he asked.

"Why, cannot you see?" She waved her biscuit at him. "I am penning a great work of fiction."

"Ah," he said. Then nothing more.

Caroline allowed herself to glance up and found him leaning a hip against the edge of the worktable. He was still wearing his dinner attire, but he had removed his coat and loosened his cravat.

And here she sat in her night attire! It was wholly inappropriate. He ought to leave.

She sat up straight and tucked her feet beneath her dressing gown.

He was watching her movements and smiling at her with an infuriatingly ironic expression in his eyes. "I should have expected to find you here after observing how little you ate at dinner."

Caroline willed herself not to blush. Of course, it did not matter if her face turned purple, she chided herself, for in this semi-dark, color was quite washed away. But indeed, she was embarrassed. It was true that she had been able to consume little at Oak Park. Her nerves had been much too strained by her circumstances. "I wish you would not observe me, Mr. Rushton. It is very rude."

His smile returned, and Caroline had the urge to remove it from his face, by force if necessary.

"May I join you?" he asked in a pleasant tone of voice.

"I wish you would not," she returned with exaggerated coldness.

"Excellent," he said as he came around the table, pulled out the chair beside hers, turned it around, and sat.

Caroline scowled at him. "A gentleman would leave. This situation is quite improper."

Mr. Rushton emitted a sort of throaty growl and said, "I would ask if you would do me the honor of sharing that tin of biscuits, but because I am certain you will respond in the negative, I find I must take them without your permission."

Before he could snatch the tin from her, Caroline handed it to him. "I would not deny you, Mr. Rushton."

She had expected him to say something mocking, but to her surprise, he said nothing, and that was infinitely worse. He merely chewed and looked at her intently.

He offered her a biscuit from the tin he now possessed.

She thought to feign disinterest, but she had come for this very purpose after all. She took one.

"And so if you will not deny me, Miss Bingley, tell me, what has really brought you all the way to the blighted north?"

Caroline stopped chewing and looked at him.

Mr. Rushton continued, "For I smell something suspicious in the air, and I must track it down. I cannot believe a woman, who so obviously desires the pleasures of town, would ever come here of her own accord."

"Can you not, Mr. Rushton?" Caroline studied him a moment and decided to deflect his line of questioning. "I should have thought a gentleman of property in the region would have reason to boast of its bounties."

"Indeed, it is a region of bounty and beauty, Miss Bingley, but have you not grown accustomed to the bustle of London?"

"I do not pretend to hide my regard for Town, but I also dearly love my mother." She lowered her eyes. "And she has brought me here."

He turned his head slightly, as if gauging the veracity of her statement and deciding he was skeptical.

"You do not believe I love my mother, Mr. Rushton?"

"No indeed, I am quite certain of your affection for Mrs. Newton," he said as he finished another biscuit, recovered the tin, and wiped his hands on his trousers. "In fact, it is one of your most redeeming characteristics."

"How very kind of you," Caroline said as she rose from her chair to look down upon him. "In you, I have found no such redeeming traits, and I wish very much that you would prevent yourself further thought on my account. I have nothing to conceal."

He had the audacity to snort in disbelief.

"You, on the contrary, seem to have a great deal to conceal," Caroline said.

He did not even possess the shame to look away under the force of her accusation. He simply stretched his legs and crossed his ankles. "You have heard the rumors then?"

"I am sure there are few who have not."

He only smiled.

"You are not contrite?" Caroline asked. How could a gentleman face the allegation of being a fortune hunter with such carelessness?

"Why should I be?" he asked with a shrug. His white shirt rose and fell with his movements, somehow exposing more of his chest. Caroline blushed again as he continued. "I have done nothing amiss. I am innocent. It is you who have chosen to believe idle gossip."

Caroline very nearly laughed. "On the contrary, I never believe idle gossip, only that which has been confirmed."

"Ah," he said with a smile. "So my guilt is confirmed then, in your mind?"

"It is."

"And what is your evidence?"

Caroline tucked her chair back under the table and pulled her wrap tighter around herself. "Every conversation I hold with you convinces me further of your unworthiness to be in my mother's household."

He laughed again and watched as she turned on her heel to depart.

"Good night, Mr. Rushton," she shot.

"Good night, Miss Bingley," he said as she swept past him toward the door.

She had almost made her escape when she heard him call out, "Miss Bingley."

She nearly ignored him, but something compelled her to look back at him. "What?"

When he spoke again, his voice was rather hushed. "I am certainly glad for whatever it is that brought you here. You amuse me, Miss Bingley. You amuse me."

"I am sorry that I cannot return those sentiments, Mr. Rushton, for you do not amuse me."

✤ Ten ✤

From the night of Lavinia's dinner party forward, Caroline could not step into the Charltons' society without Rosemary trailing alongside, keeping unending watch over her charge, but one day in late February, chance finally worked in her favor.

Rosemary had come down with a most horrifying cold, and her nose had turned cherry red. She was not fit to be seen in company, nor had she even exited her bedchamber in several days.

This offered Caroline the ideal opportunity to pay a call on Oak Park unaccompanied by her companion. And the occasion was even better than Caroline had ever dared hope, for she knew with certainty that Lavinia would not be at home that morning.

Indeed, Caroline must now seize every opportunity to associate privately with Mr. Charlton, for she could not properly woo a gentleman with her servant always about to remind her of his inaccurate reputation. And Caroline had no desire to call upon Lavinia. She went for the sole purpose of encountering Mr. Charlton.

Perhaps chance would smile upon her again and her plan would prove successful.

Caroline sat at her dressing table and studied her reflection in the mirror.

Today, she had chosen a cool blue dress that clung to her slim figure and complimented her skin tone. Her maid had worked for hours on a casual hairstyle with curls placed to frame her face as if they had fallen of their own will.

Caroline pinched her cheeks and hoped that her nose would not turn too red on the carriage ride to Oak Park. She had no wish to look as if she had fallen victim to Rosemary's cold.

Mustering her resolve, Caroline gave herself one last look in the mirror, stood, and walked quickly down the stairs and toward the waiting coach.

As she passed the sitting room door, she heard her mother call out her name.

Caroline stopped, removed all traces of annoyance from her expression, and moved to the open doorway.

"You are calling upon Mrs. Winton this morning?" her mother inquired from her seat before the fire.

"Yes, indeed."

Mrs. Newton laid aside her mending and said, "I do wish you might wait until Mrs. Pickersgill is well enough to come along."

"But why, Mama? Lavinia is my oldest friend. Surely, I do not require a chaperone to call upon her."

"Yes, you and Lavinia have long been acquainted. I only fear—" She broke off, studied Caroline a moment longer, and then seemed to change her mind about her next words. After a moment's hesitation, she said, "I fear that our Mrs. Pickersgill has not made many friends here in Kendal."

"Nonsense, Mama," Caroline objected. "She could not help but acquire acquaintances, for she has been with me every moment since we arrived."

Mrs. Newton's eyes seemed to issue a warning that Caroline could not quite comprehend, but she only said, "Yes, I suppose you will enjoy time alone with Lavinia. It is only…." Her voice trailed off.

"Only what?" Caroline said with unconcealed annoyance. The carriage was waiting, and she must hurry if she hoped to catch Mr. Charlton alone.

"Do you not find Lavinia altered since you last saw her?" Mrs. Newton asked.

Caroline stepped back in surprise at the boldness of the question. "No indeed, Mama. I find her exactly as I left her."

"Ah, perhaps I am mistaken about Lavinia then, but I do not believe the same can be said for Mrs. Pickersgill. There is a sadness about her that I do not quite comprehend. I believe she is lonely. I wish you would coax her to join us tonight at supper. It cannot be good for her to remain so long in her room."

"She is ill, Mama," Caroline said. "We must not endanger her health by pulling her from bed too quickly."

"No, I suppose not, but if she is feeling better, I think you must invite her. Company often diffuses melancholy."

Caroline had noticed no such sadness in the woman, and she certainly had no compulsion to make any effort on behalf of a servant, but she would do anything for her mother, and, at that moment, she would do anything to be in a carriage on the way to Oak Park.

"I shall do just that, Mama. Tonight, I promise."

Her mother smiled, and that pleased Caroline. "Now, be off with you, and send my best regards to Lavinia."

Caroline complied and set off in the carriage to Oak Park.

As the carriage turned onto the approach road and the house came into view, Caroline surveyed the property, all that might one day soon be hers. Of all this, she could be mistress. The thought of such prestige caused in her a strange feeling of nervousness.

This was an important visit indeed.

Caroline exited the carriage and waited on the doorstep as the coachman directed the vehicle toward the stable to wait. She raised her hand slowly to the door knocker, gathering herself, but when she knocked, it was a quick, heavy sound that indicated that she was a woman of purpose.

The door opened, revealing a plain-faced manservant.

"Good morning, madam," he said.

"Yes, good morning," Caroline said as she looked past the manservant and into the house beyond. "Is the mistress of the house available?"

"No, madam, Mrs. Winton is not at home. Would you like to leave a card?"

"Indeed." Caroline removed a card from her reticule and handed it to him, again taking the opportunity of peeking over his shoulder into the house.

A heavy step echoed through the entryway.

Then she heard a male voice. "Dash it, Peters, I can find nothing in this house since my sister arrived. Where the devil is my…. Oh! Miss Bingley, I did not realize you were here."

Caroline offered Mr. Charlton a look of surprise in return. "And I did not expect to discover you here. I have come to call upon your sister, only to find that she is not at home."

Mr. Charlton approached the door, dismissed the manservant, and then leaned against the doorframe casually. "Yes, she has gotten off to some neighbor or other. I cannot keep up with her."

"How disappointing." Caroline looked up at him through her lashes with an expression gentlemen had always seemed to prefer. "Will you not be able to offer me some sort of consolation?"

Mr. Charlton smiled at her broadly and brushed a curl from his eyes. "I was just about to walk into Kendal. Would you care to join me?"

Caroline despised walking, and she had no inclination to go as far as town in this cold.

"I enjoy walking a great deal, Mr. Charlton, but I have not the time for a walk to Kendal this morning. Shall we not take a turn about your garden instead?"

If his expression showed a bit of disappointment, he covered it quickly. "Yes, a turn about the garden would be a rather pleasant diversion. Thank you for the suggestion. I should have accomplished nothing valuable in town at any rate."

Caroline was pleased when he offered his arm, and she made certain to reward him with her most appealing smile as she took it.

"Come, let us go to the back garden. The plants appear to be a little less dead there than those in the rose garden at this time of year."

"I am certain that even your dead plants are appealing." Caroline heard herself utter those words and immediately wished to snatch them back. If she could not discover a method of showing her interest in Mr. Charlton in a less obvious manner, she would never succeed in winning him, and she would be subject to her brother's punishment forever.

They had taken one full turn about the garden, which was quite as dead as the rose garden to Caroline's eye, before Mr. Charlton spoke again.

"Tell me, Miss Bingley, do you not find yourself surprised at the changes taking place?"

Believing him to refer to the advent of spring and the transformation it brought, Caroline looked about the winter-wilted plants, and seeing no signs of life at all, she said, "No indeed, for spring occurs every year."

Mr. Charlton smiled. "Your interpretation is rather more literal than I intended."

"Oh?" Caroline asked, perfectly ashamed at having misunderstood him. "I do not care for figurative language, Mr. Charlton, but do enlighten me."

"Kendal. Have you not sensed the changes here?"

Caroline looked at him, but not in the coy manner she had used only moments ago. This look was full and questioning. Was he referring to his new status as heir? "A great many things have changed, Mr. Charlton. Do you object to these alterations?"

"I find that I do object. I quite enjoyed my life of leisure, but now I find myself pulled about by the whims of others."

"You speak rather too plainly, but I confess that I can well understand your position," Caroline said. Not caring to elaborate, she only added, "We must make of our circumstances what we can. It is useless to mope about and lament what cannot be altered."

"But changes are happening all around us. Only look at how families rise and fall in wealth. Those who were poor are now rising."

"You refer to the middling classes?" she asked with disgust.

"Indeed, I have read that one in seven people in London now account for the middling classes."

Caroline was indeed surprised. "That is a shocking number, but it changes nothing of true status."

"Does it not? Even here in Kendal, one must look only to Mr. Newton and perhaps even Miss Brodrick to observe the new stature afforded to such people. And Mr. Rushton, though he is a gentleman to be sure, had descended in wealth only to have risen again."

"Mr. Rushton is not wealthy," Caroline protested.

"Indeed, he is. Have you not seen his home in Keswick? His home in Town?" He studied her. "No, I suppose you have not. But I assure you that he has returned his family to the respectable situation it held in the past."

Caroline rather doubted this. Besides, true wealth constituted more than mere money. What of land, title, ancestry? "But Mr. Rushton has sold most of his family property, has he not? If he has no ancestral land, he cannot truly be counted as a gentleman."

"What does family land matter?" Mr. Charlton asked as he gestured broadly around him. "What does all this gain me? It is lovely, to be sure, but no one cares to work the land any longer."

"But do not you agree that land is a hallmark of a great family, of connections to the best of society through the ages? And these men of whom you speak, who have no land, they are but half-gentlemen; they have no breeding. And though they have money, they will always want for decent connections."

He looked down at her. "Yes, connections are important, as my sister has often reminded me."

"Mrs. Winton is very wise," Caroline said with what she hoped was a sage nod. "We must all cultivate our connections to our best advantage."

"Yes, yes, so she has said." He glanced around him, and when he spoke again, his voice held an edge of frustration. "She also speaks of duty and other such notions, but I cannot help but feel as if a life of freedom was ripped from me, and now I must behave in a completely new way. I wish most ardently to leave the business of Oak Park to someone more suited for the burden than I."

Caroline laughed aloud at his absurdity. "Why, Mr. Charlton, I find it utterly incomprehensible to hear you speak that way about your inheriting a barony! Only think of the advantages it provides. You may have your pick of friends and society, and any young lady would be honored by your acknowledgment of her."

Here, Mr. Charlton stopped, and again, Caroline looked at him through her lashes, letting them flutter a bit.

"Do you believe that? Any woman would be honored by me? What if I had no money at all, and only family name, reputation, and land to recommend me?" He gestured broadly at the house and land around him and then turned to Caroline. "Would you be honored by my acknowledgement of you then, Miss Bingley?" He studied her for a moment, shook his head once, and then looked toward the ground.

Caroline knew not how to respond.

"May I speak plainly?" he asked, his eyes wide and questioning.

"Of course, sir," Caroline said. She wondered if he might be on the verge of proposing marriage.

He cleared his throat and turned to face her fully.

"I have a dreadful fear that I shall destroy Oak Park when I run it without the oversight of my father and sister. I cannot seem to retain money. It slips through my grasp, and I do not quite know how. I do not wish to end a pauper."

Caroline studied him, trying not to show her surprise at this turn of conversation. Was he already losing his family's fortune?

She hoped not, but this could be a fortuitous error, for perhaps he would more quickly see her advantages if money were at stake. She did have a large dowry, and she would excel at managing Oak Park if he did not care to do it himself.

Yes, she would make an excellent baroness, especially if she had full control over the entire estate.

"Well, Mr. Charlton, you ought to use your attributes—your home and family name—to secure a wife of large dowry and leave the running of Oak Park entirely to her."

"And have you a large dowry, Miss Bingley?" he asked, his voice now a whisper. He leaned close as if hoping to catch her response, and Caroline backed away slightly.

"I do, Mr. Charlton," she whispered. Her whole body seemed to vibrate suddenly, and she could not tell if the sensation arose from hope or fear of his proposal.

He smiled and leaned closer. "And would you fancy running Oak Park?"

Mr. Charlton's lips were a breath from her, and Caroline could scarcely move enough to say, "Indeed, I would."

Her eyelids fluttered closed, and she was waiting to feel his lips upon hers when suddenly, a voice ripped across the garden. "William!"

Caroline's eyes flew open, and she jumped back, looking around for Lavinia. Had she seen her brother leaning in so closely? Had she been attempting to stop the scene from unfolding?

Lavinia was nowhere to be seen.

Caroline sent her questioning gaze to Mr. Charlton, who had righted himself. His eyelids lowered in disdain as he explained, "My sister is home and has already seen the ledger, I assume. She is likely crowing at me from the library."

"Oh," Caroline breathed. She knew Lavinia would not thwart a romantic scene between her closest acquaintance and her brother, and she felt rather silly for having momentarily doubted her friend.

"I must go," Mr. Charlton said. "I would invite you to come inside and socialize with my sister, but I fear you will not like her mood. Will you excuse me?"

"Indeed, Mr. Charlton, I would not stop you."

"I shall have your carriage sent around," he said as he took her gloved hand in his and brushed his thumb across her knuckles. "I shall call upon you soon."

Mr. Charlton then gave her a flirtatious smile and left her standing alone in the dried-up flower garden that one day she hoped to own.

❧❦ ❦❧

Caroline counted her interaction with Mr. Charlton as an unmitigated success despite his abrupt removal. She had managed to discuss all the subjects she had hoped to address with him. They had discussed marriage, and it seemed that he had very nearly kissed her.

Though Caroline's own emotions were unsettled as a result, she had lashed them tightly into place now. Sentiment was hardly a creditable reason to decline a proposal of marriage to a baron!

She would continue to put herself in his path and show herself to best advantage. From there, the logical progression for him was to consider her as a specific partner in marriage.

Caroline spent the remainder of the afternoon in her chamber at Newton House contemplating her next interaction with Mr. Charlton. Her calling card in Lavinia's salver ensured a return of call from her friend, and it was likely that her brother might accompany her, for it was he who had last received her. They had some sort of connection, though she was rather unsure how to define it.

As twilight began to fall, Caroline knew she could no longer ignore her promise to her mother to coax Rosemary out of the sickroom and into their company.

With reluctance, Caroline left the comforts of her room and knocked once on the door to her companion's chamber, entering before she was bid to do so.

She discovered Rosemary still abed.

"Mrs. Pickersgill, how do you do?"

Rosemary eyed Caroline with more than a hint of irony in her expression. "As you can see, Miss Bingley, I have not recovered."

Caroline took a moment to study the woman. Her eyes were red rimmed, her nose swollen, and her face puffy. "Yes, you do look dreadful."

"How kind of you to say, Miss Bingley," she said as she dabbed at her nose with a handkerchief. "May I be of service to you?"

"No, but you may be of service to my mother. She would like you to join us tonight if you are not too ill."

Rosemary looked away. "I do not want to disappoint Mrs. Newton, but I cannot…." Her voice trailed off, almost as if she had begun to cry.

Caroline studied the side of Rosemary's face as if it might divulge something to her.

She had never looked upon Rosemary as anything other than a servant. She had never considered that the woman experienced emotions.

She moved around the side of the bed and looked down at her. It appeared that her mother had been accurate in her earlier assessment; the woman did have a particular sadness about her. Caroline had never marked it before this moment.

This realization elicited a strange reaction on Caroline's part, for she experienced a wave of pity that nearly overcame her when she saw a tear fall down her companion's cheek.

She was suddenly almost overcome by the urge to sit on the edge of Rosemary's bed and have a chat with her, as she had done many times in the past with Louisa when they were young girls. Caroline edged closer and nearly settled beside her, but something prevented her from doing so.

Uncomfortable, she moved toward the window and pretended to look at the surroundings. She did not like the peculiar feeling that had risen in her.

"My brother would not approve of his servant neglecting her duties," Caroline said, almost by rote.

There was a silence so lengthy that Caroline finally turned again to observe Rosemary, who was staring blankly ahead, but the tears had been wiped from her face.

"Yes, he would have cause to terminate my employment today," Rosemary said and then paused. When she spoke again, her tone was rough and breathy. "I beg you would forgive me, but I cannot join your family for dinner. I cannot."

That peculiar feeling nudged Caroline forward again, and she came nearer, almost without her own volition. "What is the matter, Mrs. Pickersgill?"

"Forgive me, Miss Bingley, but I care not to share my sentiments with one who asks only out of"—she squinted up at her—"a convoluted sense of duty."

Rosemary's words stung, and Caroline was surprised to hear herself say, "I am sorry to hear that, for in my brother's absence, I am responsible for you and cannot have you skulking about and neglecting your duties."

Her companion sighed heavily, her strawberry blond hair fluttering around her face upon her exhale. "I have had a letter late this afternoon. It contained ill news."

"Ill news? Of what nature?"

"Of a private nature, Miss Bingley. I beg you would forgive me, but I cannot speak of it to you."

"But this news, it has further sickened you?" Caroline's words sounded harsher than she had intended. Of all people, she comprehended the physical effects one might experience from an emotional blow. "Was it regarding a gentleman?"

Rosemary nodded slowly. "In a manner of speaking."

If Rosemary were suffering the same emotions that Caroline had experienced over Mr. Darcy's marriage to Miss Elizabeth Bennet, well, she would not berate her.

Instead, she approached the bedside, and though it was hardly an intimate gesture, her proximity surprised them both. "I shall make your excuses to my mother."

Rosemary looked at her, and relief crossed her features. "I thank you, Miss Bingley."

Caroline, suddenly uncomfortable with her feelings, turned away. "And then you may return to your duties."

She went to the door and had nearly shut it behind her when she heard Rosemary say, "Thank you, Miss Bingley."

৩৩ Eleven ৩৩

"Shall we all not ride out?" asked Mr. Charlton. "My sister and I have come dressed for it, as you see, and our horses are at the ready. This early March weather is shockingly warm and rather appealing. What say you?"

"Oh yes, William," Lavinia said as she clapped her hands together, "what a good idea. Our ride from Oak Park was invigorating, and I do so long to take a turn around that little pond out back."

Caroline looked at her friend in abject horror. Did she not recall what had happened the last time they had ridden out together?

Likely not, for that had been years ago, and as Caroline studied her friend's countenance now, she saw only an innocent pleasure and desire to be in the saddle.

Caroline sighed. She had been pleased when Lavinia and Mr. Charlton had called upon her that morning at Newton House, but she had not anticipated such an outing. Perhaps she should have, for Lavinia and Mr. Charlton had arrived on horseback looking quite pleased with themselves.

"Oh dear. Though you are charmingly attired, I fear I am not correctly dressed for equestrian activities," Caroline said, hoping desperately that this excuse would suffice.

"Oh, 'tis nothing, Miss Bingley," Lavinia said with a wave of her hand. "We shall wait for you to don your riding habit."

"But…," Caroline said as she sought a way to avoid riding horseback. Her eyes landed upon Rosemary, who had been sitting quietly in the corner. "I do not believe Mrs. Pickersgill cares to ride."

Rosemary did not look up from the mending in her lap to see the intent expression on Caroline's face. She simply said, "I would be happy to ride if it is required."

"You see!" Lavinia said. "It is the perfect day for riding, my dear. Everyone agrees."

Caroline clenched her fists in her lap. She had no wish to ride, and she could not fathom why going about on horseback was revered as a skill a young lady ought to have. Why, that was the reason carriages were created, was it not? To prevent young women from being forced to set themselves on the back of a wild beast and gallop madly about the countryside. Yes, a carriage was much more sensible.

She sighed. She must make sacrifices if she were to win Mr. Charlton, and this must be one of them. Caroline could not turn away this opportunity to converse with him.

She relented. "Then, I suppose, we shall ride."

"Do hurry and dress, Caroline." Lavinia waved a hand at her. "You too, Mrs. Pickersgill. William and I shall await you here."

Caroline and Rosemary went upstairs, and while the maid assisted her in changing into her riding habit, Caroline thought back on her illustrious history with equestrian activity.

It was not pleasing.

It had begun when she was but a young girl and still wearing her family's newly gained wealth with all the comfort of overly tightened corset stays. Her family had only recently been able to afford to keep a donkey for the children, and Caroline had not yet found her confidence with the animal. Her father had managed an invitation to a harvest celebration on the grounds of Oak Park, and Caroline would be able to interact with the children of the upper classes for the first time in her young life.

At the celebration, the adults had been about their conversations and activities, leaving the children to their own devices. Someone had proposed pony rides, a suggestion that horrified Caroline. She was supposed to try to impress her companions by showing that she had the same accomplishments they had, but she could not ride. She also knew, however, that her hesitancy to participate would only be evidence of her status.

So she had gone to the stables with the other children, and because there were not enough mounts, they took turns riding or leading each other about the grounds. It had all been surprisingly pleasant until it had come to Caroline's turn to ride.

Caroline could not recall what happened, but she knew for certain that she had hit the ground after only a brief time on the pony's back.

The breath had left her body, and she had struggled to inhale. Tears formed in the corners of her eyes, but she did not allow them to fall. She continued to gasp as a shadow appeared above her. She wondered if it were death coming for her and closed her eyes, willing death away, and continued to attempt to draw breath.

"Caroline!" The voice was not that of death, but Lavinia Charlton, the girl she admired most in the world. Caroline opened her eyes to find her idol leaning over her. Her young face blocked out the view of the sky above her. "What is wrong with you? Relax. Just try to slow down a bit. You will soon be able to breathe."

She had only been able to cough and choke in response, but Caroline was quickly able to inhale and exhale normally, and she began to feel awkward.

"Are you well now?" Lavinia asked.

Cough. "Yes."

"Are you certain?" the girl demanded.

Caroline had nodded quickly.

"Good," Lavinia said loudly, "for I have not gotten a ride and I do not want to have to take you back to the house."

Lavinia grabbed her by the arm, yanked her into a standing position, and said more softly, "What could you possibly have been thinking? You know nothing of horses, do you?"

Caroline stared at her, and she stared back. Time seemed to freeze while her blood heated. "No."

Lavinia glowered. "You have never ridden before?"

Caroline narrowed her eyes. "I have ridden my family's donkey."

"Donkey?" She looked appalled. "You should go home. You do not belong here."

Caroline had only stood and watched as the children continued their game. Yes, she should return home. She looked down at her muddy dress. It was likely ruined, and her mother would not be pleased.

But Caroline's displeasure had come from another source. Lavinia's words had haunted and humiliated her, and she had vowed that one day she would belong amongst the elite, and then Lavinia herself would accept her.

And today, even as she allowed herself again to be swept along to the stables, Caroline vowed that she would not end on the ground in humiliation. She would devise a method for avoiding the ride altogether.

Along the way, she reviewed some potential dodges in her mind.

Perhaps she could muster a convincing fainting spell. She rejected this immediately, for she had no desire to be viewed as a swooning female.

A sprained ankle? No, indeed, for that would necessitate an undignified, unattractive limp for the remainder of the day at least. It would not do to be seen dragging about when she was trying to show herself to best advantage.

A sudden head cold? Apoplexy? Gout?

She dismissed them all.

No, Caroline was not a creator of excuses; she spoke plainly. It was a matter of pride.

She would simply have to register her objections to riding, and perhaps if she manipulated the situation correctly, Mr. Charlton would volunteer to rest with her while the others rode out.

She and Rosemary caught up to Mr. Charlton, who was walking briskly alongside Lavinia, and was discouraged to see the childlike joy in his expression. Everything about him radiated anticipation and glee. His eyes were bright, his movements quick, and even his dark curls blew about despite the tall black hat that sought to keep his hair under control. Lavinia too appeared eager to be at the stables.

"Mr. Charlton," Caroline said. "I am so pleased that you thought of inviting me to ride with you this morning."

"Ah! Think nothing of it, Miss Bingley." The stables came into view over a small rise in the landscape, and if possible, Mr. Charlton seemed to quicken his pace further as he said, "I confess that this warm weather has quite given me the desire to be outdoors."

"Indeed, it has had the same effect on me," Caroline lied. "I have found the loveliest little spot in the garden and have been many hours in the sun there."

Mrs. Pickersgill glanced sidelong at Caroline, who returned a look of defiance.

Yes, of course, it was a lie. She had not rested out of doors all week, for the wind was far too brisk, and she had not the faintest urge of damaging her hair.

"So the lure of spring has drawn you too, Miss Bingley," Lavinia said.

"A nice spot in the garden is good for the spirit, or at least our mother used to say as much," Mr. Charlton added.

"Indeed, your mother was a wise woman," Caroline said, hoping to have made headway with Mr. Charlton. "I wonder if you should care to see my little niche. I should gladly give up a ride to have the honor of showing you."

"Oh, I would not give up a ride for anything," Lavinia said for him. "And neither would my brother nor your companion, I think, for it is too fine a day to neglect the horses, is not that right, Mrs. Pickersgill?"

Rosemary smiled. "It is a fine day for riding."

Well! Caroline was going to have to resort to honesty and forget the idea of keeping Mr. Charlton behind. Their party had arrived in the stable yard, and the stench of manure, hay, and leather assaulted Caroline's senses. She was preparing to make her excuses as she approached the barn's ingress, where she discovered Mr. Rushton awaiting them.

Apparently, he was to be a part of the riding party. He stood beside his horse, a hulking grey beast, and watched her approach as if she were the only person arriving.

She did not give him the satisfaction of an acknowledgment. In fact, in recent days, she had attempted to avoid him as much as possible, a difficult task given that they were residing in the same house. But manage it she had, and they had spoken but little. Besides, he and Mr. Newton had been busy mucking about in the library and debating bridge schematics. That was hardly conversation that might interest Caroline.

"Good day, Miss Bingley," he said with all evidence of politeness, but his eyes held mischief.

Any idea of making her excuses and avoiding the ride disappeared. She would not give Mr. Rushton the satisfaction of seeing her wheedle out of their equestrian activities. He had an uncanny way of reading her motives, and she had no wish for him to witness her giving in to fear.

There was much shuffling about the stable as mounts were chosen and readied. Caroline kept herself out of the way of the commotion as well as she could, and far too soon, the horses were prepared and led to the stable yard for mounting.

Mr. Rushton found her at the back of the group and gave her a curious look.

"Allow me to present your mount, Miss Bingley." He left his horse by the fence and headed toward a small bay pony a few yards away. "This is Mossy, your mother's mare."

The pony mare looked at Caroline with dark, unconcerned eyes. Even this calm creature seemed much too big and powerful to consider sitting upon, but if her mother rode this pony, she ought to be able to manage one outing. Besides, Caroline had been able to survive her equitation lessons at the seminary. Certainly, her education would not fail her.

Caroline stood by the pony, and Mr. Rushton seemed to be awaiting her for some reason.

"Am I required to introduce myself to the creature?" she demanded.

His pale brows lowered as he considered her. "Most people give them a pat on the neck at least."

"If you insist," Caroline said as she reached out her gloved hand to the pony's neck. Mossy flinched at the sudden movement, and Mr. Rushton again eyed her.

The others had mounted, and Mr. Charlton called down to them, saying, "Mr. Rushton, assist Miss Bingley, if you please. I am anxious to be away."

Mr. Rushton hardly acknowledged the order, but he nonetheless assisted Caroline to mount Mossy. He stood on the ground beside her and watched as she fumbled to position the reins and riding crop in her hands.

"Are you well?" he asked, his blue eyes earnest. "We do not have to ride if you are unwell."

He was offering her the option of making her excuses, just as she had been scheming to do earlier, but his suggestion of it infuriated her.

"I am certainly able to ride!" Caroline snapped. "It is only that I am unused to this tack." She gestured broadly about her with her crop, hoping that "tack" was indeed the correct word for one of the things strapped to the horse.

She glanced at Mr. Charlton, hoping that he had not observed her awkwardness, and was delighted to discover that he and Lavinia were deep in conversation. Their horses strode slowly about the yard in a circle. They presented quite an elegant picture, and Caroline hoped that she looked as well as they did.

Then Mossy shifted her weight, causing Caroline to gasp at the unexpected movement.

Everyone looked at her, and she managed a tight smile. "There was a bee," she lied.

"Dashed insects," Mr. Charlton said. "Let us be off before they swarm and ruin the ride before it begins."

With that, Mr. Charlton, Lavinia, and Mrs. Pickersgill led the way out of the stable yard. Caroline urged Mossy to join them while Mr. Rushton mounted his own horse.

The mare's gait seemed smooth enough, but Caroline's feeble confidence seemed to erode with each stride away from the security of the stable.

Caroline tried to steel herself against her weakness.

Yes, fear was indeed her weakness.

Fear of exposure. Fear that her family's dubious background might haunt her forever. Fear that she might never have a home of her own. Fear that she might be flung from the back of this pony and humiliated in front of Mr. Charlton, Lavinia, Rosemary, and Mr. Rushton.

But, she reminded herself, people had been riding horses since time began. Certainly, they were no more capable of controlling the animals than she was. She could keep her seat and contain her fear on a leisurely stroll about the grounds.

Mr. Rushton had taken a bit longer to move off and was quite a bit behind her. Caroline and Mossy, as well, had fallen rather behind the others and were quite alone. Ahead, the horses seemed content. They were not snorting fire or prancing. Perhaps Mossy would take her cue from the rest of the herd.

That, however, was not the case, for suddenly, her mare seemed incapable of maintaining a slow pace. In fact, she sped up progressively. As Mr. Charlton and the ladies continued further down the wooded path, Caroline was forced to circle her obstinate pony continually in the hopes that she might calm down enough to walk like a civilized creature.

The animal remained, however, uncivil.

Caroline's hands clutched the reins, and her leg muscles ached from gripping the pommel of the side saddle as the group rounded the far end of the fish pond on their frustratingly controlled mounts.

When Mossy lost sight of the other horses, she became even more animated in her movements. Her head raised and her gait changed from smooth to springy. Caroline fancied that she could feel her pony's back muscles tense through the layers of skirt and saddle leather.

Yes, the animal was indeed tense.

This would result in no good, certainly.

Caroline looked about her, hoping to find some aid from the rocks and trees, but instead, she discovered that Mr. Rushton had ridden his mare beside her.

"Miss Bingley," he said, tipping his hat as if he were meeting her in Hyde Park for a morning excursion. His eyes held a look of superior amusement that irritated her. But almost frozen in fear, Caroline found that she could not issue a proper set down for his sardonic tone.

Instead, he continued, "I have never seen this pony become so agitated. What have you done to her?"

Something broke free within Caroline, and she snapped at him. "What have I done? What have *I* done? Sir, I can assure you I have done nothing but attempt to ride the beast. There is something amiss with this animal, not me!"

She saw Mr. Rushton set his jaw. "Stop her," he said, as if Caroline had the power to arrest the movement of a creature that outweighed her by quite a good deal.

"If I could stop her from this infernal bouncing, I would have done it long ago. I have pulled back on the reins and circled since we left the stable yard."

He looked her over from stirrup to reins and issued the following order: "Unclench yourself, Miss Bingley. You are making that pony nervous."

"Ha! I am making her nervous. Tell her to calm down first and I shall, as you say so vulgarly, 'unclench.'"

He studied the bouncing mare again, then reached inside his saddle bag and drew out a leather strap. He aligned his horse with her pony, leaned down, and fastened the clasp to her pony's bit.

"What are you about, Mr. Rushton? I do not see how another piece of leather is going to make this situation any more pleasant."

"Release the reins," he ordered. "I will lead you for the remainder of the ride."

Caroline refused. The reins were her only hope of gaining any semblance of control. "I do not think this is a wise idea."

He did not seem to be listening as he slowly reeled in Caroline's pony until its head was near his horse's shoulder, and she found her body bumping against his leg.

"Release the reins," he repeated, "and trust me to help you out of this mess."

She looked up at him. His face held no amusement now. She found that she must trust him.

So she did as he requested and dropped the reins, but she punctuated her action by grasping at the pony's mane and saying, "I do not care for horse riding."

"You are afraid of horse riding," he replied in a conversational tone.

It was the tone that disarmed her. Had he made such a comment with smugness or conceit, her hackles would have raised still further and she would have felt the need to defend herself. Instead, she allowed him to continue.

"Do not be ashamed. Many people find moving at such heights and speeds disconcerting."

Caroline could not see what Mr. Rushton was doing to the pony, but her gait was beginning to smooth, and their pace slowed. They rode along quite calmly now and were following the same course that the others in their party had taken. She could barely see their companions ahead, and this provided her some relief, for though Caroline had desperately hoped to remain near Mr. Charlton, it was better that he did not witness her ineptitude.

She and Mr. Rushton continued in quiet for some time, and eventually, Caroline was able to relax herself further. Though she felt no more confidence in her current position—being banged about on Mr. Rushton's riding boot—she began to feel a bit of her customary passion return.

"I believe my mare has calmed herself sufficiently. You may release us, Mr. Rushton."

"Indeed, I shall not. At least not until you can prove that you may control this animal without sending her into a panic."

"I can assure you that we shall be fine now. Look. We are both calm."

"You assure me of nothing until you take up the reins and show me."

So, with hidden trepidation, Caroline gathered the reins and hoped that she would not humiliate herself again.

Mr. Rushton uncoiled his leather lead, giving Caroline a bit of slack and thus the opportunity to be in control of her own mount.

She was excessively pleased that the mare did not immediately set to bouncing like a ball.

Instead, she seemed to slow down.

That did not seem such a bad prospect, and so she did nothing to encourage the pony to move any faster.

This turned out to be an error in judgment, for eventually, her pony and—by extension, Mr. Rushton's horse, for he was still connected loosely by the lead—began to dawdle beside the pond.

The ground was damp by the water's edge, and the mare's hooves made sucking sounds as she plodded along. The other horses had already reached the tree line, and she saw that Lavinia and Mr. Charlton had turned around to check their progress. Though she wished to join them and shed herself of Mr. Rushton, Caroline's mount slowed to a stop beside the tall reeds and then threw her head down, yanking the reins from Caroline's fingers, to snatch at the burgeoning grass.

Mr. Rushton appeared amused, but he did nothing to aid her. He simply allowed his horse to amble along beside Mossy.

"What is wrong with this animal?" Caroline demanded. "First, she would not stop; now, she will not go. If you have chosen this mount as a jest, I assure you, it is not amusing!"

"This is the calmest pony in the stable, Miss Bingley. I would never over-horse a rider such as yourself."

"A rider such as myself?"

"A fearful novice."

"Humph." Her embarrassment—and the knowledge that Mr. Charlton might be observing her even now—caused her to act more bravely than perhaps she ought. She put her reins in one hand and moved the crop to the other. She hesitated and then administered a very light tap to the horse's right flank.

The mare did not move. She continued to munch grass.

"Miss Bingley! I caution against the use of the crop."

Caroline ignored him.

A harder tap.

The mare's head came up, ears back. Mossy was displeased but not motivated enough to move and dove again for the grass.

Caroline grasped the crop tighter and contorted herself to give the horse a good smack. The crop hovered in midair, preparing to fall on the mare's haunches, when several ducks suddenly flapped out of the reeds.

The mare moved then.

The onslaught of ducks had caught the pony by surprise, causing her to spin sideways and trot quickly along the pond's edge away from the ducks. Caroline closed her eyes to block out the fear, and through sheer force of will and the extreme desire not to embarrass herself, she managed to keep her seat.

And then she heard a splat as if something had landed on the boggy ground. Laughter rang out from the tree line.

She opened her eyes, wondering what had happened. Mossy had already returned to eating grass as if the startle had never occurred.

Caroline looked to the tree line where Mr. Charlton, Lavinia, and Rosemary were laughing. Even from the distance, she could see clearly that Mr. Charlton was amused. He called, "Miss Bingley, do see to Mr. Rushton. We are off on a gallop."

Only then did she look down and see Mr. Rushton lying face first in the muck beside her pony, his hands still resolutely holding the lead. His horse stood alongside him, and Caroline swore his mare had a quizzical expression on her equine face, likely wondering what her rider was doing on the ground.

Caroline was wondering the same herself.

Unsure of what she ought to do, she remained on her pony, which was still grazing on the lush grass that grew alongside the pond.

Mr. Rushton began to pull himself out of the mud. For long moments, Caroline could not see his face, but certainly, he would be angry.

Gentlemen did not care for public humiliation any more than she did.

Caroline felt the familiar temptation to exploit the situation. She could offer the snide remark that came so quickly to mind, but something prevented her from doing so. And that was odd. Here was the opportunity to prove her superiority of wit. To turn the accident to her advantage.

But was not his current humiliation her doing? She had opted to ride despite her distaste and displeasure in the activity, not to mention her complete ineptitude.

Again, these thoughts were odd. Ordinarily, Caroline would refuse to admit—even to herself—any culpability in such a situation, but at that moment, she could not deny that she bore some blame for his current state of filth. But unaccustomed to offering sympathy, Caroline simply sat without speaking a word.

Mr. Rushton stood with slow deliberation, and now he looked up at Caroline as she sat on the pony's back. He had managed to keep his face from landing in the mud, but his riding coat was caked with the substance. His lower body, however, seemed to have landed on dry ground, for his trousers were largely undamaged. He wore a neutral expression, and then it began to transform.

A burst of laughter escaped him.

Caroline's brow furrowed in confusion. "You are laughing?"

Mr. Rushton did not respond except to continue laughing.

"You are mad," Caroline said.

"No, indeed," he said as he shook some muck from his hands. "I have not been unhorsed in years, and you and this little pony have managed what unbroken colts could not."

"You *are* mad."

·∞ Twelve ∞·

Mr. Rushton smiled at Caroline as he offered his assistance to her in dismounting the pony. "Come along, Miss Bingley. We shall not be joining the others."

Again, Caroline had the strongest urge to offer a set down. A lady need not bow to the whims of a gentleman. She may make her own choices. But really, did she have a choice? She could no more control this pony than she could control the weather.

"To the stables then?" she asked.

"In time," he said. "First, do allow me the opportunity of repairing some of the damage done to my pride."

From the saddle, Caroline eyed his mud-encrusted hand with disdain and chose to reject his aid. She unlaced her leg from around the pommel and slid as gracefully as possible to the ground.

"Can such a thing be accomplished out of doors?"

By the look of him, he required thorough bathing and a change of clothing.

"Not properly, no," he said as he handed her the pony's lead.

She looked at the now-docile pony and decided she would not be dragged across the countryside if she held the line.

"Now, if you will permit me, I will remove this soiled garment and wash my hands as well as possible in the pond."

Mr. Rushton did not await her permission, so Caroline did not give it. She simply watched as he removed his riding coat, turned it inside out, and stored it in his saddle bag. He wore only his white linen shirt and waistcoat, which really was not proper in the company of a lady.

Caroline ought to complain, but she found that she rather admired the way the cloth stretched across his shoulders and back. She turned away, suddenly discomfited, and cleared her throat. "It seems, Mr. Rushton, that if we may not be together without becoming embroiled in some sort of altercation, we ought not to be in each other's company."

"Altercation?" he asked as he bent to rinse his hands in the pond. "Yes, I suppose we have had our share, but this is not an argument. I find I am not in the mood to quarrel. If I had been interested in fighting with you, Miss Bingley, I would have begun this conversation by asking just what the devil you thought to accomplish by riding out when you had no business doing so."

"And I would not explain myself, of course," Caroline replied.

He stood up and shook his hands in an attempt to dry them. Water flew in all directions, catching the sunlight as it fell. "As I expected," he said.

"And I might ask why you had selected such a difficult mount for me, Mr. Rushton, if you suspected my dislike for riding."

Caroline watched as he walked slowly toward her, his gaze keeping contact with hers. "And I would remind you that you were settled upon your mother's pony, which has never so much as had a subversive thought in her head."

They were standing within arm's length now, glaring at each other.

"Then," Caroline said, "I think it best that we do not speak about it."

"Indeed," Mr. Rushton said as he brushed past her and took up both his horse's reins and the pony's lead. "Come," he said as he walked to the base of a nearby tree. "We shall sit for a few minutes."

Caroline watched as he secured the horses and then sat on the ground without so much as a cloth between his trousers and the earth.

She supposed it did not matter to him.

She, on the other hand, attempted to perch herself on a large exposed root.

"Horses are emotional creatures, and they reflect the emotions of their riders," Mr. Rushton said without preamble.

Caroline sighed. "I thought we were not going to discuss this."

He continued, "One need only look at one's mount to understand everything about the person astride."

"Oh," Caroline said, understanding his intention. "What, pray tell, does today's adventure reveal about me?"

He studied her for a moment and then looked away. "It would be impolite of a gentleman to speak of it, Miss Bingley."

"Oh, come, I have invited your opinion. You are safe."

He laughed. "Now that you have said that, I am reassured that I am indeed not safe. When a lady assures a gentleman, it is only because she believes he will then flatter her."

"And what you say shall not flatter me?" Caroline asked.

"What I say would have been the truth."

"Then, speak it."

"The truth," he said, "is better discovered oneself."

Caroline was silent for a moment, but she was determined to discover his meaning. "Do you accuse me of a lack of skill then?"

"Lack of skill?"

"I was given proper instruction in all matters equestrian. It is an integral part of every lady's education." She would never admit that she remembered very little about the endeavor.

"Yes, that much was evident." He laughed. "You knew which end of the horse to which to apply the whip."

"You jest, but I was well taught."

"I do not refer to your lack of skill." When he spoke again, his voice was soft. "Indeed, Miss Bingley, I believe there are but few skills that you have not artfully mastered."

She looked at him but could not read his expression, for he was facing forward again. His tone sounded wry, but his words were complimentary.

She hesitated and then said, "I believe, Mr. Rushton, that is the first time I have ever heard a compliment escape your lips."

He faced her now, and his expression was as wry as his tone. "Did I compliment you? My apologies. It was quite unintentional."

She laughed at him despite herself, but sobered quickly.

"You are indeed a truly accomplished performer," Mr. Rushton said. "But one may not perform when horses are involved. They have a way of revealing one's true self."

"Then they are wiser creatures than I have given them credit for being."

"Yes, Mossy has revealed quite a great deal today. I comprehend you now. Perfectly."

"Oh?" Caroline adjusted on her perch. "Enlighten me."

"Women, I find, are the finest actors. They perform continually to entice a gentleman and then drop the charade once he is caught."

Caroline spoke without thinking. "How would you suggest we behave, then, if not by showing ourselves to the best advantage?"

"You should portray yourself as you are, of course. It is foolish to perform. And it is even more foolish to overestimate one's skills on horseback. You ought to have known that."

She pointed an accusatory finger at him. "Ah, but I have heard that you, Mr. Rushton, are also a great performer."

Mr. Rushton studied her. "You have thrice laid this accusation at my feet, Miss Bingley. Why not speak plainly? I will not object."

She decided to do just that. "I have heard that you were once engaged to be married to a young lady of large fortune."

"That is true," he said, his face still open.

"And that the lady terminated the engagement when she discovered your family's true situation."

"Also true," he confessed.

"So you admit to being a fortune hunter!"

"Indeed, I do not."

"Then I fear, Mr. Rushton, you will have to explain yourself."

"I will do so happily now that you have asked and not based your entire opinion of me on supposition and gossip."

Caroline crossed her arms over her chest, waiting for him to proceed.

"My father was a proud man, and his humiliation at having sold off so much of Rushton House was complete. He vowed that before he died he would see our fortunes restored, and so with that in mind, he arranged for me to marry the eldest daughter of a wealthy London family when we were yet children. He, of course, did not divulge the status of our estate, only that I was to inherit an ancient house and land. They believed us wealthy and stable, but we needed the money desperately."

Caroline nodded.

"The old dear truly believed that my marriage would save the family, but before we reached the appointed age, my father became ill and died, making me promise that I would fulfill my vow to the lady and save our family land. I agreed, but as our wedding day approached, guilt assailed me. I could not bring myself to withhold the truth from her, so I brought her to Rushton House, which was then in quite a state of disrepair."

Caroline could well imagine the condition of the property. It would please no woman.

"Simply put," Mr. Rushton said, "she broke the engagement, and I allowed it."

"But your vow to your father?"

"I did not break it. The lady ended the engagement, and I said nothing ill about her. In fact, I said nothing at all on the subject, which is why the fortune-hunting rumor still abounds. And I did restore the family land, every piece."

"But how?"

"Through my association with Mr. Newton. Bridge building can be quite lucrative."

Trade, Caroline thought. It always seemed to return to trade.

"So you see, Miss Bingley, it was through my blatant refusal to perform—to present myself as anything other than I was—that I restored my family to rights. And I speak from that experience when I tell you that it is best not to perform for others, whether human or equine."

They were silent a few moments, and Caroline found herself watching the horse and pony as they grazed, to all appearances, peacefully.

"Mr. Rushton, you really should not pretend to have some keen insight into my character or temperament based on my interaction with unpredictable creatures."

"Horses are only unpredictable if their handler does not know their true nature." He too studied the pair of grazing beasts. "Men often experience similar dilemmas in their interactions with your fair sex. If a man does not know a woman's true nature, he cannot adequately predict what might occur next."

"Yes? And now you believe you may predict what I shall do next?"

He smiled. "I would not dare to insult you by admitting it."

She only looked at him, trying to comprehend his meaning.

Then Mr. Rushton stood and reached for her hand. "Come, I find I am quite dried out enough to attempt the walk home."

And with that, he assisted her to her feet and gathered the horses, and together, they returned to Newton House in silence.

As they walked, Caroline looked over her shoulder in the hopes of spying the others of their party, but they were nowhere to be seen.

There was no hope left of cultivating time alone with Mr. Charlton. Depressing as it was, this disastrous outing would likely be her last opportunity of being in his company for some time.

This was a heavy discouragement indeed, but such stumbling blocks only served to embolden Caroline. She may not have triumphed as quickly as she would have liked, but the game was not over.

She would have her baron yet.

༄༅ Thirteen ༅ེ༅

The best course of action, Caroline decided, was to apply to Lavinia for assistance in her quest to marry Mr. Charlton, and she must do so as soon as possible, for the London season was already in progress, and though her friend's brother seemed to show an interest in her at times, he had not yet proposed. And Caroline had the greatest wish to rejoin society as the wife of a future baron. Then her triumph would be complete, her humiliation finally forgotten, and the requirement to make amends with Miss Elizabeth Bennet nullified.

"Do get your bonnet, Mrs. Pickersgill," Caroline said into the quiet sitting room where the ladies had been reclining, "for we must pay a call on Oak Park this morning."

"Yes, Miss Bingley," Rosemary said as she rose to gather her outerwear.

Once in the carriage, Rosemary looked at Caroline with curiosity.

"You seem to be rather purposeful in this visit, Miss Bingley. Is something amiss?"

Caroline scowled and lied, "Of course not. It is a visit. Nothing more."

"Ah," Rosemary said, not sounding convinced at all.

They remained quiet on the remainder of the ride, and when they arrived, they were escorted again to the cavernous drawing room.

Caroline joined Mrs. Winton on the sofa, while Mrs. Pickersgill chose a seat on the opposite one and took a book from the nearby table, obviously giving Caroline her privacy.

After a bit of polite conversation, it was time for Caroline to reveal her motivations for calling.

"Lavinia, I have come to speak with you about a matter of a deeply personal nature," she whispered as she glanced across the room at Mrs. Pickersgill, who appeared to be engrossed in her book. It seemed safe to speak, albeit softly.

"Oh?" Lavinia asked as she leaned in, eyebrows raised in curiosity.

"I trust that we have been friends long enough that you must have already guessed what I might say."

Lavinia blinked at her and then laughed. "You could not be more mistaken, for though you are one of my dearest friends, I have not the slightest conception of what you might say."

That disclosure did not hearten Caroline. She had hoped that her friend might already be aware of her desire to marry her brother and that she would approve and assist her in that goal.

"Then, because you have not guessed already, I will speak plain. Our families have long been acquainted, and, I daresay, no one would argue that we have been the closest of friends for many years."

"No indeed," Lavinia said. "No one could argue that point, but I do not comprehend your hesitancy to speak such an obvious truth."

Caroline took heart at Lavinia's tone and pressed onward. "I hope you will not think me too presumptuous when I say that our families could only grow closer by the arrangement of a strategic union."

Had Lavinia not been one of her dearest schoolfellows, Caroline would have thought her expression momentarily registered shock. However, the look lingered but briefly, so she could not be certain that she had seen it at all.

"Union?"

This question was asked with perhaps more volume of voice than Caroline had hoped to hear. She looked quickly to Mrs.

Pickersgill, whose head was still bent over the book. She appeared not to have heard.

Caroline took a bracing breath and then spoke aloud. "Indeed, I hope I might have your support in convincing your brother, Mr. Charlton, that a closer connection between our families might be a benefit to both."

A small crease formed between Lavinia's eyes. Caroline could not tell if her friend's countenance showed her bafflement or anger, but she could certainly feel the searching nature of her look. Lavinia's intense exploration of Caroline's face was both disconcerting and more than a bit bewildering.

Could Lavinia have not guessed her motives?

"My dearest friend, tell me. Are you suggesting an"—here, Lavinia's voice seemed to catch, but she continued—"alliance of a marital nature between yourself and my brother?"

Caroline nodded.

Lavinia straightened her back and cocked her head to the side, asking an unspoken question.

Well, Caroline would explain her motives, and then Lavinia would comprehend the necessity of such a merger.

"Our association would be advantageous to all parties." Caroline watched as Lavinia's features went entirely blank. There was no joy, sorrow, or conflict to be had within her expression or demeanor. Only a confusing vacancy. "You and I would be sisters. Your brother would be wed." She lowered her voice to a whisper. "And the rumors about his proclivities of socializing with those so decidedly beneath him would be ended. And though I do not fancy my fortune to be a large enticement, it would no doubt aid in its own little way."

Lavinia's blank expression altered, and a smile slid across her features.

Yes, money was ever an enticement, Caroline thought.

When Lavinia finally spoke, her voice had taken on a new tone that was not entirely comprehensible to Caroline. "I may make one promise to you, my oldest and dearest friend: I will do whatever is in my power to ensure that both our families get precisely what is warranted."

A snort from the opposite side of the room impeded Caroline's sense of relief. She lanced Mrs. Pickersgill with a sharp stare. "Mrs. Pickersgill, if you are ill, kindly remove yourself from this chamber so that you do not infect us all."

"Pardon me, Miss Bingley," Rosemary said with a decidedly unapologetic tone. "I am not ill, and I certainly did not intend to distract you from your tête-a-tête." She then went back to her reading without the least hint of appropriate embarrassment, and Caroline reminded herself that she ought to continue to speak in hushed tones.

To Lavinia, she whispered, "I am relieved indeed to find that you favor the match."

"Indeed, I am glad to offer you some relief," Lavinia said, her head still held high.

"I hope you will direct me in the best way to convince your brother of the rightness of such unification of our families in that manner."

Lavinia reached out and patted Caroline's hands, which had been clutched in her lap for the balance of the conversation. "Do not give my brother the least thought, for I shall design the strategy myself."

⚬⚭ ⚭⚬

After their return from Oak Park, Caroline and Rosemary spent the afternoon in the cutting garden with Mrs. Newton, and Caroline had just gone to clean the soil from her hands and change into her dinner attire when a knock sounded at her bedchamber door.

"Pardon me, miss," said the rather fresh-faced young maid, "but Mrs. Newton bid me to inform you that Mr. Charlton is awaiting you in the sitting room."

"Mr. Charlton?" Caroline asked. Lavinia was an efficient worker if he had come this very day to make his proposal.

"Yes, miss," the maid affirmed.

Caroline quickly surveyed herself in the mirror. Her light blue dress had a white chevron pattern and was suitable for a country meal, but it would not do now. Not with Mr. Charlton about to make his proposal.

"Go and find my green silk gown and help me redress quickly," Caroline commanded the maid, who dashed to the wardrobe and began to search through the gowns stored there.

She did as Caroline asked, returning to her side with her finest London gown that seemed to accentuate her features nicely.

She managed to don the gown in a timely fashion, but then she realized her hairstyle would not do for such an occasion, and she demanded that the maid help rearrange that as well.

In the end, her decision to redress quickly took her almost an hour to accomplish, but when she entered the sitting room, she was pleased to have made the choice she had, for Mr. Charlton's eyes seemed to lighten upon his first sight of her.

He leapt off the high-backed chair where he had been sitting and speaking with Rosemary. "Oh! Miss Bingley, there you are."

Rosemary also stood and took in her mistress's appearance, and her eyes narrowed with suspicion. "Good evening, Miss Bingley. You look lovely."

A crease formed between Caroline's eyes as she tried to eke some hidden purpose from Rosemary's words, but who could fathom what that woman was thinking? She would do better not to try to interpret her at all. Instead, she turned her pleasure upon Mr. Charlton when he said, "Yes, indeed. You make quite a picture, just as Mrs. Pickersgill said."

Caroline stood for a moment longer so that Mr. Charlton could admire her further if he wished, and then she took a seat on the chair opposite his.

Mr. Charlton watched as she sat, and Caroline believed she might have seen a twinge of regret in his expression, but she only smiled at him and said, "We are so pleased to have you in our home this evening."

"I have been here too long already," he said as he removed his watch from the fob pocket of his breeches and glanced at it, "but I found myself quite compelled to stop here on my ride back from town."

Caroline blushed. "I am honored," she said.

"I simply could not leave Kendal without taking leave of you," he said.

Caroline's blush suddenly drained, and she felt her face pale. "Leave Kendal?"

"Yes, unfortunately, Lavinia had a letter from our father just this morning, and we have been called immediately to London."

"London?" Caroline repeated lamely. She knew she was staring at him with confusion and questions in her eyes, and that it was a most unsophisticated expression, but she could not prevent herself from looking at him thus.

On the periphery, she saw Rosemary look from her to Mr. Charlton.

"It seems a rather abrupt decision," Rosemary said into the awkward silence.

He nodded. "My sister was in a fine dander this morning and gave me barely a moment to sit, much less the opportunity to read the missive itself, before sending me on this errand. We depart tomorrow morning."

Caroline stared at him, then shook herself and managed to ask, "Has something happened to your father?"

She desperately hoped for a negative response, for it was too soon for the barony to transfer to Mr. Charlton. He had not yet proposed, and Caroline had no wish to compete for him with all the eager young ladies in Town.

"Good Lord, I should hope not, for then I would be required to take over his position," he said on a bitter laugh. Then he shrugged. "Lavinia says he is well but demands our presence. That is all I know."

"How odd," Rosemary said, again looking from Caroline to Mr. Charlton.

"When will you return to Kendal?" Caroline asked, and then, not liking the note of desperation in her voice, she cleared her throat and added, "For society will be quite tedious without your sister to lead us."

"I do not know when I shall return," Mr. Charlton said, turning his dark eyes upon her, and Caroline wondered if they didn't hold a bit of longing. "But I do hope it will be soon, for there is much for me yet to do here."

Caroline felt her skin prickle a bit. What did this signify? She managed to hold his intense gaze for long moments until Rosemary shifted in her seat.

Then Caroline felt a sudden, strange lack of emotion. She was not embarrassed at having been caught staring at Mr. Charlton, sad that he was leaving, or entranced any longer by those dark eyes.

Mr. Charlton did not make his proposal that evening, but Caroline did not feel regret at all when he stood and took his leave of her, bowing deeply over her hand.

She maintained her odd emotionless state as she looked out the window and watched Mr. Charlton's carriage disappear down the drive.

"How odd," Rosemary said again. She had been standing silently next to Caroline at the window. "How very odd."

"You repeat yourself," Caroline replied without looking at her. "Why?"

Rosemary had been holding back one of the drapes to improve her view of the gentleman's departure, and she let it slip through her fingers. The fabric swayed in front of Caroline, briefly blocking her view of the drive.

"Do you not find it strange, Miss Bingley, that only this morning you went to Oak Park to solicit Mrs. Winton's aid in winning Mr. Charlton, and now they cannot leave Kendal quickly enough?"

Caroline's face jerked toward her companion's. "You were eavesdropping on our conversation, were you?" she demanded.

Caroline's sharp tone did not appear to unnerve Rosemary, who only said quietly, "You were speaking loudly enough to be heard in Bath."

Caroline could not deny that their conversation had grown in volume as it continued, but she had greatly hoped Rosemary had not overheard. She looked out the window and let the implications of her companion's words wash over her. Caroline's plan was no longer secret. Lavinia knew her desires, as did this woman, her paid companion.

"I am not your enemy, Miss Bingley," Rosemary said, as if she read her thoughts. "But I fear Mrs. Winton is."

Slowly, Caroline turned to look again at Rosemary. Her thoughts seemed to move so quickly that they blurred within her head.

What was this woman implying?

Lavinia was her friend, her dearest acquaintance.

"You mean…?" Caroline began, but she could not allow herself to name her fear.

"That Mrs. Winton objects to the idea of your marrying Mr. Charlton? Yes," Rosemary finished. "I am sorry to say it so plainly, but I fear it is so."

Caroline walked from the window and fell into a chair. She stared at the lace trim on her sleeve, willing the pattern to assemble itself into some sort of comprehensible structure, for like her thoughts, it blurred before her eyes.

No, it could not be possible.

Could it? Could Lavinia object to her marriage to Mr. Charlton?

No, it was a ridiculous thought indeed. They were friends, and Caroline said as much to Rosemary.

"Are you certain?" Rosemary asked in a gentle voice as she sat in a chair beside her mistress.

"Yes, I am certain," she said, though questions raced through her mind.

She did not relish being forced to doubt her situation.

"I speak only as a friend, Miss Bingley. I do not want to see you injured."

Caroline suddenly felt an emotion: anger. It coursed from her feet, through her body, to her face, and she could not contain herself as she spat, "You? A friend? No, you are a servant. Lavinia is my friend, my dearest friend, and she would never treat me in such a fashion."

What Caroline did not add was that she would never allow herself to be treated as she herself had treated Miss Jane Bennet. She would never play the role of innocent victim, to have her object removed from her. No, she would never permit herself to be so fooled.

Rosemary remained silent and composed as Caroline fumed and then began to pace the room, but the older woman's calm did nothing to soothe the younger, for her ire only rose, leaving her capable of speaking only in short sentences. "You have no grounds for such statements. Your observations are flawed, and you have misunderstood everyone! You are a mere servant in this household. You are no lady of status, even if every person here pretends you to be otherwise. You are certainly not my friend."

"Indeed, I am a servant, as you have twice reminded me," Rosemary affirmed with such irritating rationality that Caroline was tempted to shout at her. "I have contracted myself to your brother's employ, not yours, and I have promised to see to your care. As such, I shall have no compunction at proving Mrs. Winton's guilt to you."

"Ha! She is guilty of nothing," Caroline protested.

"As you have said, Miss Bingley," Rosemary said, "but mark me: after this is over, you will see Mrs. Winton for what she is, and you will realize that a mere servant is the best friend you could ever hope to have."

Caroline snorted and paced the room with added animation as she began to formulate a plan. "We shall see, Mrs. Pickersgill, who is my friend and who is not, for I shall devise a method of getting us to London and back into Mr. Charlton's company. Then," she said as she whirled on her companion, "we will know who is right!"

৩৩৫ Fourteen ৩৯৯

As it turns out, the formulation of a plan was ever so much easier than actually seeing it to completion.

Desperate as she was, Caroline could not bring herself to disappoint her mother by simply declaring her intentions to leave Kendal. No, she must engineer a method for departing for London without injuring Mrs. Newton, and that would be a difficult task indeed.

First, Caroline contemplated proposing a family voyage to Town under the pretense of enjoying the gaiety of the season, but she immediately discounted that as a possibility. Mrs. Newton despised travel and would not be induced to leave Kendal for something as superficial as balls and society. Why, she could not even be convinced to attend her son's wedding in Hertfordshire, so it was rather a useless attempt to woo her mother with tales of far-flung locales.

Second, Caroline considered the prospect of utter fibs. She could claim that Rosemary had received word from her relations that her presence was required in Town immediately and that she would accompany her companion to provide support during a difficult time. Upon reflection, Caroline realized that no one would believe such a tale. It was preposterous. No one would believe that Rosemary was important enough to be needed in Town or that Caroline would accompany a servant anywhere of her own will.

Third, and oh so very briefly, Caroline mulled over the idea of claiming desperation to see her brother. Instead of taking up residence again with Charles, which he would not accept until she made proper amends, she might stay in a reputable inn until Mr. Charlton's proposal could be secured. This, however, would not do either, for Charles would never allow it. One letter from Mama and Charles would ferret out Caroline, drag her back to Kendal, and reveal her misdeeds to her mother.

That would not do at all.

Caroline quite despaired of ever contriving a reason for following Mr. Charlton to Town, and she spent her days moping about Newton House under the watchful eye of Rosemary, who must suspect that Caroline had not lost her drive to chase Mr. Charlton and might do something rash if she were not careful.

A fortnight passed before opportunity found Caroline, and this sudden chance derived from the most unlikely avenue: Mr. Newton himself.

One morning at breakfast, he declared, "I fear, my dear Mrs. Newton, that it is time for Mr. Rushton and I to be away to London to see to the commencement of the Fairmont Bridge's construction."

Mrs. Newton immediately dropped the piece of toast onto which she had been applying a liberal amount of preserves and said, "Oh no! Already? It seems as though you just returned from your last journey."

Caroline too dropped her toast, but for an altogether different reason. She picked it up quickly and dipped her spoon in the preserves as she looked around to see if anyone had noticed her slip.

Curse it, they had!

Mr. Rushton and Rosemary were watching her much too closely.

Caroline met their eyes steadily, one at a time, as she listened to her mother try to talk Mr. Newton into remaining at home just a while longer.

"I fear, my dear," Mr. Newton replied, "that we must go to London, and we must leave before the month is out, for I have had it in a letter that construction is soon to begin, and you know that I cannot bear to sit alongside while other men have the fun of working with stone and mortar."

While Caroline managed to restrain her snort of derision, Mrs. Newton picked up her toast once again, but rather than spreading condiments upon it or consuming it, she began using it as a conversational aid. She pointed the toast at Mr. Rushton and asked, "And you must be away too?"

"I fear I must, madam, though I am grateful for your hospitality. I quite agree with Mr. Newton that a designer must be present for the production of that which he has created."

"But our household will be lost without you!" she cried, flinging the toast about as she gestured.

Mr. Newton reached across the table and rescued the crumbling bread. "My dear," he said as he patted her hand in consolation, "you are most welcome to accompany me, for it would make my time in London so much pleasanter." He looked at the whole company who sat around the table, and his sideburns widened as he smiled. "You are all most welcome to join us. We would, of course, not impose upon Mr. Rushton as I often do while in Town. We could take some rooms at a hotel or perhaps lease our own home for a time."

Mrs. Newton's face fell, and Caroline knew what was forthcoming. Her mother despised travel and would not leave Kendal without great inducement.

"But it seems as if Caroline has only just arrived," Mrs. Newton said. "I could not possibly leave her or demand that she embark on another voyage so soon."

Caroline used great restraint as she said, "I would not object to a trip to Town, Mama. You know I adore it so, and I could show you all its glories."

"You would undertake another coach ride so soon?" Mrs. Newton asked.

"Yes, indeed, Mama." Mrs. Newton appeared skeptical, so Caroline added, "As much as I despise bumping along in a coach, I have always found that the discomfort is quickly forgotten once the destination is reached."

"Does my daughter speak true, Mr. Rushton?" Mrs. Newton asked.

"She is mostly accurate," he conceded, "but there is no need to pass an uncomfortable journey. We may take just as much time as you please and view the sights as we go."

Mrs. Newton turned to her husband. "Is that so, my dear?"

"Why of course, Mrs. Newton. Why do you think so many people undertake such monstrous trips? It is enjoyable and quite a delight to see new places and meet new people."

Mrs. Newton began to look pensive, and Caroline was heartened, for a conversation of travel rarely reached this point with her.

Caroline added, "Besides, the occupants of Oak Park have been in London these two weeks, so our arrival would be more like a homecoming than a trip to a strange land. We would be reunited with friends."

Caroline glanced at Rosemary as she spoke the word "friends." Rosemary rolled her eyes but added, "For my part, I shall do as I am willed, but I must say that I have no objections to such a journey."

Caroline stared. No objections? Rosemary claimed to want to protect Caroline from Lavinia, but now she had no objections to going to Town, where they would again be in Lavina's sphere? What new game was this?

"Well," Mrs. Newton said, drawing out the word, "I suppose it is rather illogical for me to confine myself always to Kendal."

Her mother's voice sounded quite uncertain, so Caroline said, "Oh yes, Mama. You must travel or else you shall miss so much of the world."

Mr. Rushton cleared his throat. "But only if you are willing, Mrs. Newton."

"Yes, indeed," Mr. Newton added. "We shall see to your utmost comfort, shall we not?" He glanced around the table to see the affirmation in everyone's eyes.

"You already know my preference for a journey of moderate pace. It is easier on the horses," Mr. Rushton said.

Caroline scarcely stopped herself from rolling her eyes at him. Who gave a fig about horses? But she would say nothing to damage the look of acquiescence in her mother's eyes.

"We shall travel quite at our leisure," Mr. Newton said as he rounded the table and knelt before his wife. He took her hand in his and gave her a pleading look. "We shall see all the best views and rest only in the most comfortable inns."

Here, Mr. Rushton interjected, "And you are cordially invited to stay at my home while in London. I would not have you at a hotel when you can rest more comfortably with me."

Mr. Newton nodded his thanks and then returned his attention to his wife. From his position on the floor, he looked up, eyes imploring, and said, "Allow me to show you the world, my dear."

"Well," Mrs. Newton said again with a look around the table. The hopeful expressions of all gathered there must have solidified her tenuous decision, for she said, "I shall be very pleased to see the world if you will all be with me!"

And so Caroline got her wish. She was going to London.

✥ ✥

Another fortnight passed before Mrs. Newton had managed to pack her necessities, and this only occurred under Caroline's constant reminder that the journey was indeed a splendid idea. After practicing continual persuasion for so many days, Caroline was quite shocked when at dawn on the day of their planned departure, it was Mrs. Newton who arrived first at the coach.

"Oh, I am so pleased that you have talked me into this voyage," she cried as the groggy travelers filed within: Mr. and Mrs. Newton on one bench and Rosemary and Caroline on the other. Mr. Rushton was astride his grey mare.

"I thought I would feel uneasy at the start of our trip," Mrs. Newton continued, "but I find myself ever so eager to be off now that the decision has been made!"

Caroline smiled at her mother, adjusting her position on the bench as the coach lurched to a start. "I too am pleased, Mama.

Our journey will be full of beauty, and the weather will only warm as we head south."

"I cannot wait to feel the sun on my skin." Mrs. Newton grinned. "I am now most pleased to be traveling to London, for I have written to your brother to meet us there if he possibly can."

Caroline forced a smile. "Oh?" she asked. "I did not know you had contacted Charles. Has he responded?" She glanced quickly at Rosemary, who also appeared curious, and then looked deliberately out the coach window as her mother spoke so that no one might see her reaction.

"No, but I told him where we were to stay, and I am certain the letter will find him in his travels and he will come to see his mother."

Caroline nearly sighed in relief. The letter might take weeks to reach Charles, and then, it might take yet more weeks for him to travel to London. By then, Caroline would most certainly have won Mr. Charlton, for he seemed almost near to proposing on at least one occasion already, and now she had Lavinia's aid, despite Rosemary's contrary opinion.

Outside the coach, the sun slowly melted the dew from the grass, and Mr. Rushton rode beside them, looking very much pleased with himself. Caroline scowled as he tipped his hat to her in greeting.

"Why does he insist on riding horseback when there is a perfectly good coach?" Caroline asked.

Mr. Newton laughed. "He is a young fellow and ever in want of exercise and sun. He will join us inside only in the event of foul weather."

Under her breath, Caroline added, "Then I shall hope the sun remains for the duration of our trip."

◈◈ ◈◈

This hope, of course, proved fruitless, for after nearly a week of blessedly dry weather, the Newtons' coach encountered precipitation: a soft spring rain accompanied by a moderation of temperature.

The rain began after their noontime stop for victuals and fresh horses, and Mrs. Newton become quite anxious for Mr. Rushton's health. She leaned out the carriage window and waved at him as he rode alongside.

"Mr. Rushton!" she called. "Do join us in the coach, for I fear you shall catch your death of cold out there in all that moisture."

Caroline watched as Mr. Rushton turned to respond. Though the rain appeared to be but a mist, he seemed quite damp indeed. His coat adhered closely to his upper body, revealing his outline in alarming detail. Caroline forced herself to look away from his broad chest and instead followed the line of his body to his head, discovering that even his hair was flattened to his forehead, and his hat appeared limp.

Mr. Rushton's face glistened with rainwater, but his eyes danced brightly.

"There is no need for fear, Mrs. Newton," he insisted. "I am quite well."

Mrs. Newton leaned back in the coach to appeal to Mr. Newton. "Do make him come inside! That rain is cold, and I would much rather have him snuggled inside with us."

Caroline winced. She did not relish the idea of a warm, wet Mr. Rushton snuggling amongst them.

But Mr. Newton did as his wife bade and leaned out the window. "Come, Rushton, do not be foolish. Join us before you become soaked through. There is adequate room, surely, for I purchased the largest coach available." He turned toward Mrs. Newton. "I knew the decision would prove fortuitous one day."

"I find myself quite comfortable," his wife said with a look around, "but I do worry about poor Mr. Rushton."

Caroline watched as poor Mr. Rushton's shoulders moved into a shrug and he relented, saying, "If you insist, I shall join you."

Mr. Newton rapped on the top of the coach to alert the driver to stop, and Caroline watched as Mr. Rushton reined in his horse and dismounted. He disappeared around the back of the coach, likely to tie up the great beast, and then reappeared at the door.

"Where shall I sit?" he asked, surveying the arrangement.

Rosemary, cursed woman, was asleep again, so she would not be moved from her place on the bench. Mr. and Mrs. Newton quite took up one full bench on their own, so there was only one spot available: between Rosemary and Caroline.

Caroline thought to poke her companion, for she suspected Rosemary was feigning slumber. Who could sleep through all that yelling and jostling as the coach ground to a halt? But Mrs. Newton pointed out, "There is adequate space there between Mrs. Pickersgill and Caroline."

And that is just where Mr. Rushton deposited himself.

Then he smiled at her, quite aware of her discomfort, she realized.

"Do slide to the right, Mr. Rushton," Caroline demanded. "I do not want my gown ruined by your damp clothing," she said as she pulled her lap robe higher.

But Mr. Rushton did not move.

ᵉᵍᴸ Fifteen ᶿᵉᵃ

"Miss Bingley."

The voice tickled her ear.

Caroline attempted to rub it away with her hand.

She heard a soft chuckle in response, but it faded so quickly into the pleasing sound of raindrops tapping on the roof that she wondered if she had imagined it. The gentle rocking of the coach lulled her, and slowly, all sound began to recede once more.

"Miss Bingley," the voice repeated, softer this time. "Wake up."

Caroline's eyes slowly slid open to find Mr. Rushton looking at her. She gazed back at him for long moments, enjoying his closeness before she realized she should be affronted by it.

Then she experienced a moment of horror at the thought that she might have fallen asleep on his shoulder, but as she took stock of the situation, she realized that she had been reclined against the side of the carriage. She righted herself and looked about her to discover that Rosemary, her mother, and Mr. Newton were asleep. The interior of the coach seemed muted, casting Mr. Rushton in softness, which must account for the fact that she had no urge to scoot away from him even though he was sitting so close that she could feel him along her whole side.

Slightly discomfited by his nearness, she turned her head and peeked out the window to find that the clouds had gathered so closely that they blocked out the sun, making it appear to be as dark as a moonless midnight though it was not yet suppertime.

Everything seemed calm, warm, and safe. The coach seemed to cocoon her.

Why, then, had Mr. Rushton awakened her?

"What?" Caroline demanded in a harsh whisper.

His eyes narrowed slightly. "I know I should have followed my own good judgment and allowed you to continue sleeping, but you were whimpering."

"Whimpering?" Caroline repeated, slightly louder than a whisper. "I was most certainly not whimpering. I do not whimper."

"Indeed, you were, and indeed, you do," he insisted.

Caroline crossed her arms in front of her.

Mr. Rushton smiled pleasantly as if she had just said something kind. "Were you dreaming?" he whispered.

Was I dreaming? Caroline wondered.

"I do not know," she whispered back.

Mr. Rushton watched her expectantly, and Caroline looked away as she tried to recall what she might have dreamt. She closed her eyes and attempted to forget Mr. Rushton's proximity as she focused on the sound of the wheels sliding across the muddy roads.

The wind gathered in intensity outside, and the images of her dream returned from somewhere within the confines of her mind. If it was true that she had been whimpering, then she expected the dream to have featured Mr. Darcy, but surprisingly, her brother's vexed face appeared in her mind. She could not hear his words, but he was making broad gestures with his hands, forcing her to walk backward, away from him. Suddenly, she was standing outside Pemberley with the door closed and locked solidly in front of her.

Caroline opened her eyes to discover Mr. Rushton still watching her.

"I cannot recall the dream," she lied. "And I most certainly did not whimper."

"Ah, now those are lies, Miss Bingley," he said in a disarmingly conversational tone. "Come, I have told you my secret. You must share yours. What has made you so sad?"

Caroline had not the least intention of telling him anything, but as she turned to rebuff him, his countenance was so sincere, the carriage so warm, and the rain so soft outside that she found herself saying more than she meant.

"I dreamed of my brother Charles," she confessed.

"Yes?"

"We argued."

"Ah."

"And he sent me away."

Mr. Rushton studied her for long moments as the carriage rocked them. "That was more than a mere dream, was it not? That is what truly occurred to bring you to Kendal?"

Caroline sighed and looked at her mother, who was still asleep on Mr. Newton's shoulder. "I told you once I came out of love for my mother, and I do love her, but yes, the truth is that I was forced to come."

"But why?"

"Charles and I argued."

He cocked his head sideways and waited for further explanation.

"I opposed Charles's choice of bride," she heard herself say. "Jane is a sweet girl, but a fortune hunter nonetheless."

Mr. Rushton considered her for a moment. "We are all fortune hunters, Miss Bingley, in our own way. Society tells us that marriage is the only way to gain or secure a fortune, but it is not true."

"Oh, but it is true!" Caroline whispered. "Though I have 20,000 pounds, I have nothing! I must follow my brother's wishes as he has control over my allowance. I must marry, but then my husband gains control of the whole." Caroline looked him directly in the eyes. "So you see, in order to have anything, Mr. Rushton, anything at all of my very own, I must marry. Only then will I have any sort of power over my life."

He did not speak but kept his eyes on her.

She sighed. "Miss Jane Bennet had nothing. No wealth, connections, or land. I knew precisely what she was about, and I only wanted to save Charles..." She thought of Mr. Darcy and her desire to marry him. "To save myself."

"That is perhaps the first honest remark you have made since arriving at Kendal, Miss Bingley," Mr. Rushton said with soft eyes. "I only wish it were the whole truth, but I shall forgive you for withholding, for it is clear that you are wracked with guilt."

"Guilt? No, I was innocent," she protested. "My attempt to separate them was just and fair. I was in the right."

Mr. Rushton's next words surprised her. "I believe you probably were, Miss Bingley, and your protest was meant to protect your brother, but your proclaimed innocence seems doubtful."

"You are speaking nonsense," she said, still in a whisper, as she leaned away to take in his full facial expression. "Whatever do you mean?"

"Take, for example, the charges against me. They were true. For a time, I was a fortune hunter."

"But you released your object when given the choice."

"Indeed I did, but until that very moment, I would have proceeded with the marriage. I was behaving as my father expected—even as society required. I was in the right, but still far from innocent."

Silence descended as Caroline contemplated his words. Their gazes met and the intimacy of the coach intensified. Around them, their companions slept on, and they did not witness the moment when Mr. Rushton's head leaned further toward her, their faces drawing very close, his lips a whisper away.

Caroline did not move. She could not, though she knew she should have. Instead, she closed her eyes, expecting any moment that his lips would touch hers.

So when his fingertips brushed her cheek, her eyes flew open.

Mr. Rushton remained as close as before, watching her carefully as his fingers trailed down the length of her neck. She sucked in a breath at the unexpected warmth that flooded her, and try as she might, she could not look away.

"No, not innocent," Mr. Rushton whispered. "We are, neither of us, innocent, are we?"

"No," Caroline breathed as his fingertips stroked the back of her neck and then disappeared back into his lap.

A protest rose within her, but not at his words. She had the oddest desire to object to the removal of his hand, the ending of the intimacy they had shared.

As if sensing her protest, he smiled. "Do not fear. I will hold you again once all your secrets are made plain to me, for I believe, Miss Bingley, that London shall reveal all."

৩৫ Sixteen ৯৯৯

Mr. Rushton's words had shattered the coach's intimacy and ended the odd détente between him and Caroline, and soon after, the coachman pulled into their final stop of the day.

As the carriage jarred to a halt, its occupants awakened to find Caroline's back turned as much as possible to Mr. Rushton, and so they perceived no change in the relationship between the two. And when Caroline elected to take dinner in her private chamber, no one found it out of character.

But now Caroline felt a spark between herself and Mr. Rushton, and she was not convinced that once ignited it would erupt into anger, as it should have, rather than into something altogether more terrifying. And that caused her great tribulation indeed. She could not experience romantic sentiments for a tradesman. No indeed!

Much to her relief, the sun soon returned, and with it Mr. Rushton had been restored to his saddle, so Caroline had been able to avoid him quite successfully for the remainder of their journey.

In a coach and four, the trip from Kendal to London should have endured six days, but with Mr. Newton's overly cautious care of his wife and Mr. Rushton's dislike of overtaxing horses, it took ten.

When at last they arrived in London and the coach halted in front of the town home Mr. Rushton owned in Grosvenor Street, Caroline was both overjoyed and overwhelmed.

She had not expected Grosvenor Street, one of London's finest. Indeed, the house's grand presence evoked awe and a bit of jealousy within her. An intricate pattern of cream-colored Portland stone and elegant sash windows graced its façade, and it seemed to tower above the adjoining homes. It made her sister Louisa's town house, which was no less charmingly designed of red brick, appear inconsequential in comparison.

Mr. Rushton was either wealthier than Caroline had believed or more deeply in debt. Either way, it mattered not to her, for he would always be a tradesman. She must remember that.

"Do come in," Mr. Rushton said as he bounded up the staircase to the front door. Caroline followed at a sedate pace and attempted to appear apathetic to the home's splendor.

Rosemary, who walked along beside her with her head down as if the steps might move beneath her feet, turned slightly to Caroline and whispered, "You did not tell me that Mr. Rushton's home was in this precise location."

Caroline's eyebrows lowered. "That is because I did not know its precise location. Why should it matter where the house is located?"

"I suppose it does not," Rosemary said in a halting tone. "It is only...well, this is Grosvenor Street!"

"Yes, one of the finest in London." Caroline turned to her. "I am shocked as well. I did not know they would allow tradesmen to lease on this street. I had expected to stay in Cheapside."

She regretted at once her mention of Cheapside. The very name called to mind Miss Jane Bennet, who had resided in that section of Town with her aunt and uncle when she came to London in pursuit of Charles.

She looked again to Rosemary and despised her for insinuating that her current situation held any similarity to Jane's. Lavinia had most certainly not removed Mr. Charlton to prevent a union, and her installation in Grosvenor Street must be a sign that her London excursion would not end as Jane's had. Caroline would win her object immediately and go about Town as the wife of a future baron. There would be no drama, no attempts at concealment. All would go smoothly.

She was about to speak again to Rosemary on the subject of fashionable addresses and her good fortune at staying on this street, but a maid appeared and escorted the group to their chambers.

Caroline followed the maid's precise footsteps up the house's main staircase and then to a fine guest chamber that overlooked the street. From her vantage point, Caroline could see Grosvenor Square and everyone who walked nearby. The chamber was ideal, for she would be able to accost Mr. Charlton whenever he happened by, and everyone came to Grosvenor Square eventually. Caroline would simply wait and seize upon him.

Rosemary was stationed across the hall, but she soon rapped on Caroline's door.

"Have you come to assist me with this gown?" Caroline asked upon Rosemary's entry.

Rosemary paused. "Yes, indeed I have."

Her companion crossed the room and began helping Caroline remove her dusty traveling attire. Her careful fingers worked the buttons and at length she said, "It is a lovely house."

"Yes," Caroline agreed on a sigh, "but I shall never comprehend how Mr. Rushton was able to purchase it. There must have been some error in drawing up the papers that allowed him to afford it."

"Hmm," Rosemary said. She was prevented from saying more until Caroline's dress had been removed and laid aside.

"Will you be much out in company while in London, Miss Bingley?" her companion asked as she slipped Caroline's wrapper onto her shoulders and then crossed the room to regard the trunks, which a manservant had delivered earlier.

"Of course! What is there to do in Town but be in company?"

"I see." Rosemary began to rearrange some items in one of Caroline's trunks. "And I shall be required to accompany you?"

Though she had no wish for the woman to follow her about Town, Caroline did not like the idea of a servant choosing her own duties. Rosemary was here to act as Caroline's companion after all. "Do you object to performing your duties in Town?" she asked.

"No indeed." Rosemary turned, faced her, and then lowered her eyes. She fidgeted with the hem of her sleeve and then said, "I do know now what I was thinking in coming here. I had hoped…. Miss Bingley, there is something I must confess."

"Oh?" Caroline sat on her bed, curious about what might cause the woman so much consternation. It could be nothing of true consequence, surely.

"I am known in Town," Rosemary said flatly.

"Known? Whatever do you mean?"

Rosemary raised her eyes and looked directly at Caroline. "I mean that people know me."

Caroline also raised an eyebrow and crossed her arms. "You have developed a reputation?"

"Yes, Miss Bingley. I have a reputation of sorts."

"Of what sort?" asked Caroline. Now she was imagining the worst. Had Charles hired a companion who was nothing more than a fallen woman of poor character?

"It is nothing as immoral or reprehensible as you must be imagining, but I thought it best to warn you that people may find my return to London rather interesting."

"Are you a fallen woman?" Caroline demanded.

"No, I am not wicked! I am merely known."

Caroline could not fathom what her companion was going on about, and she said, "Explain yourself clearly or leave me, for I am too tired to listen to more of this prattle tonight."

"I will tell you only that I am neither wicked nor dissolute, and that must provide enough comfort, for I shall only reveal my secrets if I am required to do so."

"And if I required you to speak?"

"You could not. Only my circumstances can induce me to speak."

Caroline could see very well that she would make no progress with Rosemary, and she was eager to rest, so she said, "Leave me, please."

Rosemary opened her mouth as if to protest, but then she obeyed her mistress and left the room without another word.

◦◦ ◦◦

Caroline awoke the next morning to the sound of iron horseshoes striking pavement.

After so many days of travel and so many nights in different coaching inns, for a moment Caroline could not remember where she was. She sat up, letting the bed linens fall away as she peeked out the window.

She was not in a coaching inn, but in London, in Grosvenor Street of all places, and now she must be about the business of discovering Mr. Charlton and Lavinia.

And so she passed a full week at her original plan of watching passersby as they visited Grosvenor Square. Neither Lavinia nor Mr. Charlton appeared, and on the first day of the second week, Caroline was forced to take more aggressive action.

She would have to go out and search for them herself.

On that morning, she rang for a breakfast of meats, bread, jam, and a small pot of chocolate, and after consuming her meal, she again rang the bell for assistance in dressing herself and coiffing her hair. Her appearance today was crucial. She could not meet Mr. Charlton without looking her very best.

As the maid went about her duties, Caroline found that she could not help but approve of the manner in which Mr. Rushton's household was being run. The servants obviously respected their master despite his acerbic wit and lackadaisical temperament, and they performed their assigned tasks without requiring much direction.

She had not expected Mr. Rushton to keep a respectable household.

Descending the stairs, Caroline steeled herself to encounter the gentleman in question, for she had not felt quite comfortable with him since their conversation in the coach. Still, she forced herself to smile as she entered the breakfast room with her reticule clutched tightly in her hand. "Good morning," Caroline said to the gathered party. "Please keep your seats."

Mr. Newton and Mr. Rushton, who stood despite her injunction against it, both bowed their greetings and then returned to their chairs.

"Will you not join us for breakfast, my dear?" Mrs. Newton asked. She seemed perfectly comfortable, even so far from Newton House and in the home of another, and Caroline could not help but be pleased. She had not expected her mother to fare so well in London.

"I have breakfasted in my chamber, and now that I am quite recovered from our long journey from the north, I find I am eager to walk about the streets as soon as Mrs. Pickersgill is ready. Mama, would you care to join us?"

"Mr. Newton, Mr. Rushton, and I are bound for Fairmont Bridge this morning," Mrs. Newton said. "We were hoping you would come along."

"Oh, it is a kind invitation, but you are well aware that I have little interest in bridges. I shall keep to my plans and have a nice walk about the city today, and perhaps I will visit some shops."

"Oh, well, I am disappointed, but I cannot chastise you, for we all have our own interests, do we not?" Mrs. Newton took a sip of her morning tea and gestured at a vacant chair with her cup. "Only do sit a moment and allow me to tell you my news."

Caroline did as she was bid, taking the empty chair beside Mr. Rushton, who smiled at her expectantly.

Feeling concern rise in her at Mr. Rushton's expression, she frowned back at him. He seemed to be taunting her without speaking. He knew something, and she did not like it. Deliberately turning away from his smirking face, she asked, "What news, Mama?"

"I have had a letter from your brother!"

"Oh?" Caroline asked, though she did not wish to hear what she knew must be forthcoming.

"He received my letter and is even now en route to London with his friends."

Caroline sat back in her chair as this news descended upon her. How had her mother's letter reached Charles so quickly? He was traveling she knew not where. It should have taken months for her mother's missive to find him.

Worse, his friends were coming with him. His friends!

Caroline forced a smile to her lips. "What friends?"

"Your former traveling companions save your sister and Mr. Hurst. They remain in Devonshire."

"I am sorry to hear that Louisa will not come," Caroline said and then, though it cost her, added, "but I am pleased that you will soon meet your new daughter."

"Oh yes!" Mrs. Newton said with a clap of her hands that fairly shook the dining table. "I long to meet our Jane!"

Mrs. Newton's eyes had filled with joyful tears. Her happiness was too pure to be trifled with, and so Caroline nodded in agreement. "She is sweet. You will approve Charles's choice."

"I am certain I shall!"

"Have you not forgotten something, my dear?" Mr. Newton prodded.

"Oh!" Mrs. Newton exclaimed as she picked up the letter that had been lying neglected on the table. "Charles included a letter to you, Caro."

Caroline watched not without trepidation as her mother removed a smaller letter from within the larger missive and passed it across the table to her.

Caroline looked at it, wishing very much not to read it in company, for she had a good notion of what it might contain. But everyone was regarding her, so she broke the seal and began to read silently. The words were scribed in her brother's nearly illegible handwriting.

Dear sister—

Please forgive the brevity of this letter, but I see little need in wasting ink when we are to be together soon. I do not know how you convinced Mama to leave Kendal, but as our party is traveling so near to Town on our return trip to Pemberley, I could not pass this opportunity to introduce her to my bride.

I dearly hope this visit will prove to be a harbinger of reconciliation for our family, but that joy, my dear sister, depends entirely upon you. I bring with me those with whom you currently claim an uneasy acquaintance, and I hope these relationships might be restored to their former states.

I hope you shall not force me to explain why you are no longer welcome amongst your former friends.

I trust Mrs. Pickersgill has been an adequate companion and that you are treating her with the respect she deserves.

Until we meet,
Your brother,
Charles Bingley

"Well?" Mrs. Newton asked, her eyes still bright. "What does he say?"

Tears clogged Caroline's throat. She refolded the letter and stuffed it into her reticule as if concealment of the object might also hide its message. Charles and his party were coming too soon!

None of Caroline's plans had been accomplished, and now she would be faced with the uneasy prospect of either winning Mr. Charlton very quickly indeed or making amends with Miss Elizabeth Bennet, for she refused to disappoint her mother by causing so much tension amongst her relations.

But oh how she detested the very idea of their arrival!

"Are you quite well, Caroline?" Mr. Rushton asked, leaning closer as if to measure her countenance.

Caroline looked directly at him. "Why would you ask such a thing?"

"Suddenly, you appear quite pale," he responded.

"Indeed, you do," Rosemary added. Her gaze was suspicious.

Caroline looked around the table to find Mr. and Mrs. Newton watching her expectantly.

"It is only that I am overjoyed at the news of his arrival," she managed to say. "Charles says," she cleared her throat, "that their party is on the way to Pemberley."

Pemberley! The symbol of all her hopes and dreams. If she did not do something very soon, she would be excluded from that great house again.

Rosemary pushed away from the table, and though Caroline could not quite say why, her companion had a definite air of determination about her. "I am prepared to go wherever you wish," she said.

Caroline also stood. Resolve, for she would not call it desperation, swelled within her. Today, she would find Mr. Charlton and extract a proposal at all costs.

As she and Rosemary said their goodbyes to the group assembled at the table, Caroline wondered how compliant her companion would be once she discovered where she planned to walk and with what purpose, but she did not speak of it yet. She only donned her finest bonnet and departed the house with her companion on her heels.

Once they were a good distance from Grosvenor Street, Rosemary asked, "Are we to call upon Mrs. Winton and Mr. Charlton then?"

Caroline gaped.

"Come, Miss Bingley. I may not yet have grasped all the particulars of your circumstances, but I do comprehend why we are here."

Caroline had not expected herself to be so easily readable, but she nodded. "I do intend to call on them, but first, we must discover their location."

"Ah, Mrs. Winton did not tell you where she was staying?" Rosemary's words were not exactly a question, even though her inflection implied it. They seemed more of an indictment against Lavinia.

"No," Caroline said, "but that signifies nothing."

"London is a large city, and we will likely spend days in search of them."

"You are mistaken, Mrs. Pickersgill, for the fashionable residents of London haunt only the most particular locales. We shall start with the shops and confectioners on Bond Street."

And so they walked in that direction, and after spending hours darting from one establishment to the next, Caroline finally settled into a dressmaker's shop, which she felt certain Lavinia would frequent.

Her friend would approve of this sort of enterprise, for it was the most elegant in town. The large main chamber featured high ceilings, and tall built-in cabinets of fabrics and other notions lined the walls. The main table displayed sumptuous silks and cottons, which were being perused by ladies in the most stylish dresses Caroline had seen since her arrival. Yes, it was a fine establishment.

Besides, she had the greatest need for a new gown for her time in London.

Ordinarily, Caroline would have relished a shopping venture in town and spent hours in thrall at the newest fashions of the season, but that day she took no pleasure in the atmosphere of excitement, and when she finally exited the shop, she was only slightly pleased with her purchase.

She had a fine gown on order, but her true object had not been accomplished: they had not discovered Lavinia.

Caroline decided to make one last attempt and led Rosemary down Bruton Street toward Berkeley Square, where she hoped to chance upon her friend.

When she and Rosemary arrived at their destination, however, they discovered not Lavinia but Mr. Charlton, the gentleman himself, leaning against the park square railing. He faced away, looking into the greenery beyond the railing, but she recognized his long, lean—almost thin—form and dark curls.

Upon seeing him lounging there, Caroline took a swift breath. The first encounter was crucial.

He must seem to have recognized Caroline first. It must not appear as though she sought him out, and he certainly must never know that she had undertaken this trip to London in order to find him.

But first, she must rid herself of Rosemary. She turned to her companion and said, "You will rest here for a quarter hour, Mrs. Pickersgill, while I speak with Mr. Charlton privately."

Rosemary looked beyond Caroline to observe Mr. Charlton at the railing. She narrowed her eyes. "I will do as you ask, Miss Bingley, but I do not trust him, and neither should you put your faith in him. He has too much of the upper-class disregard for morals."

Caroline glared. "You speak utter, utter nonsense. Besides, what care I for the opinion of a servant? I trust him, and that is all that matters." She gestured at a shady spot further down the railing. "Wait over there until I return."

Rosemary went, leaving Caroline to formulate her plan.

She would simply walk past, and certainly Mr. Charlton would notice her and turn.

She began to stride toward him, taking care to walk with grace and poise, but he neither noticed nor turned, so when she reached the end of the rail, she approached again, this time allowing her fingers to trail along the vacant rail until she neared him.

And again, Mr. Charlton did not offer her so much as a glance as she passed.

She sighed, turned, and repeated the process. Still, he refused to take note of her.

After several more failed attempts, Caroline decided to change tactics and take up a position at the rail a short distance away in the hopes that he still might notice her first.

She walked to the rail slowly with as much of a regal bearing as one who had just spent the past ten minutes walking back and forth in the same spot could possibly achieve.

She stood not ten feet away for another ten minutes without him so much as turning his head before she finally relented and said, "Oh! Mr. Charlton, whatever do you do here?"

Finally, the gentleman turned and looked at her. Recognition sparked in his eyes.

"Miss Bingley?" He walked closer and bowed to her deeply. "I am shocked! Shocked, but pleased to see you here. How is it that you have come to London?"

Caroline smiled and let her eyelashes flutter closed for a moment. "Did you not know that my family had planned a trip here?" she lied. "Mr. Newton and Mr. Rushton have some business or other in Town."

"Oh? I was unaware that you were to travel to this destination," he said with a bright smile. "I am so pleased, for

Lavinia hauled us to Town so quickly, and matters between you and me remain unfinished, do they not?" he asked softly.

Caroline lowered her gaze demurely and did not respond. Caroline sensed that Mr. Charlton was tempted to take her hand; his fingers fairly twitched within his fine gloves. She watched him look about and knew the precise moment he saw Rosemary. His hands drew into fists.

"We are not alone, I see."

"No," Caroline said.

"I have had to elude my sister for a few moments' peace as well. She has been with me every moment since we left Kendal. It is most frustrating."

Caroline nodded in agreement.

"Then we must find a method of gaining some privacy," he said, "and the best technique, I have found, is to be in the largest crowd possible. My sister and I go to Vauxhall Gardens tomorrow."

"A pleasure garden?" Caroline asked, though she had not meant to. She had often been in company of the fashionable people who frequented such places, but Caroline had never lost her distaste for them. London was quite littered with such gardens, and though they all attracted a different sort of clientele, they had one commonality. All were known for their romantic assignations. In fact, she knew that private niches had been designed for the very purpose of encouraging such liberties to be taken. Vauxhall, though the most prestigious of these gardens, was also the most notorious, and Caroline had never had the least wish to venture within.

After hearing tales of young women quite ruining their reputations or, barring that, being snatched away from their companions and taken into the darkness to be molested by some gentleman or other, the very idea of such a place assaulted Caroline's sensibilities, leaving her rather aghast that a lady of any social class would frequent them.

"Indeed, Miss Bingley," Mr. Charlton said on a laugh. "A pleasure garden. Is not that the most wonderful invention?" He studied her and must have read the uncertainty in her countenance, for he added, "You will not allow your time in the country and its backward manners to restrain you, will you?"

Caroline set her jaw. No, she would not allow her past to determine her future. She would not permit anything to prevent her from a union with Mr. Charlton, especially now that her brother and Mr. Darcy were on the way to London.

"No," she said, "I shall not."

"Excellent!" cried Mr. Charlton. "Then join us tomorrow for supper, and perhaps we may sneak away for a few moments of privacy."

Before Caroline could officially accept or decline his invitation, he took his watch out of his fob pocket and sighed. "I must go. My sister will be waiting for me. I shall see you tomorrow at the Grove."

Caroline watched as he disappeared into the crowded street and wondered how she would ever manage to get away to Vauxhall, for her mother would most certainly not approve.

Well, Caroline thought as she turned back toward her companion, she would do it! Her object was so close. She would find a way, even if she had to go to the reprehensible Vauxhall and drag Rosemary with her.

Rosemary was currently resting where Caroline had commanded, but she was not alone. She had also encountered an acquaintance, a wealthy-looking woman with a regal bearing and a gown too fine to be worn for a day of idle shopping. Caroline quite envied that dress, and she was rather curious as to the woman's name and relation to her companion. Her mien and bearing were of polite society, and that was quite incongruous with Rosemary Pickersgill. How were they acquainted?

She must discover all.

Caroline approached them but remained on the periphery to feign a study of a shrub, as if she were suddenly entranced by the local flora.

"I must say I am all astonishment!" she heard the unknown woman say with a sly laugh.

Rosemary said not a word in response to the woman's remark, but her eyes flickered to Caroline, and she turned her body slightly to invite her into their circle.

"Oh, Miss Bingley," Rosemary said with a tight smile. Her tone was strained, and Caroline could not tell if she were adding to her companion's tension by joining the conversation or if she had relieved it. But tension or not, she was determined to discover the other woman's identity.

Rosemary looked back to her acquaintance and asked meekly, "Will you allow me to present my friend?"

The woman turned to Caroline, noticing her for the first time, and swept her from head to toe in one quick glance. Caroline raised her chin at this blatant assessment. Then the lady nodded once with great condescension, and Rosemary began her introduction, saying, "Viscountess Middlebury, may I present Miss Caroline Bingley."

Viscountess?

Now it was Caroline who was all astonishment. This woman was not the wife of a commoner or a lowly knight, baronet, or even baron. Rosemary was speaking with the wife of a viscount.

How utterly shocking.

After Rosemary completed the presentations, Lady Middlebury proceeded to ignore Caroline completely, and for her own part, Caroline barely prevented herself from looking between the other ladies in bewilderment. How had Rosemary become acquainted with the wife of a titled gentleman?

"Whatever do you do in Town?" Lady Middlebury said on a laugh of disbelief. "It is quite brave of you to appear. I had thought we would not see you here so soon given your predicament. I told Lord Middlebury that we should never think to see you again." The woman's tone was so haughty that even Caroline, who was used to consorting with the proudest and most arrogant in society, was momentarily taken aback. Her feelings were clear; she did not care for Rosemary Pickersgill.

Rosemary only managed a weak, "I…"

Rather startlingly, a new wave of emotion sneaked upon Caroline. She felt suddenly protective of her companion, and so without pondering the reasons for this, she lifted her chin and said, "You will pardon me, Lady Middlebury, for speaking out of turn, but Mrs. Pickersgill and I are due back on Grosvenor Street even now."

Lady Middlebury turned her proud face and hawkish eyes upon Caroline, who did not shrink back.

"Who are you?" Lady Middlebury asked with a wave of her hand. "I have already forgotten."

"Caroline Bingley, my lady."

"Ah. And who is your family?" she asked. Lady Middlebury inclined her head as if interested, but really, the posture was designed to intimidate. The feathers on her bonnet blew in the breeze and almost hit Caroline in the face.

"My brother, Charles Bingley, is the head of our family." Upon the shake of Lady Middlebury's head, Caroline added, "He travels often with Mr. Fitzwilliam Darcy of Pemberley."

"Ah! Yes, I have heard of Mr. Darcy of course. A fine family and so very rich—"

Caroline had not the patience to hear her next words. "You will excuse me," she interrupted, "but we must be off this minute."

"Of course, be off," the viscountess said and then turned to Rosemary to add, "I shall make your presence in Town known, my dear. There are some who will be rather anxious to find you."

Caroline took Rosemary's hand, and together they walked down Davies Street and turned onto Grosvenor Street before they broke their silence.

"Thank you, Miss Bingley," Rosemary whispered, though there was no one about to overhear her.

Caroline pulled her hand away and wheeled on her. "I do not know what I was thinking to adopt that tone with a viscount's wife! I should never have spoken as I did."

"Still, I thank you," Rosemary said softly. "You have no idea the embarrassment you saved me."

Caroline could also not guess the motivations for her own actions. She was no great friend of Rosemary, but seeing her thus abused had been too much! If anyone were to abuse her, by rights, it ought to be Caroline herself.

"What is this great embarrassment?" she demanded. "I must know."

Rosemary began to walk again, leaving Caroline to trail after her. "I would prefer not to say."

"I insist that you do, for I did not just insult a titled lady for no reason."

"I did not ask it of you, Miss Bingley; nor shall I share my secrets unless it is absolutely required. And it is not yet absolutely required."

Caroline stopped and stared after Rosemary, who continued to walk all the way to Mr. Rushton's house and disappeared within.

Caroline sat on a vacant bench and wondered at herself. Ever since her brother had banished her to Kendal, she had begun to say and do the oddest things. She had confessed part of her secret shame to a tradesman and defended her servant before a noble. It was as if she were suddenly possessed and unable to control her impulses. The Caroline of old would have ignored the tradesman and taken up the part of the titled lady, but she had done the opposite.

Caroline was quite put out to discover the resurgence of her country morals, especially the day before she was to visit Vauxhall Gardens with Mr. Charlton.

✤ Seventeen ✤

"Good morning, my dear," Mrs. Newton said as she entered Caroline's bedchamber the following morning, dismissed her maid, and took up the task of helping her daughter prepare for the day. "I am so very pleased that you insisted I come with you to London. Now that I have left Kendal, I am eager to see more of our fine country."

"I am so happy, Mama, that travel agrees with you."

"Tonight, Mr. Newton has promised to take me to the theater," she said as she added pearl-encrusted combs to Caroline's hair, "and though such entertainments have quite a reputation, he assures me I will be diverted. Will you not join us?"

"I fear I cannot, Mama, for Lavinia has asked me to dine with her this evening," Caroline said. It was not quite a lie, but also not the truth either. Undoubtedly, she would dine with Lavinia at Vauxhall, but Mr. Charlton had issued the invitation and not his sister.

"Oh?" Mrs. Newton smiled. "I did not know you had spoken with her since arriving in London. I am so pleased that you have found one another."

"We met yesterday at Berkeley Square," Caroline lied again.

"And Mrs. Pickersgill? Does she dine with you as well?"

Here was Caroline's opportunity to shed herself of her companion. It would be simple to tell her mother that the invitation had not been extended, but something within Caroline prevented her from saying so. And she despised that part of her—that country aspect—that niggled at her.

She had no wish to navigate Vauxhall, with all its dark walks and hideaways, on her own. It was all so distasteful, though she would never admit as much aloud.

Oh! She clenched her fists at her own turn of thought. How she wished to conform to polite society!

She simply could not manage it completely.

"Yes, Mama," Caroline said on a sigh of surrender, "she will dine with us as well."

"I am pleased to hear it, but…" Here Mrs. Newton trailed off and then began again. "Our Mrs. Pickersgill has seemed rather odd since our arrival in London, do you not think?"

Caroline pondered her mother's words as she stood to check the fall of her gown in the mirror. "Indeed, now that you mention it," she said, feigning indifference, "there have been some odd occurrences."

In truth, Caroline had not stopped wondering about the mystery surrounding Rosemary's exit from London.

Mrs. Newton patted Caroline's hand. "I do hope you will watch over our Mrs. Pickersgill and protect her, for she has been such a good friend."

Caroline wanted to protest the appellation of "friend," but she did not. She thought back to their encounter with Lady Middlebury at Berkeley Square. She had already defended Rosemary as only the most devoted friend might.

Beyond what most friends might do, in fact, but she would not tell her mother of her actions. It was all too embarrassing.

However, Caroline may as well admit to herself that she had developed a tenderness for the woman. She replied, "I will not allow any harm to befall her."

In actuality, Caroline feared that Rosemary might harm *her* when she discovered their destination for the evening, but her companion would relent and accompany her. She had no choice.

And that is precisely what happened.

As evening fell, Caroline ordered a servant to hire a hackney carriage to transport them from Grosvenor Street to Vauxhall.

"I do not like this," Rosemary said as the hackney whisked them southeast toward the Thames through the lingering evening heat.

Indeed, Caroline did not much approve of their destination either, but she would not fall prey to her country upbringing by agreeing. Instead, she said, "Oh, do not be so difficult, Mrs. Pickersgill. Vauxhall is a fashionable place. Why, the prince regent himself can often be found there."

Rosemary cut her eyes to Caroline. "That does not provide encouragement, Miss Bingley."

"Well, I do not care whether or not you are encouraged, for we are dining with Mrs. Winton and Mr. Charlton, and that is all there is to it."

Caroline's words were meant to reassure herself as well as Rosemary, and she could think of nothing more to say and only sat quietly as the hackney traversed the streets of London and then rumbled across the Vauxhall Bridge. As the wheels struck the stone, Mr. Rushton's face entered Caroline's mind, but she shoved the image of him aside. She must concentrate on her object: Mr. Charlton.

The hackney deposited its occupants at the entrance to the gardens, and the view within its walls quite took away Caroline's breath.

"It is lovely," she said as she peeked through the entrance. She had not expected it to appear so enchanting. Trees lined a long walkway, and lanterns dangled from their branches. Their light swayed with the breeze and cast a romantic, ever-moving glow across the walkers below.

"And crowded," Rosemary added.

Indeed, the garden teemed with people. The line to enter the garden was quite long and would take many minutes to navigate.

As they waited among the other would-be revelers, Rosemary stood with her head bent, again looking as though she thought the ground might suddenly shift beneath her feet. At length, they reached the front of the line, and Caroline paid the entry fee before proceeding along the tree-lined trail toward the Grove, which was located at the intersection of the four principal gravel pathways at

Vauxhall. The garden was a blur of motion, glittering gowns, and dark gentlemen's attire. Around her, Caroline heard snippets of conversation and laughter, and she detected an orchestra tuning in the distance.

As Caroline navigated the path, she wondered at the multitude of people from all social classes mingling together and found herself quite certain she would never locate Mr. Charlton amongst them all, but she need not have worried, for Mr. Charlton found her.

"Miss Bingley," he cried from the path behind them. The ladies turned to see him already bowing low. "You have arrived at last. Come, Lavinia will be so pleased to see you."

He offered Caroline his arm, which she accepted, and the three of them walked toward the Grove, where the random sounds of the instruments became louder.

Mr. Charlton led them through the colonnade, where a hundred supper boxes had been arranged, and they followed as he wound deftly to the one they would fill that evening.

Lavinia noticed their approach, and a look of horror spread across her fine features, but it disappeared quickly, leaving Caroline confident that she had misinterpreted it. Her friend's face must have registered surprise only.

Lavinia swept forward to welcome them, but Caroline met her halfway and spoke first, as if she were the hostess of the event and not her friend.

"Ah, Lavinia," she said with a regal curtsey. "You may be certain of our pleasure at your invitation to join you for dinner here."

Lavinia curtseyed too, but she seemed a bit taken aback at Caroline's choice of greeting. When she spoke, however, her voice hinted at no discomfort or confusion. Her tone was regal as it ever was when she said, "Though I am quite shocked to find you in London, you are most welcome to dine here."

The party seated themselves around the table, and conversation flowed, albeit not freely, and Caroline could not tell whether the strain was due to Lavinia's distant behavior or to the fact that the orchestra had begun to play, rendering hearing difficult.

Around dusk, a strangely minimal tray of victuals had been brought to the table. The cold ham, which was supposedly intended to feed four, would barely cover a piece of bread, and the chickens were the size of underfed pigeons. But Caroline could not be disappointed because she had become entranced by the orchestra.

The notes of George Frideric Handel danced around her, and Caroline had the greatest urge to put both elbows on the table, rest her chin in her hands, and listen the whole night through. But she sat bolt upright, allowing her pleasure to show only as she tapped her toes beneath the table linens.

Her enchantment endured until she chanced to see Lady Middlebury in a nearby box.

She leaned toward Rosemary. "Is not that the lady with whom you spoke at Berkeley Square yesterday?"

Rosemary looked and then winced. "It is."

"Oh dear," Caroline whispered, "I hope she does not spot us. After I behaved so rudely, she cannot help our situation."

"What are you speaking of?" demanded Lavinia. "I must know."

"Oh," Caroline hesitated and then chose to reveal the truth. Perhaps hinting at an association with a viscountess might spur Lavinia into more jovial conversation. "I was just pointing out to Mrs. Pickersgill a mutual acquaintance."

Lavinia looked around pointedly. "Who?"

"Lady Middlebury," Caroline responded.

"Well, how exceedingly interesting," Lavinia said as her eyes alighted on the woman herself.

Caroline could hardly guess why and was about to ask when Mr. Charlton stood. "Will you walk about with me, Miss Bingley?"

Taken slightly aback by the suddenness of his invitation, Caroline managed to smile and nod, but Lavinia said, "I do not think it wise, William."

"Oh come, sister, we shall keep to the lighted pathways. Rest here and our Mrs. Pickersgill will divert you."

And with that, Caroline found herself, quite without her companion, being escorted down the main path deeper into the garden and leaving a sputtering Lavinia behind.

Though she ought to be experiencing jubilation and triumph at this precise moment, Caroline felt only confusion.

This was the moment for which she had been waiting! She was on the arm of a soon-to-be titled, wealthy gentleman, and she was perched on the cusp of rising to the status of baroness, forever removing herself from the pall of her family history and never again being forced to depend on anyone else—not her brother, Mr. Darcy, Miss Elizabeth Bennet—to secure her place among the best society.

Yes, she must focus on that and not on the feeling of unease within her.

She forced herself to smile at Mr. Charlton.

"Vauxhall is lovely, is it not?" he asked.

She looked about her, noticing again how the lighted lanterns swayed among the tree branches, bathing the pathway in semi-light and moveable shadow.

"It is rather lovely," she agreed. The giggling walking parties and love-struck couples they passed along the path reminded her all too forcefully of its reputation.

Still, she allowed Mr. Charlton to lead her further into the garden, and as the sounds of Handel faded into the background, they met fewer groups of walkers. Soon, they encountered only couples, hanging upon each other in a manner that would be inappropriate in polite society.

Despite the idealistic setting, Caroline did not feel the thrill of her closeness to Mr. Charlton. Her hand rested along his forearm, but she felt only her glove beneath her fingertips. He elicited no response from her at all. She thought briefly of Mr. Rushton and of her reaction to him in the carriage, but she quickly removed him from her mind.

She ought to feel the same thing for Mr. Charlton, should she not?

Some sort of twinge in her heart? She had heard such sentiments described at boarding school, this feeling she should experience. It had always sounded a bit like indigestion, and that did not seem pleasing. But after her experience with Mr. Rushton, she had been forced to reconsider. This strange indigestion was rather pleasing. Still, she felt nothing in the vicinity of her heart when she looked to Mr. Charlton.

Caroline continued to examine her emotions as she looked up at him. He did not return her gaze, but only looked forward as he led her deeper into the shady hollow, and she studied him with immunity.

What was the matter with her?

He was handsome, well dressed, and rich. He had ancestors of note. He would be a baron.

Despite all these inducements, her heart was obstinately uninvolved.

Her mind, however, rejoiced over her position on the arm of the future baron. Yes, her plan was working itself out shockingly well, even if her heart seemed to be attempting a coup.

When Mr. Charlton stopped, they were standing alone at the edge of an even darker, more intimate section of garden.

"I confess," said Mr. Charlton, "that I could not listen to another note of that orchestra. Could you?"

"No indeed," Caroline lied.

"And I do have the greatest desire to speak privately with you, but I dare not drag you any farther into the dark. I do not want to ruin your reputation, Miss Bingley. Perhaps," he lowered his voice, "you could meet me at the ruins." He pointed down the dim pathway. "Just follow that corridor in a quarter hour or so and you shall find me."

With that, he dashed off, leaving Caroline quite alone among the trickle of visitors along the path.

Caroline looked around and then took a deep breath.

What could she be thinking?

Here she was in Vauxhall, preparing for her first assignation.

Well, not really her first assignation. She had allowed Mr. Rushton to touch her intimately in the carriage after all.

But this was her first moonlight assignation.

And it was with a future baron, not a tradesman.

It would mean the end to all her worries. She would never again fear that her past might be discovered, and she would no longer be required to apologize to Miss Elizabeth Bennet in order to return to the best society. Finally, she would be completely free of it all.

So Caroline waited fifteen minutes and then marched down the dark path to meet her future.

༄ঙ্গ ঙ্গ৯

The classical temple was composed of columns that supported a domed stone roof. Long drapes of a filmy material hung in the spaces between the columns and blew gently in the breeze. To the side of the temple stood a small flower garden, which was surrounded by a trellis of clinging vines that quite obscured the view within.

Caroline approached the structure but did not enter. Her determination had waned as she marched, then walked, and finally dawdled along the path toward the rendezvous point. Now, she found that she could only manage to look at the temple, and as her eyes adjusted to the muted light, she detected Mr. Charlton's figure behind the sheer fabric. He seemed to be speaking with someone.

Confused and thinking perhaps she had come upon the wrong ruins, Caroline edged closer, but by the time she drew near enough to hear the conversation, the pair had disappeared. And so she followed, quietly stepping into the temple.

She looked around the columned room and discovered that the attached trellis actually formed a sort of walled walkway, and she followed it, passing under the flowered vines that hung above her head. She was just about to round the corner to the entrance to a small interior garden when she heard a giggle.

A girlish giggle.

That was odd.

Then, even odder, she heard Mr. Charlton's voice. She could not decipher the words, but then there was another snigger.

Abruptly, Caroline realized what sort of scene she had come upon, and though she had no wish to see the particulars, she peeked around the corner. She could see nothing of the woman, however, without revealing her position in the garden.

But the scene was plain enough. Mr. Charlton was seated on a low stone bench, and the girl, whomever she was, was seated on Mr. Charlton.

Caroline shrunk back, horrified and enraged.

She had heard the rumors about Mr. Charlton and his habits; he had, in fact, confirmed them. But somehow, she had not believed him.

Of course, she was acquainted with the ways of polite society, but she had always been fortunate to remain in the company of those—her brother and Mr. Darcy—who had adopted a higher moral code and who would never lower themselves to such dissolute displays.

Now she was witnessing Mr. Charlton's debauchery for herself. It was true; he was fond of titillating maids.

Caroline's first instinct was to confront him, for fighting was part of her nature. He was supposed to be meeting her to propose marriage after all! She ought to be in the place of the dissolute woman!

She peeked again around the corner and very nearly stepped into the open, but then she thought the better of it.

Making a scene would benefit no one.

Besides, this behavior should neither shock nor offend her, for as she had so lately reminded herself, it was the way of their class, and if Caroline desired to fit in amongst them, she must learn to accept it.

As she turned and retraced her steps to the entrance of the ruins, Caroline felt the full force of her discovery. It was the strangest sensation. Here she was attempting to convince everyone—including herself—that she belonged as mistress of Oak Park and wife of a baron, but her soul cried out against the very thing her mind wanted.

Could she truly live with a gentleman who would behave in such a manner?

Or was her bourgeois upbringing causing her to view the situation in too moralistic a manner?

These morals were hallmarks of the middling classes, so was not her current state of mind to be blamed on her unfortunate background?

Caroline could no longer think. She simply crunched along the path back toward the Grove where she had left Rosemary. Her mind was in a whirl of emotions and thoughts, and she could not settle upon one or the other.

She simply continued to walk toward Rosemary, and when her companion saw her pale face and shocked expression, she asked, "Miss Bingley, are you well?"

"Oh yes," she said. "Why do you ask?"

"You look pale."

"Yes, you look dreadful, dear. Will you not sit?" Lavinia suggested, but she did not move to aid Caroline to a chair. Instead, she just stared at her.

"No," Caroline said. "I shall not sit. We must be away."

"What? So early?" Lavinia asked, sounding completely unconcerned.

"I am afraid I have had quite enough of Vauxhall for one evening."

"Yes?" Lavinia asked. "Well, I suppose my brother is still amongst the revelers."

It was more of a statement than a question, but Caroline responded anyway. "Indeed, he is."

ᵉᵉ Eighteen ᵉᵉ

Caroline and Rosemary rented another hackney and returned to Mr. Rushton's home in Grosvenor Street in silence. If in fact Rosemary had attempted to begin a conversation, Caroline had not noticed, for her mind was too full and confused to allow one more thought to enter.

She only wanted the forgetfulness of sleep to come and take away her tumultuous worries, and when Caroline's bedchamber door finally closed behind her, she sighed aloud. Although almost all the energy had drained from her body, she managed to walk across the room and sink onto the dressing table stool.

She looked at the mirror, but she did not see her own reflection. She only began removing the pins from her hair by rote, dropping them in a small pile on the table and then combing her hair absently until a knock at the door arrested her.

She decided to ignore the sound.

It came again.

"What?" Caroline asked. She had hoped to speak the word with a biting tone, but her voice came out weak and breathy.

"May I enter, Miss Bingley?" The voice that floated through the barrier of the closed door issued from Rosemary Pickersgill.

"No, you may not."

The pause was so long that Caroline thought—or rather hoped—that Rosemary had gone away, but then the door opened and her companion entered unbidden.

Caroline did not even bother to turn around when she said, "Did you not mark me? I said you may not enter."

"I apologize, Miss Bingley, but I felt the strongest urge to speak with you tonight."

Caroline glared at her in the mirror.

Rosemary continued, "Do not make me regret my decision."

"I find I do not have the vigor to protest. What is it you must say to me?"

Rosemary seated herself on the edge of the bed and looked at Caroline in the mirror. "What happened with Mr. Charlton this evening?"

"Nothing you ought to concern yourself with," Caroline said.

"He has not proposed?"

"No."

"I have already warned you that his sister may not be your ally, but—" she began.

"I will not hear such talk!" Caroline's fist descended on the dressing table, causing the hairpins to jump.

"—I ask because," Mrs. Pickersgill hesitated. "Because I do not want to see you suffer as I did."

"Do not compare yourself to me. We are nothing alike."

"We are more similar than you realize," Rosemary insisted as she rose to stand behind Caroline. "I too was raised in the arms of the middling classes—"

"I will not hear my family so degraded!"

Rosemary held up a hand and their eyes met in the mirror. "Allow me to finish, Miss Bingley, and then you may rail at me as much as you please."

Caroline crossed her arms before her and said, "Hmph." But she listened, eyes locked on Rosemary's reflection.

"I was once just as eager as you to rise in society, and one day, I caught the eye of a gentleman, a wealthy gentleman, and I believed all my tribulations were at an end. I married him, Miss Bingley, but as you see, it did not gain me one measure of enduring status, for here I stand, nothing more than a paid companion."

The two women stared at each other in the mirror's reflection, but Caroline had no will left in her to fight or even question the woman's story.

"Leave me," she begged.

"Yes, I shall leave you in a moment." A long pause ensued, but Rosemary did not depart. Finally, she said in a quieter voice, "Miss Bingley, you must understand this about me: I was not born to this station."

"Yes, yes, as you said."

"I was a gentleman's daughter and more."

"I hardly believe that," Caroline said. This woman could not possibly be what she claimed.

"I care not for your belief in my veracity, Miss Bingley, for your perception cannot alter the facts. I have experienced all that you fear and more. I have fallen in the eyes of society, and yet I live on, and I have even managed to be tolerably happy even if I have been reduced to being the companion of a pretentious young lady."

"Insolence!" Caroline said, though her voice lacked venom. "My brother will hear of this when he arrives."

"Your brother knows precisely what I am, Miss Bingley, and until this very day, I was willing to accept my fate. But you have taught me something valuable. Watching you persist no matter the obstacle, even when it was a foolish attempt, has shown me how easily I have given in to my circumstances. Well, no longer! Mark me. I will do anything to return to my station."

Rosemary turned on her heel, her strawberry blond hair shaking loose from its pins with the vehemence of her spin, and exited the chamber, leaving Caroline to stare at herself stupidly in the mirror.

Caroline knew not how long she remained in that position before lying down in an attempt to sleep, but she could not manage to drift off. She was angry, confused, and most of all hungry. The food at Vauxhall had not filled her.

She flung the bed linens from her, donned her wrapper, and stomped across the room toward the door. Here, she managed to mute her steps as she headed toward the kitchen in search of something to eat. She stole a slice of bread and a hunk of cheese, and for fear of encountering Mr. Rushton in another of his own midnight meals, she took her plate to the library, where the fire would likely still be smoldering and provide her enough light to read.

She opened the door and the voice she had hoped not to hear said, "Ah, Miss Bingley."

Caroline discovered Mr. Rushton lounging sideways on one of the Grecian sofas, his back propped against an armrest and a book splayed open across his chest. Such shocking posture! A gentleman ought not recline, but sit up straight.

His next words were also a shock. "How did you find Vauxhall this evening?" he asked.

She nearly dropped her food, but she managed to retain her hold and place her plate on the small table beside the unoccupied sofa as she forced herself to speak to him.

"Vauxhall?" she asked innocently. "Why would you think I went there?"

"My manservant hailed your hackney. Did you expect him to lie when I asked its destination?"

Caroline sighed, lowered herself to the sofa, and said, "Yes, I went to Vauxhall, and I did not enjoy myself if you must know."

"I suspected you would not, for though you claim no influence by your past, you will never be able to mount such a flagrant disregard for morals as does most of polite society."

Caroline selected a piece of bread, bit into it, and did not reply.

"And did Mr. Charlton make his proposal?" He asked this question in an altogether different tone. It was almost vulnerable, and so Caroline suspected immediately that he must be about some sort of trickery. "Do not bother asking how I discerned your desires in that direction, for you have hardly been subtle in your arts."

She thought to argue with him, but managed only to say, "How kind of you, Mr. Rushton."

But in truth, it was likely that only her trusting mother and Mr. Newton remained oblivious to her schemes, so she admitted, "No, he did not make an overture, but it is only a matter of time."

"You will be a fool indeed to accept him," he said.

"I thank you for opining on this topic, sir, but if you will forgive me, I will make my own decisions."

"I may forgive you, but will you forgive yourself? I thought you a great many things—foolish among them—but I dearly hope that you will not condemn yourself to the sort of life Mr. Charlton will offer."

She laughed. "He can provide all that I require."

"That is where you are wrong, Miss Bingley. He may cast an image of himself as a wealthy, carefree soul, but he is not unlike others of polite society who disregard their debt and gamble at every opportunity."

To Mr. Rushton's list of charges against Mr. Charlton, she could add dissolute debaucher, and he had confessed to being poor at money management, but she had heard nothing of his gambling. But what did that matter? It was entirely natural for the upper classes to behave that way, for they were born to their wealth and status and could not lose it. They could show no economy or moderation and indulge until their coffers emptied, and it was the duty and privilege of the lower classes to uphold them, was it not? After all, had not the landed gentry upheld them for years as tenant farmers?

It was only right, and it was the way of society.

But what of her father? He had earned his fortune with no aid from the titled landowners in the county. And the elder Mr. Rushton? He had lost his, and no amount of kindness on the part of his creditors had saved him.

It ought to be so simple. The titled were wealthy, and the poor were poor. That is how it used to be, but now trade and title were blurring, a most confounding condition. Caroline sighed. She simply could not understand the way of the world.

So instead of pondering that subject, she studied Mr. Rushton as she ate. He was still lying on the sofa opposite hers, and though his posture appeared relaxed, he radiated a sort of anxiety that Caroline could not comprehend.

Now finished with her small meal, Caroline stood. Hoping to intimidate him using the advantage of height, she loomed over him and said, "Your words do you no credit, sir, for I have heard nothing amiss about Mr. Charlton outside of what is expected of the aristocracy."

"Neither do your actions, Miss Bingley, do any credit to you." He looked at her with stern eyes. "I see you. I see exactly what you are thinking."

She shook her head, realizing that her hair fell loosely about her shoulders in a most improper manner. "You cannot presume to know my intentions, and moreover, you are very rude."

"I am well respected both in London and in the country, Miss Bingley, and that means I may be as rude as I desire and say whatever I choose, and still people defer to me and seek my good opinion. It is a most charming—and maddening—arrangement."

Caroline leaned down until she was much too close to him. "Charming or not," she whispered into his ear. "I would never seek your good opinion, so please do not endeavor to give it. And if you wish me to defer to you in any matter, you may as well abandon that hope immediately, for it shall never happen."

"Miss Bingley, you will fail in your quest."

Caroline blinked at him slowly as she formulated her retort. Finally, she said, "Indeed, I wish you would not think on my endeavors, Mr. Rushton, for it only leads to conversations of this nature. We are always at odds, and I fear you are not up to a true battle of wits."

"And you intend to supply these wits?" he snorted. "How amusing."

Caroline returned to her full height. "I wish I could say I found your behavior amusing, but alas, our reacquaintance has taught me to expect the contrary."

Upon those words, she spun on her heel, but before she could step out of his sphere, a hand grasped her wrist and prevented her from stalking away. Caroline whirled around prepared to spew angry words upon him and discovered that Mr. Rushton had risen from the sofa.

Worse, she found herself drawn even closer to him than she had ever been, even when he had caressed her face in the carriage. Now his eyelids were lowered in an expression she had only once seen on his face and still could not precisely identify.

Her face heated.

Traitorous blood, Caroline thought.

"If you find my behavior shocking, you would indeed be surprised, my dear Miss Bingley, if you could read my thoughts."

"I doubt very much that your thoughts would be appropriate for a lady to know," she whispered.

"You are correct." His voice had softened, and he released his grip on her arm and stepped back, but somehow, his presence still overwhelmed her. "It is best to keep my thoughts to myself, for you are too genteel to be acquainted with them." His words were laced with a particular sarcasm that told her he did not find her genteel at all.

Caroline stepped back too, eager to put more distance between them. His gaze was too intense. "Yes, it is best that you do not speak," she said. His intensity did not waver, and she added more weakly, "For you never speak a word of sense."

"Well, I will endeavor to do so for the first time now, Miss Bingley." His voice had returned to its normal tone, setting her at ease just a bit. "You must realize that Mr. Charlton is not suited to a woman of your ilk."

Caroline gawped at him, unsure whether he was complimenting or insulting her.

"Your marriage to him would be most unhappy."

"That is simply not true."

Mr. Rushton's face took on a sardonic bent. "So you desire a husband who, rather than admiring your impudent and independent spirit, would choose to take your inheritance and then ignore you?"

"Mr. Charlton would do no such thing," Caroline protested.

"I wager you would be living in separate abodes before the first year of your marriage concluded. He wants a wife who will bring him a fortune and then foolishly turn her back as he fritters it away at cards and women. You, Miss Bingley, while certainly wealthy and foolish, are something more." He gave Caroline the most intense look. "You are something more."

The combination of his countenance and his words caused Caroline to turn and flee to her bedchamber, where she passed a restless night in trying to discern his motives.

ഏ Nineteen ഇ

Caroline was quite shocked when upon rising late the following morning, taking a prolonged breakfast in her chamber, and finally descending the staircase of Mr. Rushton's town home well after noon, she discovered a red-faced Lavinia awaiting her.

She caught sight of Caroline as she descended the stairs and marched over to face her.

"Good God!" Caroline blurted, completely flummoxed by her friend's vexed demeanor, and then added more civilly, "I did not realize you were here."

The entirety of Lavinia's being radiated agitation. Even the feather in her hair seemed to quiver with anger. Lavinia, always calm and dignified, was more distraught than Caroline had ever observed her.

It was a fearsome sight to behold.

"My brother. He has not been here?" she demanded, her shrill voice echoing through the entryway.

Caroline's confusion deepened. "Mr. Charlton? No, we have not had the pleasure of seeing him since Mrs. Pickersgill and I were in your company last evening. Come," she said as she led her friend to the privacy of the sitting room, "we can speak in here."

"You saw him last at Vauxhall?" Lavinia demanded as she followed Caroline.

"Yes," Caroline said as she shut the door behind them. "At Vauxhall."

"After your assignation, no doubt?"

"What? No! I never encountered...."

Obviously not listening, Lavinia began to look around the room in anger, as if considering which decoration she ought to hurl into the fireplace. "Why did you come to London?" she demanded. "Why would you even think to? Are you that thoughtless and imprudent?"

Caroline stepped back at Lavinia's words. "You have me at a disadvantage," Caroline said, deliberately forcing her voice to project calm, as if she were dealing with a small child in the midst of a temper tantrum. "I cannot think of what has caused you to become so distressed. Do sit down and tell me what has happened."

"I shall not sit!" Lavinia said, and as if to punctuate those words, she began pacing the room with heavy steps. "My brother thinks to propose to you!"

"Of course, was this not the object all along?" Caroline asked, confused.

"No." Lavinia turned and looked at her with unapologetic directness, and then she spoke as if to herself, saying, "My plot to separate you has been a dismal failure. You have proved bolder and more cunning than I imagined."

Caroline took another step back. "What plot?" she whispered.

"Oh come. I contrived an occasion for us to come to our father in London so that William would not wed a woman as vulgar as you, *my dear Caroline*."

The venom with which she unleashed her last phrase immobilized Caroline. Her friend had never spoken of her in such a way before.

But were these the words of a friend?

Caroline felt suddenly slow and dim. Could Rosemary have been correct? Was she now reliving the exact circumstances she herself had inflicted on Jane Bennet? Caroline thought back upon her interactions with Lavinia since her return to Kendal—the long wait for her first call, her initial seating arrangement at the Oak Park dinner party, her insistence on riding when she knew Caroline despised it, and apparently, her desire to remove her brother from her sphere. Were these the actions of a friend?

No indeed, Caroline realized as she looked upon Lavinia with a newness of understanding.

Dash it! Rosemary had been correct. Standing before her was the enemy.

Caroline's altercation with Mr. Rushton the night before had prepared her for battle, for though stunned and distressed, she straightened her back and took a few steps closer to Lavinia. Her friend did not back away, but her eyebrows drew down and her lips tightened. Anger in its purest form radiated from her countenance.

Caroline's astonishment at the unconcealed malevolence in her oldest friend was complete, and she would not allow it to remain unanswered. "You accuse me of vulgarity?" she said as she again stepped closer. "You invade this residence and then charge me with conduct in which no upstanding woman of quality, sense, education, and breeding would engage, and you expect me to accept your unfounded malice? It shall not be borne."

"Do you deny that you had hoped to entrap William into a marriage?" Lavinia demanded.

"I had no wish to entrap him. If I had intended to be subversive about the match, would I have come to you for assistance in bringing about the union? I hardly think so."

Lavinia's eyes had narrowed further and her lips drew into so tight a line that wrinkles formed at the corners of her mouth, but she did not speak. The two women eyed each other for long moments until finally Lavinia spun away.

Caroline was pleased to have set her down so completely, but her victory was not to be, for though her back was turned, Lavinia said to her quite clearly, "I may content myself, at least, with the knowledge that he has not succumbed to your machinations and eloped with you. That would have been the height of folly."

"Folly!" Caroline felt the burn of humiliation on the same scale that she had first experienced upon Mr. Darcy's wedding to Miss Elizabeth Bennet, but she used that fire to respond in kind. "Though your opinion of me in general is no longer a secret, your accusations are unjust. I would never lower myself by participating in an elopement. If Mr. Charlton ever disappears with a female, you ought to check within your own household, for he has a famous reputation for titillating the maids!"

Lavinia, purple with rage, whirled on her. "You cow!"

Caroline felt a slow smile spread across her face, for the use of derisive appellations was a sure sign of an opponent's defeat.

Lavinia gave one great tremble and then stamped a foot in impotent rage. "I will have nothing further to do with you, Miss Bingley. I will no longer recommend you to society or allow you to use my good name for your benefit. Our friendship, such as it was, is finished."

"Excellent," Caroline said in a shrill voice. "I have been desirous of ridding myself of you as well," she lied. Truly, she had no wish to lose an ally of the magnitude of Lavinia, and she would have much preferred to have succeeded in her plan to marry a baron, but one must retain one's dignity.

"Oh, do be honest, Caroline," Lavinia said. She seemed to have recovered her wits somewhat and now walked toward Caroline slowly. She spoke in a soft, patronizing tone that grated Caroline most thoroughly. "You can have no hopes for social improvement now. I know the genesis of your family's wealth, and I will not conceal my knowledge any longer." She completed her tirade by sighing and saying, "It shall be a relief to be shed of you, for I could hardly view you as more than a pet."

Caroline's mortification was complete. To be called a pet....

But still, Lavinia continued heaping hot coals upon her.

"For a time, I took a great deal of pleasure from introducing you into the finest society. I quite flattered myself that I was responsible for every positive change I perceived in your address and countenance after you had been in the company of acquaintances from my rank. It was a bit like teaching a mongrel a series of interesting tricks. The cur is appealing to watch, but when dinner is served and everyone is seated according to their rank, the dog, though he performed well, is still required to sit on the floor and scavenge the crumbs that might fall from the table."

Caroline felt tears leap to her eyes. Did they originate from anger or despair? She could not be certain. Nor could she allow those tears to fall.

Instead, she lashed her emotions tightly down into a small, dark place within her, and when she spoke again, she was satisfied with the modulation of her tone. "You were pleased for me to associate with your friends, but you balk at my association with your brother."

"Quite so, my dear," Lavinia said with disdain, "we have ever been unequal acquaintances. You must comprehend that I cannot allow you to have designs on my brother. It would sully the family name."

"I see," Caroline whispered, all the fight suddenly gone from her body. She desired nothing more than for Lavinia to leave her in peace to contemplate what had just occurred.

As if sensing her opponent's defeat, Lavinia came closer and sneered at her. "Oh," she said as she patted Caroline's hand in mock comfort. "Do not appear so injured. Even you have confessed to having attempted to remove an unworthy woman from your brother's realm. So I have only followed your lead, my dear."

Lavinia laughed and then exited the room in a swirl of skirts and superiority. All at once, realization struck Caroline. As she stared at Lavinia's retreating form, she observed what no amount of wealth, no quantity of the finest silk, and no title might conceal: the pure hatred of a shallow creature.

Dreadful as it was to see her former friend in this new manner, it was the next realization that struck her most forcefully.

Caroline had indeed done nothing less when she attempted to separate her brother from Miss Jane Bennet. She could not deny that she would do—and in fact had done—something very similar in the name of family protection.

She walked across the room and positioned herself in front of one of the large windows that lined the walls. Caroline stared blindly at her own reflection in the glass for some time, and when her eyes finally focused on it, she was shocked.

Before her was a frightened, powerless woman who, though financially stable, had managed to deny herself every other joy of society that was available to her sex.

A tear ran down one cheek, and though she quickly dashed it away with the back of her hand, she felt angry at her uncharacteristic lack of control.

But she could not blame herself, for it is difficult to ascertain one's true nature for the first time.

ᴗᴥᴖ Twenty ᴖᴥᴗ

It was upon this very thought that Caroline heard her mother's voice say, "Your brother and his companions have arrived, my dear. Do come and greet them."

Good Lord, Caroline thought. How had they arrived in London so quickly? They must have been only a day's ride behind the mail coach! To be so soon in the company of Miss Elizabeth Bennet and Mr. Darcy and to know that her brother would be eyeing her closely, wondering if she would make amends, was simply too much. How would she survive the moments to come?

She could not fathom a method. She must simply endure it as best she could.

"Yes, Mama," Caroline called back in a controlled tone that contradicted the turmoil within her. She must take a bit of time to gather her scattered wits.

Caroline looked through the window, saw Mr. Darcy's carriage at the entrance, and wondered how she had managed to ignore its arrival. She had been so focused within that she had entirely missed the happenings in the world around her.

She took a deep breath and refocused on her reflection. She looked strained and bloodless. She pinched her cheeks and smoothed her hair, but it did little good.

Her jangled nerves nearly prevented her from turning and walking toward the entryway to greet the new arrivals, and she did not approve of this sensation at all. Nervous complaints were the hallmark of weak-willed, silly women everywhere, and Caroline had always been proud not to count herself among them. Now, here she was having some sort of apoplexy at the thought of encountering her own brother and a gentleman with whom she had traveled extensively.

But how could Caroline possibly face any of them now?

She was an abject failure.

Lavinia would see to it that she never met with Mr. Charlton again. He would not propose. She would not be the wife of a baron.

All hope of escaping her brother's injunction to make amends with Miss Elizabeth Bennet was now lost. If she wanted to escape the prison of the north, then she must depend on her brother. And now that she understood Lavinia's feelings toward her, she must not return to Kendal.

Ever again.

Resigned to her fate, Caroline entered an empty foyer. While she had been summoning her courage and contemplating her appearance, the guests had already been greeted and ushered into the drawing room, which had more seating than the small sitting room she and Lavinia had occupied, and by now, her mother was no doubt attempting to recount every happening in Kendal since the day Charles had left it all those years ago.

As Caroline drew nearer to the chamber, she saw that the double mahogany door was ajar, allowing her to distinguish the voices of the room's occupants from her position in the hallway.

Truly, she was preparing to make her entrance when she heard Mr. Darcy speak, and suddenly, she felt quite immobilized.

His voice had once been the audible symbol of all her hopes and dreams, and hearing it now in the wake of her greatest defeats was nearly more than she could bear. She could only stand and listen to its modulated tones and wish for what could not be.

With such strong emotions coursing through her, Caroline took the cowardly option and peeked through the open door instead of meeting her former companions with her usual boldness. They were all charmingly arranged about the room, but Caroline's eyes sought Mr. Darcy, and she discovered him standing behind the sofa. A deep brown coat covered his broad back, and he appeared to be quite at his leisure, for he leaned against the back of the sofa in a relaxed posture. When she observed that his hand was resting so that his fingertips could with great subtlety brush the shoulder of the woman—his wife, Miss Elizabeth Bennet, as Caroline would always think of her—who was seated before him, Caroline could not bear the unfairness. Miss Elizabeth Bennet had every tangible need met, and she had love as well.

On that thought, Caroline strode into the chamber prepared to be just as cold to Miss Elizabeth Bennet as ever and just as attentive to Mr. Darcy as propriety would allow.

The gentlemen all stood at her sudden entrance, and her mother was forced to break her litany of local news. "Oh Caroline, my dear, there you are. Do come and greet your brother, his wife, and their friends."

Caroline did as she was instructed only because it was precisely what she had intended to do.

"Charles," she said as she grasped his hand in both of hers. "How happy I am to see you looking so hale after your travels."

Her brother returned her greeting and gave her a searching look, as if attempting to gauge her intentions with one mere glance. Caroline offered him her boldest smile, which caused his eyebrows to draw down in confusion.

He may as well share in her perplexity, for she was acting without fully knowing her own aims.

She then smiled at Jane, who was eyeing her with a mixture of suspicion and openness. Jane's visage transformed into a look of honest pleasure that surprised Caroline.

After having just experienced the same suffering she had inflicted on Jane, Caroline could not imagine offering such an open expression to Lavinia Winton. No indeed.

But Jane had always been a kind-hearted girl, and now Caroline must admit that she was twice as good as herself.

"My dear sister," Caroline said. "I am also happy to see you here."

Jane smiled with ever-increasing openness. "Thank you. I am happy to be here."

Caroline then turned to Jane's sister Elizabeth, who was eyeing her with only suspicion and no openness at all. Caroline squinted at her, believing in her mien a certain level of suppressed anger. Possibly there was also a hint of superiority.

Caroline forced the smile to remain upon her lips, intent upon paying Miss Elizabeth Bennet every arrear at civility. "Mrs. Darcy, you are welcome too."

The woman only smiled and inclined her head.

Finally, Caroline looked to the gentleman who remained at her shoulder. "Mr. Darcy…" she began, and to her horror, she found that words failed her.

In the past, perhaps she would have uttered a caustic remark about the tedium of long journeys, but today, she could not think of a word to say.

Mr. Darcy bowed to her, looked away, and the moment was over.

The guests returned to their former positions, leaving Caroline in want of a chair.

She turned toward the fire, where she discovered Mr. Rushton lurking by the poker.

She looked to the pianoforte and considered seating herself upon the stool, but out of the corner of her eye, she saw Mr. Rushton gesture to the wooden chair beside him, clearly offering her a place.

She glared at him, unleashing upon him the venom she must conceal from others. What a blessing to have him here, for she could be just as rude to him as she liked. Yes, she would take the seat he offered.

Mr. Rushton had the audacity to smile as she approached, prompting her to say sotto voce, "Mr. Rushton, I did not realize you were to be a part of our family party."

"I might remind you that this is my house," he returned softly, "but I am certain you recall that already."

She glowered happily. She knew very well why he had installed himself in the chamber. He had come with the dual purposes of eating the food intended for their guests and of gathering information, for he must suspect that an explanation for her sudden arrival in Kendal would lie with her former traveling party.

"Yes," Mrs. Newton said, having not heard Mr. Rushton's reply. "We quite fancy Mr. Rushton a part of our family, and Mrs. Pickersgill as well, though she has been called away abruptly this afternoon. You will meet her soon, I am certain, for she is a dear friend of Caroline's."

Then she turned to her daughter and said, "My dear Caroline, do attempt to convince your brother to stay here in Mr. Rushton's home, for he has already issued the invitation." Caroline glared again at Mr. Rushton as her mother continued. "But Charles says they are to stay at a hotel. A hotel!"

Relief flooded Caroline. They would not stay at Grosvenor Street. Thank heaven. She did not think she could bear any further discomfort, but for her mother's benefit, she must attempt to persuade them.

"Mama," Charles protested, "it is a fine hotel: Grillon's."

"Well, it sounds very…French." Mrs. Newton turned to her daughter and said, "Caroline, convince him to stay here."

Caroline restrained a sigh. "Yes, Charles, do stay here if you possibly can and eat just as much of Mr. Rushton's food as you like." She glanced about the room to find everyone looking at her rather oddly. She must get control of her tongue and her emotions, for she was quite making herself appear the fool. "Mama has the greatest desire to acquaint herself with my new sister."

Caroline smiled at Jane, whose face brightened at the prospect of deepening her relationship with her new maternal figure.

"Indeed, I must become acquainted with my new daughter," Mrs. Newton said. "And Mr. and Mrs. Darcy as well, you must stay, for you are family too, are you not? I understand from Caroline that the two of you are sisters."

It was Mrs. Darcy who responded, saying, "Yes, Jane and I are indeed sisters, both in family lineage and in heart. So I suppose…" She looked at Caroline with a rather grim set to her mouth. "We are family."

"Then you must stay here so that we may all get to know one another, and I may as well begin now." She smiled broadly. "Jane, my dear, I do believe you have already brought goodness to my son's life."

"Oh, Mrs. Newton," Jane said as a blush graced her classical features, "it is kind of you to say, but quite unnecessary."

"Unnecessary? I think not. Only look at my Charles. He has quite come into his own since your marriage, I must say."

"I could not possibly claim credit for such a change," Jane demurred.

"I am as I always have been, Mama," Charles said, though he appeared a bit proud of himself.

"No, no, I sense a new confidence in you, Charles. Do not you agree, Caroline?"

She looked at her brother. In truth, she agreed wholeheartedly with the assessment, though he was exercising his new bravado in a most inappropriate way. Let him order about his servants, not his sister.

Caroline did not see, however, that such an admission in this company could do her any justice, so she said, "I sense in him only that he is a bit more thick-headed than usual."

"Oh, Caro!" Her mother laughed, and the rest of the room followed suit, albeit uneasily. "Do not tease your brother so. You must admit that he has chosen his wife wisely. He has not, like so many gentlemen these days, chosen his bride based on frivolity or greed. He has chosen from his heart, and that, I find, is the best way."

"I have indeed," Charles said, causing Jane to blush.

"And these are the things we must discuss," Mrs. Newton cried, "and why you must stay here."

"Mama," Charles said with great patience. "I believe we will all be more at ease if we stay at the hotel as planned." He turned to Mr. Rushton and said, "We will be pleased to accept your invitation to dine with you on Wednesday evening, however."

Wednesday evening?

That was a mere two days hence!

That gave her little time to....

To what?

What course of action was open to her now?

While Caroline was attempting to conceive a sensible reply, she was conscious of Mr. Rushton's movements on the periphery.

Caroline could think of nothing worse than to have to dine in company on Wednesday, for now she had no choice but to relent to her brother's desires. Her plans had all failed, and she may as well concede defeat. She was staring at the floor as if it might provide a polite response when a booted foot emerged in her field of vision. Then, a teacup appeared before her.

Reflexively, she took it and then looked to see who had carried it.

The hand was Mr. Rushton's.

Had he come to torment her from a closer distance?

No, his expression, instead of holding mockery, seemed to convey a sort of strength.

She decided she must have wished the expression onto his face out of her need for support, and so she sneered and attempted to return the cup and saucer to him. "I thank you, but I find that I am not thirsty."

He returned her sneer but did not retrieve the teacup, and he said quietly, "Take it anyway. Perhaps it will warm that chilly soul of yours."

Before Caroline could issue the appropriate response, her mother called, "What are you two talking of over there?"

Caroline rolled her eyes, but Mr. Rushton looked at her mother with a pleasant expression. "Why, we were merely discussing how warmth and comfort may often come from an unexpected source."

❧❧ ❧❧

Caroline would never admit to experiencing comfort from Mr. Rushton, and she certainly received no reprieve from her own brother when he cornered her in the drawing room alone when the others had been preparing to see their guests to the carriage.

Charles approached her with caution, his questioning eyes immediately meeting hers as he glanced at the open door behind him.

She knew what he was about, but she would not aid him in his quest. She only sat silently and watched him pace the room.

Finally, he said, "Time has passed."

"Yes," she agreed. "Time has a way of doing just that."

He sighed in exasperation. "Time offers the chance of reflection."

Caroline must not seem to give in to him so easily, so she deliberately chose to misunderstand him. "Are you saying that, upon your own reflection, you see how wrong you were to insist on my guilt and removal? That you understand now how you have overreacted by insisting on having your will done?"

Charles turned around, eyes wide, saying, "What? No. I mean only…that…perhaps you had altered your opinion."

She remained seated like a queen on her throne, all the while feeling like a pauper in the gutter, and looked at Charles with feigned superiority. "My opinion remains unchanged, and as long as it remains thus, I shall never apologize," she bluffed.

He appeared surprised. "That certainly makes our visit here awkward." He paced a few steps. "Dash it, Caroline, this will be dismal if you do not relent."

"Well, that is your own fault. I did not ask you to bring the Darcys here, and as you cannot remove me from another gentleman's house, you shall have to suffer the consequences of your own choice."

Charles let out an exasperated sigh. "I had assumed you had seen reason."

"Reason?" Caroline asked a bit too loudly. "There is nothing reasonable about apologizing to someone whom I have not wronged!"

Indeed, Caroline would admit to having wronged Miss Jane Bennet egregiously, but Miss Elizabeth Bennet was another matter entirely. Here, Caroline was still in the right.

"Then I must appeal to your desire to restore family harmony if reason will not tempt you."

"I am not the person responsible for having destroyed family harmony; therefore, I cannot restore it through any action."

Charles shook his head. "That is utter nonsense, Caroline, as you are well aware."

"I am not aware of any such thing."

Tension lanced the air as brother and sister stared at each other.

Charles turned away, and when he spoke again, it was in a soft voice. "Caroline, be logical. Do you not want to retain your invitation to Pemberley?"

"You know I do," she whispered.

"And do you not want to continue traveling with your sister and me?"

"Nothing would provide greater pleasure."

"Then, can you not forget your pride and do what I ask, for my own sake if not for yours?"

"I do not know," she answered honestly.

Charles stood before her, his eyes holding a mixture of pity and indignation, and said, "I know how difficult this must be, Caroline, but it is difficult for me as well. And that is precisely why I must demand that you make your amends before our dinner Wednesday evening, or we will leave London, and your opportunity will have disappeared along with us."

Charles turned to leave the room, and out of desperation, Caroline leapt from her seat.

"Charles…please…wait," she pleaded, but his steps did not hesitate. He walked resolutely from the drawing room and toward the front door where the coach was already waiting.

Caroline yearned to follow her brother, to stop him from handing down such an ultimatum, but she knew it would do little good. His back was stiff and straight with determination as he bid their mother farewell. She would not convince him now.

In the entry hall, Caroline hesitated. Politeness required her to join Mr. and Mrs. Newton on the stairs of Mr. Rushton's house to bid adieu to her brother and his party, but she simply could not do it. Instead, upon exiting the drawing room, she turned in the opposite direction and fled upstairs to her bedchamber.

Finally, shutting the door solidly behind her, Caroline threw herself onto the bed and buried her face in the linens. She had expected to burst into tears the moment she gained some privacy, but she could not cry.

Her emotions had endured such wild changes that her body seemed no longer able to react properly. She had passed so quickly from anger to horror to sorrow and back again that she seemed to have run through all her reserves, leaving her completely and utterly numb.

As she lay with her face hidden against the soft bed coverings, she tried to take stock of her situation. Lavinia despised her, and Mr. Charlton would certainly not propose marriage now. Her brother had arrived and demanded her final decision regarding her apology to Miss Elizabeth Bennet. Her mother seemed suspicious, Rosemary was absent, and Mr. Rushton seemed to be enjoying her circumstances entirely too much.

After enduring the day's events, Caroline felt as if she really ought to be suffering from nervous complaints and demanding smelling salts, but she felt nothing. In the space of one day, the entire world had crashed around her, and yet she was a void. Her only concern now was to think of what must be done in order to extricate herself from the rubble and debris.

But what could be done to remove herself from the wreckage of her own life?

She knew very well that nothing could be done.

Lavinia would never allow her into Mr. Charlton's sphere again. Caroline had not the least hope of becoming the wife of a baron, thereby raising herself out of the mire of trade and into the glory of polite society by her own actions.

She must again depend on others.

She turned her head and sighed. She was glad that Rosemary was not at home, for this was just the sort of time when the woman would appear and moralize over the situation. She would gloat about having accurately assessed Lavinia's motives in taking her brother to London, and she would remind Caroline that her current circumstances were entirely of her own making.

She did not need to be reminded of these truths, for she was all too aware of them as it was.

Now, the prospect of returning to Kendal loomed before her. Once the Fairmont Bridge was comfortably in progress and their sojourn in London ended, her exile in the north would continue indefinitely.

But upon her return, her situation would be altered. Lavinia would ensure that she was no longer welcomed into good society there, and Caroline would be forced to explain matters to her mother, which she could not bear.

She could not admit her failures—either of action or of character—to her mother. She would not. She did not want to see the shame and sorrow in her mother's eyes when she discovered that Caroline had been the cause of the split between all her children. She, who saw no real value in associating with the wealthy and titled, would look upon her daughter with new eyes. She would see Caroline for who she was.

Yes, Caroline could admit it. She always wanted to be seen as better than she was.

It was a failing indeed.

This was too much. Truly, Caroline ought to be shaking or crying or screaming.

But she was just lying on the bed. Her body had given up, and now her mind was beginning to yield as well.

She may as well face the painful truth of her circumstances and concede defeat. It was time for her to surrender. Her desires in the matter were irrelevant. Whether or not she believed in her own guilt, she must now capitulate. She had no choice.

Tomorrow, she must make amends with Miss Elizabeth Bennet.

✺ Twenty-one ✺

Caroline repeated this truth to herself as she fell into a fitful sleep, and when she awoke, they were the first words that entered her mind.

Today, she must make amends with Miss Elizabeth Bennet.

Yes, it had to be done.

Caroline sat up slowly, feeling unbalanced, and attempted to orient herself. She had dozed off precisely where she had thrown herself the night before and had not bothered either to position herself correctly on the bed or pull back the linens. She lay exactly as she had fallen.

She managed to stand and look about her. The curtains had not been drawn, and light streamed into the room. It was later than she had expected, probably well after noon.

Caroline sighed and turned from the window only to be faced with her own reflection in the mirror. Her hair, which she had not bothered to take down or brush, resembled a bird's nest, and wrinkles marred the fabric of her dress.

She ran her hands down the front of her skirt, but her efforts were to no avail. She shook her head, ashamed at herself for having fallen asleep in the clothing she had worn the night before.

What was becoming of her?

Caroline supposed that this is what happened to women once they reached such a hopeless state. They simply fell apart.

Well, she may have no hope of rising in society or of ever attaining any control over her own life and fortune, but she would go into her hopelessness with as much pride as possible.

She would go to Grillon's and be done with her apology, but she would do so looking like a queen.

Caroline rang the bell, first for nourishment and then again for assistance in her preparations for the day.

As the maid arranged her hair, she sat listlessly at her dressing table and attempted to compose her speech to Miss Elizabeth Bennet, but the words simply would not arrange themselves.

What could she say?

Yes, I attempted to separate your sister from my brother, but they are now married and I must accept her as one of my family. That at least was the truth.

Yes, I disliked you, but it is all over now. That was less true.

Yes, I wanted your husband and his home for myself. That was true, but far too humiliating to admit.

Caroline sighed aloud and realized that the maid had completed her coiffure and left the room while she had been engaged in her own thoughts.

Well, she may not know how precisely she would issue the apology, but she may as well go and be done with it.

She stood, opened her bedchamber door, and crept down the hall. She felt quite foolish creeping about during the daytime hours, but she greatly hoped to sneak out of the house and complete her errand with no one, especially her mother, the wiser.

Caroline met no one in the hall or on the stairs, and she had the front door within her sights. She must only walk a few more paces to be out of Mr. Rushton's home and into the anonymity of London's streets.

"Miss Bingley," a male voice said.

Curse it! She had been caught.

Thoroughly embarrassed, Caroline turned slowly to discover Mr. Rushton's butler standing at the foot of the stairs regarding her with scarcely concealed curiosity.

"Yes?" she demanded in her haughtiest tone. "What is it?"

"A letter, miss," he responded.

"Well, bring it to me."

He crossed the room and handed her the letter. Caroline did not thank him, but simply snatched the folded paper from the silver tray he held and disappeared into the sitting room, shutting the door behind her.

Out of habit, Caroline crossed to stand beside the escritoire as she stared at the unfamiliar handwriting and wondered who could have possibly written. The lettering was bold and neat, but she could not place it. She tore open the seal and began to read.

My dear Caroline,

Long hours did I await you in the ruins that night at Vauxhall. Did you become lost? Or did you meet another gentleman instead?

It matters not, for nothing could prevent me from composing this letter to you, my darling, not even my sister's ire. I refuse to concede to her wishes, for my desire for you overwhelms me and I cannot restrain myself from speaking. Will you marry me, my dear, and run Oak Park?

If you wish to make me the happiest of gentlemen and answer in the affirmative, then you must come away with me immediately. Meet me at dusk where first we encountered each other in London.

All my affection,
William Charlton

Caroline plunked down onto the wooden chair beside the writing desk. Her breath was coming short and quick, and for a moment she thought she might swoon.

Laughter bubbled within her, and though Caroline covered her lips with her hand, a giggle escaped.

Mr. Charlton had proposed!

Last night, Caroline had lost all hope, and suddenly, with the dawning of a new day—or at least with the noontime sun—her dreams and schemes had come to fruition.

Here was her salvation, and it came at the last possible moment. No longer would she be required to apologize to Miss

Elizabeth Bennet in order to rise in society. She could ascend on her own and under her own power.

Caroline sat for a moment, basking in this sudden turn of events.

Of course, there was the question of Charles. He would be angry at her disappearance, but eventually, he would relent and welcome her again into his company. And if he did not, she would at least gain her own place in society.

Caroline smiled at her next thought: she would have the additional benefit of evicting Lavinia from Oak Park.

The laughter suddenly died on her lips.

If she married Mr. Charlton, she would have all these things, but at what cost?

Her husband would be unfaithful always.

Proper society would look away, but could Caroline?

And she would run Oak Park, but Mr. Rushton had hinted that he gambled as well. Was she capable of risking her only power, her money?

But finally, she would have a home of her own.

She would always have her own place.

She did not know how long she sat at the writing desk contemplating her situation before she heard the door to the sitting room open.

Caroline glanced over her shoulder at the new arrival.

Rosemary Pickersgill.

If she were to succeed in sneaking away to Mr. Charlton, Caroline must not allow Rosemary to discover the proposal. She turned her back to her companion, intent on concealing the letter as quickly as possible.

"Mrs. Pickersgill," she said as she folded the paper with silent fingers and then slid it under the desk blotter. "I have not seen you since yesterday. Wherever have you been?"

"That is a fine greeting, Miss Bingley, but there is nothing you may say to me today to ruin my spirits."

"Oh?" Caroline asked as she thought of the marriage proposal hidden beneath the blotter. That might shake Rosemary's joy, but Caroline would not speak a word of it.

She turned to face her companion more fully. Yes, she did appear nearly overcome with joy. Her eyes fairly shone with vigor, and she seemed years younger somehow.

"Tell me," Caroline encouraged as she moved to join Rosemary on the sofa, "what has brought you such joy."

"I have just had a most successful meeting with my solicitor."

Caroline could not conceal her shock. "Your solicitor?" She laughed. "Why would you have need of a solicitor?"

Rosemary did not seem at all affronted by Caroline's mocking laughter. She only said, "You recall, Miss Bingley, that I once told you I would share my secrets at the proper moment."

Caroline nodded slowly, unsure whether to continue laughing or give way to the feeling of unease that rose within her.

"This is the proper moment, for Lady Middlebury has spread the news of my arrival and my name will soon be gracing the gossip columns, I fear."

"Tell me then, Mrs. Pickersgill," Caroline said, still unable to believe that anything this woman might say would be worthy of such anticipation.

"I do not mean to shock you, Miss Bingley, but I fear we have not been properly introduced."

"Have we not?"

"No, for before you, you see Rosemary Pickersgill, paid companion and thorn in your side. But not so long ago I was Lady Braye, wife of Mr. John Pickersgill or Baron Braye."

Caroline's eyebrows dropped in confusion. "I do not comprehend…" Her voice trailed off as she stared at Rosemary. Sitting before her, apparently, was the Dowager Lady Braye. She ought to be tucked away in a secure country estate and consuming chocolates, but she was here in London acting as a mere servant. "You? The wife of a baron?"

Caroline meant the question as an insult, but somehow it fell flat.

"Indeed, Miss Bingley, close your mouth. Do not appear so shocked."

"But…"

"How did I come to be your companion?"

Caroline nodded.

"My husband John died two summers ago." A shadow passed over Rosemary's features. "I was devastated, for I truly loved him. He was the kindest and best of men, and he also loved me. You see, Miss Bingley, he married me, the daughter of a country gentleman without a great dowry, land, or any relations of consequence.

"As you might imagine, I was thrown into an utterly new society when I came with him to London those first years, and John was generous both with my inheritance and my allowance. I admit to having indulged more than I ought to have. I had the finest gowns and attended the grandest balls. I had attained the pinnacle of social delights and I reveled in it. Until John died."

"But your inheritance?" Caroline demanded. "What of that?"

"Patience, Miss Bingley." She paused to clear her throat. "We had no children and thus no heirs upon whom to bestow the title after John died, so the barony passed to his brother James. At first, James invited me to remain in his household and was generous with my treatment, but I fear his wife had no wish to share her home with a dowager, and so she used her influence to remove me, inch by inch, from her sphere." Rosemary shook her head sadly. "I feel rather foolish. I trusted them and did not realize what was occurring until I had lost everything."

Caroline could hardly think how to react, and her mind seemed stuck on Rosemary's true identity. It made no sense. How could this woman be the Dowager Lady Braye? How had she lost her fortune and come to this place? And how could Caroline have not recognized a lady of quality in her own household?

Rosemary continued, "James, the new Lord Braye, became quite intoxicated by his power and position—an easy transformation, I can assure you—and his wife preyed upon this weakness. She convinced him that I was a drain on their household and, in fact, that I had extorted John into marriage in order to gain his fortune. Then, through some legal machinations and deceit, I was out."

"Out?" Caroline repeated.

"Yes, all that was rightfully mine was removed, and I was quite alone and poor. Rumor circulated through London that I had been declared a fortune hunter, and as such, I had been legally disinherited. It was quite a scandal."

"But surely you had friends or relations who would come to your aid, despite the lies?" Caroline demanded.

Rosemary's face softened and then transformed into regret. "I did, but after a time, I began to recognize that my dependency on them could not last, and that was when Charles mentioned his need to find a companion for you."

"Charles knowingly sent the widow of a baron to be my paid companion?" Caroline could hardly believe her brother would be so foolhardy.

"He thought it would appeal to you to have a former baroness in your entourage." Rosemary offered a hesitant smile. "And I needed employment. Truly, I had no other option. John's family would have no part of me, and it was not in my nature to rely forever on my friends."

"And why tell me this now?" Caroline asked. "Has something altered?"

"Do you recall the tears I shed that evening you entered my chamber at Newton House?"

Caroline nodded.

"I had recently received a letter disclosing all the rumors that had been circulating about me in Town. I was a fortune hunter and extortionist, and my marriage was a fraud. This news quite broke my heart, for John and I loved one another. I did not want my marriage to be so abused."

"And so you hired a solicitor?"

"Yes." Rosemary looked at her directly. "Thanks to you, Miss Bingley."

Confused, Caroline only stared at her.

"Watching you fight these past months to attain your own goals—no matter the cost to you—has inspired me to fight for mine," Rosemary explained. "I have returned to my solicitor and am attempting to reverse the decision against me. Their charge against me—that I coerced John into marriage in order to gain his fortune—is unfounded. Such an accusation only has legal merits if the gentleman in question is a youth. There is no legal precedent for me to be disinherited for that reason."

"And you expect to win?"

"Indeed I do."

Suddenly, matters became very clear to Caroline. Rosemary had always displayed a comprehension of manners and etiquette beyond the station she was presumed to hold. She had also shown a great deal of dignity in her bearing.

Though Caroline had not been able to see it until now, Rosemary had always shown herself to be a lady of class and distinction.

The truth was that everyone else—her mother, the occupants of Oak Park, and even Mr. Rushton—seemed to have suspected something of Rosemary's history based on her comportment alone.

Only Caroline had remained oblivious. She felt like an utter fool. She had mocked, insulted, and tortured this woman, who ought to be inflicting the same kind of pain upon women of Caroline's class.

Why had Rosemary allowed it? Why had she concealed her identity?

"I see the questions in your eyes, Miss Bingley. You feel I betrayed you by not sharing my past, but I did not. I am no longer of the titled class, and so my status could have no bearing upon you." Caroline was about to protest when Rosemary continued. "Besides, you shared nothing of your own past with me."

Caroline was silent.

"Mr. Bingley summarized your actions and his reasons for sending you away, and I admit that I quite agreed with his decision. I had once been in Mrs. Bingley's position, after all, and as such, I had no great fondness for you."

"I do not see how this conversation is helpful," Caroline said.

"Do you not? Well, allow me to continue." Rosemary's tone was airy and light, but her next words were harsh. "Though you have done little to endear yourself to me, I believe I have been enough in your company to see that Mr. Bingley has overreacted. He has overlooked two crucial aspects of your character: fear and misunderstanding."

Embarrassed and angry at Rosemary's words, Caroline snapped, "You take upon yourself too much power, Mrs. Pickersgill, for you are still in my family's employ and thus dependent on me, no matter who you used to be."

"That is not precisely true, as I shall later explain, but allow me to finish my speech, for this is something you ought to hear." Rosemary did not await Caroline's permission. "You fear that one day you will be in my situation. You will be exposed as the daughter of a tradesman and a social climber, and you will do anything if you believe it will ensure your safety, including the pursuit of men who would never truly show you love. But the worst of it is, Miss Bingley, that you misunderstand the ways of the world."

"Indeed I do not!"

"You believe that a marriage to a man of fortune or title will ensure your entire future happiness, but as you see in the example before you, that is not necessarily the case!"

Upon this pronouncement, Rosemary seemed quite content to leave Caroline to her contemplation. In fact, Caroline was so lost in her own thoughts that she hardly recognized the moment when her companion left the room.

Could this be true? Had Caroline been searching for her future happiness and security in vain? Would a marriage to Mr. Charlton prove so fruitless?

৩৫ Twenty-two ৯৫

No, Caroline thought, she could not be so utterly incorrect!

All her experiences told her that money, title, and land were her best opportunities at protection and status. It was the way of society, and society could not be argued with, could it?

No indeed, it could not.

She leapt from the writing desk, determined to find Rosemary and demand further explanation of her meaning when she chanced to look out the window and notice that dusk had already begun to fall.

Dusk!

How could she possibly have remained so long in the sitting room? She had not even had the opportunity to pack a trunk for her elopement, and yet the time was upon her to meet Mr. Charlton. She must be at Berkeley Square even now.

Briefly, she considered dashing upstairs and throwing some necessities into a small bag, but she decided against it.

Impractical, unwise, foolish: they described her decision with accuracy, but time had quite run out.

She must forget all practical questions and act. No bag, no note, no goodbyes. She must leave before someone caught her and attempted to talk her out of the decision.

Besides, Mr. Charlton was wealthy and would purchase any article she required. Yes, all would be well once she met with him.

Caroline had left Mr. Rushton's house before she remembered the proposal letter, which was still hidden under the blotter.

Well, no matter. By the time anyone discovered it, she would be safely wed to her baron.

No one—not Charles, Mr. Darcy, Miss Elizabeth Bennet, and certainly not Rosemary Pickersgill and her cautionary tale—would be able to stop Caroline from finally removing from herself the stench of trade and freeing herself from following the whims of others. She would be Lady Charlton, and as such, she could do just as she pleased.

Lady Charlton. Caroline repeated the name as she traversed the streets toward Berkeley Square in the day's waning light.

As she walked with determined steps onto Davies Street, Caroline contemplated her first acts as Lady Charlton.

She would announce the marriage to her brother, officially removing herself and her fortune from his control. No longer would Charles be able to insist she take any action against her will.

Though Caroline would do her best to repair matters with Jane, who was now family, she would have no need to make amends with Miss Elizabeth Bennet, for Pemberley would no longer mean a thing to her. She would have her home and her fortune at Oak Park, and she would never again have to rely on Mr. Darcy to bring her into society. She would be a baron's wife!

And Caroline would delight in throwing Lavinia out of Oak Park on her ear. She laughed aloud and then sobered.

Lavinia.

And her son. The next in line for the barony.

The woman despised her. What would happen to Caroline if Mr. Charlton were to die before an heir could be produced?

Lavinia's son would become the baron, and Lavinia herself would certainly have no pity on Caroline.

Would Lavinia, like Rosemary's relations, remove and disinherit Caroline?

Would she marry a baron only to end a paid companion?

Caroline's steps slowed as she neared Berkeley Square.

What if she had misunderstood Mr. Charlton as she had Lavinia and Rosemary?

She must know the truth.

With renewed purpose, Caroline completed her trek to the square and spotted Mr. Charlton leaning against the rail precisely where she had first seen him.

Only this time, he saw her when she first approached.

"Miss Bingley," he whispered. "You are here."

"Yes," she agreed. "I am here."

"Come," he said, as he attempted to lead her along the rail. "My carriage waits for us at the street." He glanced at her, confused. "Have you a bag?"

"Wait," Caroline said. She refused to take another step though he pulled at her arm.

"We ought to be away, for my sister may discover my absence."

"Yes, we ought to discuss your sister," she said as she extracted herself from his grasp.

"I wish you would not think of her!"

"She despises me and would object to this union if she knew of it."

He sighed. "Yes."

"And yet you still wish to marry me." She narrowed her eyes at him. "And because you have always spoken so very plainly about your inheritance and even your faults, you must also speak plainly now. Tell me why."

He hesitated, looked at the ground beneath his feet, and said, "Because I love you."

Caroline laughed and Mr. Charlton's head snapped up.

"That is not the truth, is it?" she demanded. "Before I step foot into your carriage, Mr. Charlton, I demand to know your motives. Do you seek revenge on your sister?"

"No," he said quickly and then added, "Yes. Well, somewhat."

"Explain."

He exhaled and then his words came: "You know how much I hate this barony nonsense. I am terrible at managing my own finances much less those of an entire estate or country! I have lost quite a bit of money already, and I cannot allow Lavinia or my father to learn of my folly. I must pay my debts quickly and quietly, and then I must find someone to keep Oak Park from falling into shambles."

Caroline sighed. So it was her fortune that attracted him. Only a few weeks ago, that fact would not have seemed half as reprehensible to Caroline as it did now.

She would marry him, and in the process lose her money and the only small shreds of power she had.

"It is a good plan, is it not?" Mr. Charlton asked, his voice shockingly logical. "You will have Oak Park and a title, and I shall wipe the slate clean and remove my sister from her place in the household. You shall manage the house and keep me from complete ruination. It could not be more agreeable to either of us."

Caroline eyed him. "And if you were to die, I would be left with nothing. No money, and Lavinia would throw me out and install her son in Oak Park as baron."

He looked at his boot. "It would not happen that way."

"How can you be certain?" she asked.

He seemed to have no answer.

Caroline sighed, and, suddenly tired of the nonsense, she spoke with utter candor and no rancor at all. "You are wrong, Mr. Charlton, for I object to the very idea. I fear you will have to marry someone else in order to accomplish all you desire. Though I harbor you no ill will, for only recently I would have believed this the ideal solution for both of us, I cannot marry you."

The couple looked at each other for long moments, assessing.

"I am sorry to hear that, Miss Bingley." He sighed too. "Now I must find another wealthy young woman with whom to elope in order to save my family."

"I wish you luck, Mr. Charlton, and you must do the same for me, for I must now lower myself by apologizing for a crime I did not commit and thus save my own family."

৩৩ Twenty-three ৩৩

Grillon's Hotel stood only two streets over from Berkeley Square, and Caroline resolved to walk the distance as quickly as possible before reality intruded upon her and she realized what she had done and what she must do.

The hotel was large and grand, but beyond its size and scale, Caroline hardly noticed it. She simply forced herself up the stairs and into the building, past the plush rugs and wall hangings to the first liveried servant she saw.

"Mrs. Darcy," she demanded. "I must speak with her immediately."

The servant did not appear shocked by her rudeness but only said, "She is in a private sitting room, miss. Do follow me."

Too soon Caroline was announced and ushered into the presence of the lady herself.

There, reclining on a sofa, was Mrs. Darcy. Charles, Jane, and Mr. Darcy were nowhere to be seen.

Elizabeth stood abruptly, and Caroline thought she saw her wince ever so slightly at discovering the identity of her guest. Then she recovered herself enough to say, "Miss Bingley, you must be in search of your brother. He is above stairs, I believe."

Caroline hesitated only a moment in the doorway before steeling herself to do what she must do.

"No, I come in search of you, my dear Mrs. Darcy," she said as she walked farther into the room and heard the servant close the door behind her. Even to her own ears, her voice sounded contrived and awkward. "You are alone, I see."

Elizabeth returned to her seat and picked up the book she had been reading. Then she smiled. "Yes, Miss Bingley, as you see, you have caught me quite alone here."

Caroline advanced further. "You are reading."

"Yes," Elizabeth said with another rather smug smile. "Jane and I are reading this book of poems upon my sister Kitty's suggestion."

"Ah. How does your younger sister do?" Caroline asked, though she could not remember if Kitty was the moralizing Bennet sister or the giddy, silly sister.

"My sister is well, thank you, Miss Bingley, but I do not think you came here to speak of my relations."

"No," Caroline agreed. There was a long pause as she mustered her waning resolve. Finally, after two aborted attempts, Caroline managed to say, "I find I owe...."

There, she had begun the apology, but it died suddenly on her lips.

Caroline had been quite determined to get the apology done with, but now, she was experiencing a nagging feeling of her own conscience. An apology would remedy all her problems, save one: she could not live with herself if she made it.

She simply could not do it.

Caroline could not apologize for something any woman—and indeed Miss Elizabeth Bennet herself—might have undertaken in her situation.

"Oh, I simply cannot do it." Caroline sat down across from Elizabeth. "I must speak frankly, Mrs. Darcy."

Mrs. Darcy raised a suspicious eyebrow. "Must you?"

Caroline continued with all honesty. "My brother is quite anxious that I conceive a way of making amends with you. He has suggested an apology, but I find it a pointless endeavor."

Elizabeth appeared amused, and her eyes brightened as if she had heard a diverting joke. "Do you?"

Caroline felt Elizabeth's amusement as if someone had boxed her ears. She did not appreciate her obvious display of pleasure, but she forced herself to continue. "You cannot be unaware of the reasons for my actions all those months ago regarding your sister and my brother."

Elizabeth nodded. "I believe I have a full understanding of what transpired."

"And you also must know that your husband was the chief instigator in separating them."

Again, she agreed. "Mr. Darcy has confessed as much and asked forgiveness."

Caroline leaned forward, desperate for Elizabeth to comprehend her. "But as a devoted sister yourself, you must understand why I cannot make apologies as Mr. Darcy has."

Elizabeth's amusement did not seem to wane at all as she laughed a bit and said, "I have always believed that one might make an apology whenever one has committed a wrong."

"And that is precisely why you will understand my refusal to apologize." She looked Elizabeth full in the eye. "I have done nothing wrong."

Annoyance briefly crossed Elizabeth's features before amusement seemed to claim the victory. "Have you not?" she asked, smirking.

"Consider, Mrs. Darcy," Caroline said with all seriousness, "your own actions regarding your sister Miss Lydia."

Elizabeth's amused expression faded. "I caution you not to speak ill of her in my presence."

"My intention is quite the contrary, I assure you. Though I know not all the particulars of what transpired, one thing is perfectly clear to me: you believed your sister to be in danger, and you would have undertaken any action to save her."

Elizabeth studied her for a moment, her face completely devoid of emotion. "Miss Bingley, I do not comprehend what you expect this line of discussion to gain for you. I—"

"I only refer to this uncomfortable matter to remind you of your own sentiments for your family. You would have done all that was necessary to save Miss Lydia, and that is all I did. Only I did not fully realize my brother's love for your sister, and I am pleased for him now."

"You admit you were in the wrong?" Elizabeth asked, eyes wide.

Caroline hedged. "I admit that he loves her, and he has married her. Now my objections are at an end. She is my family now."

Elizabeth continued to look at her with a level gaze. Caroline returned it.

"I do not know how you view Mr. Wickham now that he and Lydia are married, but I hold your elder sister in highest regard. Truly, I do." And Caroline's words actually were true. She did like Jane.

Elizabeth watched her in silence as if deciding whether or not to argue some salient point.

But Caroline pressed onward. "That is but one half of the issues that must be addressed, for there are other impediments to our ever being friends, as you well know."

The ladies regarded each other carefully before Elizabeth said with all frankness, "Yes, you desired my husband for yourself."

Elizabeth's forthrightness startled Caroline, and she knew not how to respond.

After a moment's thought, she said just as bluntly, "In this circumstance, you cannot expect me to own such a thing aloud. No woman would."

More hesitation.

"No," Elizabeth agreed. "I suppose you are correct."

"And," Caroline said, "you are too astute not to realize that we shall never be friends, apology or not."

Elizabeth nodded slowly. "Such a thing would be well nigh impossible."

"And if I were to venture an apology," Caroline added, "you would not believe me."

"No, indeed," Elizabeth said. "If you were to make your apologies, you would certainly not mean it."

"No, indeed, I would not."

"Then we are at an impasse."

Caroline shook her head. "This, Mrs. Darcy, is my proposal. For the sake of family harmony, we may as well agree to become indifferent acquaintances."

Elizabeth appeared to consider her words and then said hesitantly, "It would be folly to attempt friendship."

Caroline nodded with vigor. "Indeed."

Elizabeth indulged in a few more moments of thought before saying, "I do not like to disappoint Mr. Bingley, for he is the best of men, and it would be so much easier on your brother and my sister if we appeared to have put aside our grievances."

"Yes, I do not like to disappoint my brother either, and as I said, I have already made amends with your sister."

The two women sat in mutual silent contemplation before Elizabeth finally said, "Then, Miss Bingley, for the sake of our families, I believe we have struck an agreement."

The tension Caroline had been carrying about her shoulders and neck suddenly dissipated. This unpleasant situation might actually resolve itself to everyone's satisfaction.

"Yes," Caroline said. "I will treat you with courtesy and respect."

"And I shall do the same."

"For the sake of harmony, we will tell Charles that all is well between us…"

"…but we will not push the endeavor to friendship," Elizabeth supplied.

"No, indeed."

Elizabeth smiled.

Caroline returned it.

There, the matter was settled.

Family harmony was restored.

ஓஇ Twenty-four ஓஇ

Caroline returned to Grosvenor Street while the household was at dinner, but she could not bring herself to join them. Instead, she meandered without definite purpose to the pianoforte in the drawing room and settled herself on the stool.

After leaving Grillon's, Caroline had spent the whole evening in contemplation, and now her mind felt sluggish. All her plans had been overturned and all her hopes dashed. She had lost two gentlemen—both Mr. Darcy and Mr. Charlton—and had come to see the painful truth of her friendship with Lavinia Winton.

In the past year, she had lost quite a great deal indeed.

But she had, at the very least, the comfort of having regained her family. She realized now, however, that she must resign herself to spinsterhood and to being without any control over her own future. Evidence showed that she was not the sort of woman with whom gentlemen fell in love, so she ought to face the prospect of never having a home of her own or of enjoying the benefits of her fortune on her own terms.

Why, she may as well return to her mother's home and live there for the rest of her days. She would at least enjoy observing Lavinia's daily horror at hearing whatever chit Mr. Charlton married addressed as Lady Charlton.

That would be some consolation.

Caroline could not say she felt either pain or pleasure at her future prospects. She felt precisely nothing. Perhaps she was still overwhelmed.

And that is why she went to the pianoforte. It seemed to calm her as her fingers stroked the keys. She was in the midst of a lovely, soft piece, and her mind felt peaceful and serene as a result, when she heard a voice behind her.

"Miss Bingley." The voice was warm, but still it startled her, and she craned her neck to see who had entered.

Mr. Rushton stood in the doorway, smiling as if he understood something secret about her. Slowly, he approached, his eyes focused on her.

Caroline managed to pull her hands from the keys and then sat on the stool completely immobile.

"Caroline," he said. His eyes suddenly seemed hooded and more intense than she had ever seen them appear.

She clasped her hands in her lap and forced herself to maintain eye contact.

"I…" he began, stopped, and surveyed her from head to foot.

Caroline stifled the urge to check herself for wrinkles or to straighten her hair. No, she would not allow him to disconcert her with his boldness. Instead, she crossed her arms over her chest and raked over his appearance with equal boldness.

"You are not dressed for dinner," Caroline said.

"No, I was out."

"Ah," she said, not knowing how else to respond.

"I was searching for you."

Caroline's eyebrows drew down in confusion, and there was a long pause as the two looked at each other.

"I found this…." Mr. Rushton's voice trailed into silence as he pulled a folded sheet of writing paper from his coat pocket. "Under the blotter."

"Oh," she said, "I had forgotten about that."

Caroline watched as he refolded the note and returned it to his pocket. Then he gestured toward the pianoforte.

"That was," he said, as he came ever closer, "the most unguarded moment I have ever witnessed."

Caroline looked into Mr. Rushton's face, and then she heard herself saying, "I do not take your meaning, sir."

"Of course, you do not take my meaning, for no one has ever complimented you on your honesty and vulnerability."

"Can vulnerability be an asset?" she whispered.

"Asset or not, no person is without it."

"Even you, Mr. Rushton?"

Here, Mr. Rushton came around the pianoforte and positioned himself beside Caroline's stool.

Out of sheer habit, she turned to face him fully. He hovered above her, and although he was not so close as to make it feasible, Caroline imagined that she could feel the heat of his skin and the stirring of his breath as he said, "Even me."

His expression was rife with meaning, but still, Caroline could not comprehend it.

An unfamiliar—and not altogether uncomfortable—sensation ripped through her body as the focus of his gaze lowered from her eyes to her lips.

She licked them, but she had not meant to do so.

Heat flooded her face, and, embarrassed at her reaction to a gentleman such as Mr. Rushton, whose family had been brought low, Caroline shot to her feet.

Too late, she realized that a standing position only brought her closer to him. Now she actually could feel the warmth of his skin and the stirring of his breath.

They stood still, their bodies close and their gazes locked together.

And with shocking suddenness, Caroline comprehended the absolute truth of her vulnerability as she faced the full level of her attraction for him for the first time.

Somehow, his proximity had done queer things to the dimensions of the chamber, for it seemed much smaller. Not only had it diminished in size, but it had also warmed considerably.

"But tell me, you have not eloped with Charlton, have you?"

"What?" Caroline stared at him. "Eloped?"

"Yes, eloped. Have you?"

"You ought to know that I would never consent to such a method of matrimony! Besides, there was not time for an elopement."

He shook his head as if attempting to understand her. "So you are not married?"

"No, indeed," Caroline said, her voice suddenly gone soft.

Mr. Rushton took a step closer, and all the noise from the busy street vanished into sheer silence.

"Come," he said, "you must admit that you do—or did—have designs on that gentleman."

Caroline would not deign to answer. She would not even look at him, for such a task seemed far too difficult in this small, warm, intimate room.

In response to her obstinate silence, Mr. Rushton lifted her chin with his forefinger. Their eyes met, and she knew that there was no concealment deep enough to obscure her true motives from him.

"Quite so," he said, with a shake of his head. "I have no need of your reply, for I see very plainly that my supposition is true. But Miss Bingley, you must see that Mr. Charlton is a man who is ruled by something other than sentiment. He has other motives."

Caroline sighed. "What does it matter? No gentleman would fall in love with me."

"No, my dear Miss Bingley, that is not the case. I am certain that some unlucky man will offer you his heart, and for his sake, I do hope that you will be generous with it."

"I am not generous, as you well know."

"Indeed, therefore it is fortunate that you are not the type of woman with whom such men fall in love. Your attempts at pretense and accomplishments are so very blatant. Your machinations so transparent. Most gentlemen would be put off by you and lured by a woman of more subtle arts."

She glared.

"I see you are more hurt that your machinations are so obvious than you are distressed that this gentleman will never love you. You do not love him."

Caroline blushed, but she did not demur. "No, I do not love him."

Mr. Rushton's hand was still on Caroline's chin, but she did not feel trapped. She felt strange, almost immobilized by his touch. "And you did not love Mr. Darcy either."

"No," she said, speaking the truth aloud—and perhaps truly realizing it—for the first time. "I did not love him."

Mr. Rushton was looking at her so intensely that she let her lashes flutter lower in an attempt to avoid his searching gaze.

"Caroline," he said. "Look at me."

She found she could not.

"If you will not look at me, then…" He paused and slipped his hand to the nape of her neck. "You must allow me to experiment…"

Caroline looked at him then.

His face had drawn very near to hers, and the unfamiliar sensation intensified.

Perhaps it was the intimacy of their location in that empty room that was affecting her good judgment, but she did not pull away or attempt to rebuke him verbally. No, she stood quietly and watched through lowered lashes as he came ever closer.

She felt his breath stir the loose hair at her temples as he said, "Be still, Caroline, and allow me to…"

He had not needed to say it. She could not move.

She felt his left hand come to rest on her hip.

When Mr. Rushton's lips brushed hers, a frisson of incomprehensible feeling skittered through her, and without realizing precisely what she was doing, her hands came to grasp at his coat.

He pulled away with the apparent intent to gauge her reaction—to discover the results of his experiment—but Caroline was in no humor to be studied or gauged.

She pulled back, and he let his hand slip down Caroline's arm, but he did not let her break their contact completely. "Caroline, you must marry me."

Had he not maintained a firm grip on her fingertips, Caroline would have retreated as far as was possible within the confines of the chamber.

"No," she said flatly.

"Do not be absurd, woman. You know very well that we are perfectly suited for each other."

She jerked her hand away from his grasp. "I know no such thing."

Tears had sprung to her eyes, but through sheer force of will, she did not allow them to fall. Truly, she had never experienced the level of emotion she had felt with Mr. Rushton, but she could not bear to fail to follow her father's wish that she—and all his children—marry people of status.

"I have understood you as I have understood no other woman, and, I believe, you comprehend me better than any woman of my acquaintance. We, neither of us, play at false modesty or hide our true motives."

"If you are aware of my true motives, you know that I will never marry you."

"No, I know no such thing, for if you would but allow yourself to be influenced by something other than your fear, then you may just find that your material concerns will be taken care of."

As he spoke, he had been approaching slowly, and now he was again upon her. Her calves were pressed against the stool, and she could not retreat further.

In truth, she did not want to.

She desperately wanted to allow her feelings to guide her, perhaps only this one time, so she abandoned herself to her sentiments.

When she kissed him, it was not tentative or experimental, but desperate and full of passion. The kiss encompassed her embarrassment at being rejected, her fear of being alone, her rage at society's strictures, and her despair at the knowledge that, no matter what, she must not marry beneath her intended status. Yet, the kiss was something more. It was rife with long-concealed anxiety and unattainable hope.

And it was the first moment of uncensored emotion she had ever experienced.

But it was not to last.

"Caroline!"

The word barely registered upon her first hearing it, and only upon its second pronunciation did Caroline tear herself away from Mr. Rushton.

In the open doorway stood her mother, staring at her with a completely incomprehensible expression.

Caroline could only watch as her mother closed the door with measured control.

"I would ask what you are about in the drawing room," Mrs. Newton said as she approached the couple. "But it is quite apparent."

"No!" Caroline fairly shouted in protest at the whole situation. Her cheeks were hot as a newly stoked fire, and she stepped forward, though not quite certain whether she ought to attack Mr. Rushton for putting her in this circumstance or object to her mother's catching them.

Mrs. Newton spoke to Mr. Rushton, who was standing close behind Caroline. "You do realize the predicament you are in, sir."

"I fear that I do." Caroline turned to glare at him as he ran a hand through his blond hair. "And yet it is worse than you know, Mrs. Newton."

Mrs. Newton turned to her daughter. "What have you done to him, Caroline?"

Caroline sputtered. "What have *I* done to him? Mama! How can you ask me such a question? I have done nothing. Nothing!"

Her mother smiled oddly, but said not a word.

Caroline continued, "Mr. Rushton has taken advantage of me. Your daughter!"

Mrs. Newton looked at Mr. Rushton. "Is that true? Have you taken advantage of my girl?"

"No indeed," he said with shocking frankness. "She has taken advantage of me."

Caroline gasped. "What?"

"But it is worse than that. I am in love with her."

"Oh good God!" Caroline said with a horrified glance at her mother's pleased expression. "This is not to be borne!"

Mrs. Newton looked between Mr. Rushton and Caroline, and her face transformed from pleased to exultant as a wide smile spread across her face.

"I comprehend very well," she said to Mr. Rushton. "My daughter will never admit to her true feelings, and based on the circumstances in which I found you, she certainly has them."

Mr. Rushton looked sidelong at Caroline and replied, "Yes. She has them."

"The two of you ought not to presume to tell me what I do and do not feel," Caroline said. She took a few steps toward her mother, hands outstretched. "I certainly experience no sympathetic emotions for this person."

"Poor Caroline," Mrs. Newton said, taking both her hands. "She has spent her whole life searching for home and she does not recognize it when it is standing before her."

"I do not understand," Caroline whispered.

"Then allow me to speak plainly. You are violently in love with Mr. Rushton."

"No," Caroline whispered. "I most certainly am not."

"But you realize, of course, Mrs. Newton, that it is hopeless," Mr. Rushton said in a tone of irritating practicality. "She will marry only a gentleman of large fortune, a title, or both. And as far as she knows, I have none of these attributes."

"You speak as if I would marry you, even with those enticements," Caroline spat.

"Ah, but you shall marry him, Caroline," Mrs. Newton said. Her face held the strangest combination of seriousness and glee.

"I shall not." Caroline's anger burned and she thought to walk out, but her mother's expression alone seemed to block her way. "Only I may decide what is for my own benefit, and I can say with utmost certainty that Mr. Rushton can have no worthwhile influence on my opinions."

"And that is precisely the problem," Mrs. Newton said. "You allow the wrong people to influence your opinions: Mr. Charlton, Lavinia, even to an extent your dear father. I have seen you work to please those who care not a fig for you and conceal your heart from those who love you."

Caroline had not realized the depth of her mother's understanding of what had transpired between herself and Lavinia and Mr. Charlton.

"Yes, I know everything. I surmised that something was amiss when Lavinia and Mr. Charlton left Kendal, and that alone persuaded me to take this trip to London. I knew you would find a way to Mr. Charlton, and this seemed the best method to ensure your safety while you saw for yourself what he is. But now, I have watched you suffer enough." Mrs. Newton held up a hand to prevent Caroline from protesting again. "I am afraid you have compromised yourself with Mr. Rushton, Caroline, and I shall not conceal that fact from anyone."

"Mama! You know very well that Mr. Rushton is at fault...." Caroline allowed her voice to trail into silence. Only to herself did Caroline acknowledge the lie. She could have forced Mr. Rushton to leave, but she had not wanted him to go.

Though Caroline had not spoken aloud, Mrs. Newton looked at her as if he could see into her heart and mind. It was so disturbing that Caroline was forced to avert her eyes. She was a wanton hussy, and everyone in the room—including her own mother—knew it.

Lord! Whatever had she been thinking to allow a gentleman to embrace her like that? Worse, she had craved it. She had thrown herself back at him.

Now, she must arrange matters so that she could escape unscathed.

She mustered all her strength and willed her voice to be forceful and authoritative. When she finally spoke, she was the Caroline of old, the Caroline of twenty minutes ago, before she had allowed Mr. Rushton's advances. She rose to her full height, and her voice was terrifying, even to her, when she said, "I shall not be forced into a marriage to *him*." She jerked her hand toward Mr. Rushton.

Here, Mrs. Newton approached and took Caroline's hand in her own. "What I am about to say, I say for your own benefit and because I love you."

Caroline could not fathom what might next spring from her mother's traitorous lips, and she was truly shocked to hear her words. "You are ruined, my dear girl. You have been glimpsed in an intimate posture with a gentleman in an empty chamber. Now, you must either face life as a ruined woman or marry the man with whom you committed the indiscretion."

༄ Twenty-five ༄

Caroline did not dare to speak at that precise moment, for her rage and embarrassment were burning too brightly within her. She had disappointed herself and her entire family in indulging in such an emotional display with Mr. Rushton, and now she was being maneuvered into a marriage to a gentleman of whom she could not approve.

Caroline had nothing left within her but a broken spirit and a heart of dashed hopes. It was time to admit the truth.

Gathering herself, Caroline spoke in a painfully modulated voice. "I admit to having failed to attain all I have attempted. It seems I have taken the wrong path at every turn, and the best I can say for myself is that I was only hoping to gain that which every other woman attempts to achieve."

Caroline looked to Mr. Rushton, realizing she may as well accede to the wishes of her heart, and said, "Please leave us, Mama."

There was a pause and then her mother smiled, causing Caroline to stare in disbelief.

"You must be aware, Caro, that my departure will only solidify your ruin."

"I understand, Mama. My decision is made."

Mrs. Newton smiled again and then grasped Mr. Rushton's hand as if welcoming him to the family. "Ten minutes," she said as she turned and left the chamber.

Caroline waited until she heard the door shut behind her mother and then she spoke. "Mr. Rushton, it appears I have no choice but to accept your proposal."

She turned to face him again, but found that she could not read his expression at all well. His next words surprised her.

"That is not precisely true, Miss Bingley," he said, but he stepped closer. "For those who are truly motivated, there is always a method of escape."

"Oh?" she asked with feigned innocence as she reached out tentatively to touch his sleeve. "And what method would you propose?"

"Your mother has concocted this scheme for your own benefit, and if you truly do not wish to accept my proposal, she will not speak ill of us, no matter how deeply we deserve it. Mrs. Newton hopes only to give you ample excuse for doing something that heretofore your pride would not allow."

How accurately he summarized her, except on one score.

"It is not solely pride that has been the root of my actions, Mr. Rushton. It is also fear, as you are well aware. Have you not told me as much on numerous occasions?"

"I confess I was not aware that you marked me."

"You may rest easy in your comprehension of me, for at first, I did not listen. I believed you to be utterly incorrect," Caroline admitted.

"And now?"

"Now, a fearsome prospect is before me," she said as she ran her hand up his coat sleeve to his shoulder. "I have entangled myself with a gentleman who is quite opposite of the husband my father envisioned for me and whom I imagined for myself. I will fail at raising my family's status."

"But you shall have all the benefits of my fortune, ill gained though it may be." He paused to wrap an arm around Caroline's waist. "And you will have love."

"Yes, and that, Mr. Rushton, is my greatest fear."

His eyebrows met in confusion. "I do not believe I comprehend you."

"I will be required to open myself to you, to become vulnerable to your searching gazes, to admit the abject failure of all my schemes. I do not know if I could bear such an admission."

"Your schemes have already failed. Your admission changes nothing."

"But worse, I must become a love-struck puppy. I must laugh at your every joke, hang upon your every word, and spend my days in thrall of your wit. I do not believe I could bear the lies. As you are aware, my life has been built upon them, and I find it quite tiresome to uphold them any longer."

Mr. Rushton smiled.

He comprehended her.

Yes, he understood.

"Caroline, you harpy, I know very well that your personality has no chance of improvement, and I fully expect you to pick and prod at me for all the days of my life."

"But it is too late for you, for you have already confessed your love, have you not?"

"I fear I have."

"And I must confess as well," she said with a sly smile. "I despise you." Caroline knew quite well that her face revealed the truth of her feelings. Her cheeks were rosy, and her eyes were moist with unshed tears. Here was a gentleman who understood her. A gentleman she truly loved.

His arms came around her waist, and when he spoke again his voice was soft. "I despise you too."

❧ Epilogue ❧

Caroline's return to Kendal led to the revelation of secrets she had not realized the sleepy little hamlet held.

Mr. Charlton, as it turned out, had indeed eloped, but his partner was Miss Brodrick, the daughter of a local pencil manufacturer. On a purely practical level, Caroline could not disapprove of his choice. Perhaps the sensible young lady could manage to rein in her new husband and prevent him from depleting his family's fortune.

On a more wicked level, the marriage had provided great joy to Caroline, who felt no compunction whatsoever at her pleasure over Lavinia's embarrassment. Yes, she could just imagine her former friend's expression when she discovered the truth of the matter: her brother had eloped with someone even lower on the social scale than Caroline Bingley!

And upon her brother's inheritance of the barony, Lavinia would be required to hear Miss Brodrick called Lady Charlton.

Caroline's amusement over Lavinia's condition was tempered, however, when she discovered the truth of her friend's situation.

Her husband, Mr. Ralph Winton, was not the genial, selfless gentleman who had sacrificed to allow his wife to return to Kendal to help during her family's time of crisis.

No, indeed.

Mr. Winton was happy to see her go.

Her absence gave him complete discretion in pursuing his own dissolution. He had already gambled away their fortune, given his mind in exchange for the dubious pleasures of whiskey, and traded his marriage vows for the comforts of a mistress.

Had Harold Charlton not had the courtesy to die of consumption when he had, Lavinia would have been required to return home in disgrace, as just another victim of a dissipated, purposeless man. As it was, she had been able to claim a nobler motive than merely escaping a wretched husband.

Mrs. Pickersgill was making successful strides in her legal battle with her husband's heirs and had left the matter entirely in the hands of her solicitor in order to return to Kendal for Caroline's wedding.

Days before the ceremony took place, she received a letter from her solicitor that indicated that documents were being drawn up to finalize the return of her jointure, including her monetary inheritance and her retention of her late husband's small town home, which he had always intended for her. She would be able to return to London in triumph due to her willingness to fight her own family.

A new understanding had built between Caroline and Rosemary, and their friendship was growing stronger as her former companion helped her prepare for her wedding to Mr. Rushton. For the first time in her life, Caroline knew what it was to have a true friend, one who was not interested in gaining anything from an association with her and from whom she did not hope to gain anything in return.

Caroline's agreement with Mrs. Darcy had pleased Charles greatly, and he promptly invited her to rejoin his traveling party, which was bound for Mr. Darcy's home in Derbyshire. Though pleased to return to her brother's good graces and to have retained her welcome at Pemberley, Caroline declined his invitation and instead requested his presence at her wedding, which was to take place upon their return to the north some weeks hence.

৵৻৶ ৾৶৶

Upon the eve of Caroline's wedding, she received a letter borne by courier and carrying an unfamiliar seal.

She had almost chosen not to open it, believing it could contain nothing that needed to be read at such a moment, but upon Mr. and Mrs. Newton's prompting, she did so.

The seal belonged to a solicitor in London, and Caroline scanned the document from top to bottom. Her eyes landed upon Mr. Rushton's signature and beside it, her brother's. She looked to Mr. Newton for clarification.

"What is this?"

"Mr. Rushton and your brother completed the matter of your marriage settlement, I presume," he said with a broad smile.

Caroline sat down and read the document once and then again.

"The money Father left me." She looked at Mr. and Mrs. Newton with wide eyes. "He has allowed me control of it all, from the first moment of our marriage."

"Yes," Mr. Newton said. "Mr. Rushton spoke of it to me. I knew you would be pleased. Does she not seem pleased, my dear?" he asked his wife.

Mrs. Newton nodded. "I believe pleased and shocked." She turned to Caroline. "He is a good man."

Caroline looked away from her mother to regard the letter again. It made no sense. Who but a fool refused a fortune of 20,000 pounds? She greatly hoped that she was not engaged to a fool.

"But why?" Caroline asked.

Mrs. Newton smiled. "He has no need for it, dear. I think he wanted you to understand that his proposal was about something more than your fortune."

Caroline stared down at the letter.

Upon their nuptials, her fortune should, by all rights, become legally his. He should control it and, thereby, control Caroline as well.

And at that thought, Caroline understood him perfectly.

His wedding gift to her was the very thing around which all her striving had been centered. He was giving her lasting security by eschewing his legal right to her fortune.

No longer would she have to scramble up the social ladder, for even in the event of her husband's death—when most women, even Mrs. Pickersgill, were vulnerable to being left penniless and thus falling upon the mercy of relations or friends—Caroline would never find herself in that predicament. She was no longer slave to appearances or social whims or gossip. She depended on no one for her future security.

Caroline Bingley was finally her own mistress.

And that meant that she could finally give herself wholly to Mr. Rushton, the only gentleman she had ever loved.

⚜ ⚜

The barouche carried Mr. and Mrs. Patrick Rushton with inexorable swiftness toward Rushton House, and within its confines, its occupants sat rather stiffly for a bride and groom on their way home from their wedding breakfast.

Having not found an opportune moment to mention her inheritance all morning, Caroline now could not seem to find the words to express her feelings on the subject, or on any subject at all.

She found only the courage to make furtive glances at her husband, who, she must admit, looked handsome indeed in his fine black suit. She could not manage to meet his eyes, but looked at Mr. Rushton whenever she believed him to be focused elsewhere. When their gazes did chance to meet, she felt heat rise to her face and a flutter building in her chest.

Caroline blamed this odd behavior for the feeling of tension mounting within her.

She clasped her hands in her lap, willing them to remain still, but she jerked visibly when Mr. Rushton finally broke his silence, saying, "There is no need to conceal your anxiety, Caro, for I know very well that you must feel it."

Caroline faced her husband, but she could not yet admit her feelings aloud, so she responded with her usual sarcasm. "What can you possibly mean, sir? What cause have I to experience anxiety?"

"Come," he said. His blue eyes showed some internal pain. "You are aware of my family's fall from fortune. Though you have seen my home in town, you must harbor some fear regarding the condition of my ancestral estate."

Caroline looked at him for a long moment, and then, over his shoulder. They were coming upon the stream that she knew formed the boundary to his property, or had at one point.

"How far are we from the house?" she asked.

"What?" he replied, confused.

"The house: how close is it?"

Mr. Rushton lowered his eyebrows at her but then looked outside to discover where they were. "Not a quarter mile."

"Excellent, have the coachman stop the carriage," Caroline said, delighted at the confusion on his face. "I should like to walk."

His blond eyebrows dipped even lower. "But you despise walking."

"Yes, but if I am entering a new life, I intend to do so of my own volition and under my own momentum."

Mr. Rushton nodded, did as she bid him, and stopped the carriage. He assisted her to the ground and sent the driver on.

They stood together in the grass as the cloud of dust dissipated in the wake of the barouche's disappearance. Their eyes were locked, as if each were trying to read the other's thoughts, and then Mr. Rushton offered his arm.

She took it, and they walked slowly toward the stream.

"I suppose it is natural for you to desire to meet your future on your own terms and under your own power. You had little choice in the decisions that led to this point."

Here, Caroline laughed aloud. "Little choice? What can you mean?"

Mr. Rushton looked upon her as one might regard a lunatic.

"Oh, you refer to the circumstances of our engagement," she said.

"Indeed."

"Well, you may cease being concerned about them, for I can assure you that nothing has occurred that I did not truly desire in my heart, though I hesitate in sharing that truth with anyone, especially you, husband, for you shall undoubtedly enjoy wielding this new power over me."

He smiled broadly at her and then sobered. "I should think you understand by now that I love you. And it should be abundantly clear that I have no desire for power over you." He referred to the solicitor's letter, Caroline knew.

She desired to speak, but she had never been easily able to understand her own heart, much less share its content with others.

So the couple walked on through the summer green grass as far as the bridge across the stream.

Finally, Caroline stopped. "I know that you do not act for dreams of power. Your actions—your repudiation of my fortune—revealed to me your love in a way that your words may never have."

"I wanted you to understand that my motives were not the same as other gentlemen's may have been."

"All my life, I have labored under the misapprehension that society's values were correct. That a person ought to be born to his position and inherit his fortune, but Mr. Newton, my own father, and even you have shown me that perhaps English society is changing."

He offered her a look of mock shock. "Do I understand you correctly? Have you finally abandoned your preoccupation with society and its whims?"

Caroline laughed again. "No indeed! I shall always seek the best company and purchase the finest of every item available, but I shall no longer be ashamed of my past. I will not make my every decision based on my fear of its discovery, and I shall never look down upon tradesmen again."

"Never?" Mr. Rushton asked, clearly dubious.

"Well," she hesitated. "I shall not look down upon them overmuch as long as they behave with civility."

"So have you changed at all?"

Had she?

No, Caroline thought not. She was still the same woman who enjoyed music, good company, and society parties. She would never be a soft, submissive creature, and she would speak her mind at every opportunity. No, that much remained the same.

Still, she had indeed learned something from the events of the past year.

"I have said only that I realize that society may be changing. It would be foolish—would it not?—to deny that fact, to refuse to understand it. And so, you must tell me," Caroline said, gesturing toward the bridge at their feet, "about this structure before me. Mr. Newton informed me that it was one of your early designs. And it appears more complicated than throwing some logs across a stream as I previously believed."

Mr. Rushton gave her a smile, but he did not respond to her invitation to explain its design and construction; instead, he only took her hand in his and led her across it.

Still, she understood his meaning. The bridge served its purpose, and it was a thing of beauty to behold as its stone slabs sparkled in the afternoon sun. This bridge was a product of his mind as well as his hands, and it had saved his whole family from poverty. For Mr. Rushton, it was an object of pride, not shame.

And it ought to be for her as well.

She looked at this man—her husband—beside her. He was smirking. "So tell me, Caro, for we have danced about this subject, do you think you shall ever admit how desperately you love me?"

She returned his smirk. "I had not thought I was required to speak those words to you, husband, for my actions revealed the truth, even before I realized it myself. Did not I allow you to take advantage of me and compromise my reputation?" Caroline felt herself blush, but she continued. "Did not I throw myself into your arms like a wanton woman?"

He turned so that they were facing each other, their hands still joined between them. His blue eyes were wide and clear, and in their expression, she was surprised to observe what in any other gentleman she might have described as uncertainty. But that could not be, for Mr. Rushton was perhaps the surest individual she had ever encountered.

"Yes, but did you not know that a gentleman likes to be assured of the love of his wife?" he asked. "He does not care to speak his feelings aloud if hers remain hidden. So you must speak."

"You ought to realize early in our marriage, husband, that I have no interest in doing as I am told." Her lips stretched slowly into a smile as she stepped closer until their bodies were very nearly touching. "If I choose to let my actions speak for me, then you shall have to learn to accept it."

Caroline raised her free hand to her husband's neck and allowed her fingers to trail toward his collar. His expression had turned hungry, and it seemed he could remain still no longer. Mr. Rushton pulled her flush against his body, causing a little gasp to escape from her lips. Pressed against him in the middle of the road to Rushton House, Caroline felt as if she had finally found her home, and it was not in the house that awaited them at the end of the drive. No, it existed in something else entirely.

Caroline realized in that moment that she could not date her falling in love with Mr. Rushton upon her first sight of his beautiful grounds at Rushton House—although they turned out to be lovely indeed—but upon her understanding of the depth of his character and upon her comprehension of her own heart.

ುಲಿ ಲಿಡಿಲಿ

✣ Author's Note ✣

I am most indebted to Jane Austen for her creation of the wonderful world and characters of *Pride and Prejudice*. I would also like to thank my family and friends who contributed to this book and to my life in general: Bert Becton, Marilyn and Robert Whiteley, and Octavia and Ed Becton. I am grateful to my editorial team Beverle Graves Myers and Kelley Fuller Land, both excellent editors and writers. Though any errors within this text belong solely to me, I will—as usual—do my best to foist them upon someone else.

✣ ✣

❧ About the Author ❧

Jennifer Becton has worked for more than twelve years in the traditional publishing industry as a freelance writer, editor, and proofreader. Upon discovering the possibilities of the expanding eBook market, she created Whiteley Press, an independent publishing house, and *Charlotte Collins: A Continuation of Jane Austen's* Pride and Prejudice, her first historical fiction novel, was published in 2010 with great success.

She also writes thrillers under the pseudo-pseudonym J. W. Becton. *Absolute Liability*, the first in the six-book Southern Fraud Thriller series, became an Amazon Kindle Best Seller, and *Death Benefits* (Southern Fraud 2) will be out in January 2012.

❧ ❧

Connect with Jennifer Online
Blog: http://www.bectonliterary.com

Facebook: http://www.facebook.com/JenniferBectonWriter

Twitter: http://twitter.com/JenniferBecton

Southern Fraud Thriller Series: http://www.jwbecton.com

❧ ❧

Printed in Great Britain
by Amazon.co.uk, Ltd.,
Marston Gate.